OUR BATHTUB WASN'T IN THE KITCHEN ANYMORE!

Gerade DeMichele

Our Bathtub Wasn't in the Kitchen Anymore

Author: Gerade DeMichele

Copyright © 2020

ISBN 978-1-54399-972-3 (softcover)
ISBN 978-1-54399-973-0 (ebook)

To Pasqualina, Amadeo, Philomena, Donald, and Peter

"Change your thoughts and you change your world."

–Norman Vincent Peale

Contents

Author's Note

While this book is indeed a work of fiction, it includes many stories based on fact. The names of characters are fictional except for those in my immediate family and closest friend. It is in part a memoir since the events in this book are based on my personal recollections of fifty to sixty years ago, and the story lines approximate reality. The places mentioned, with a couple of exceptions, are real. Morris Avenue, 152nd Street and the Melford Club all existed, as described. Our Lady of Pity grammar school, Cardinal Spellman High School and Hunter College are real.

While quotation marks are used in the dialogue, these conversations are fictional but reflect actual exchanges as best as I can remember them.

A colleague of mine who read an early draft suggested that it would be interesting to know who and what are real and who and what are fiction. I decided to add a supplement that provides a chapter by chapter notation of real people, places, and events referenced. Anything not mentioned as true in this supplement can be assumed to be fiction. I thank the colleague wholeheartedly for this suggestion as I believe it adds signfiicantly to this work.

I have authored or co-authored sixteen books of non-fiction, so the writing process is not new to me. I can assure you that the task of writing non-fiction is very different from the effort I had to put in here. While this book is essentially an individual's story about growing up in the Bronx in the 1950s and 1960s, my goal was also to provide the reader with a window into a neighborhood and a culture that ceased to exist as the borough and the country underwent great demographic and societal changes. In this respect, social historians, sociologists, and urbanists might find some of the descriptions interesting and important.

Lastly, I thank Chet Jordan and Deborah Greenblatt for reading earlier versions of this work. I also am most appreciative of Elaine Bowden's significant contributions to the final version.

–*Gerade DeMichele*

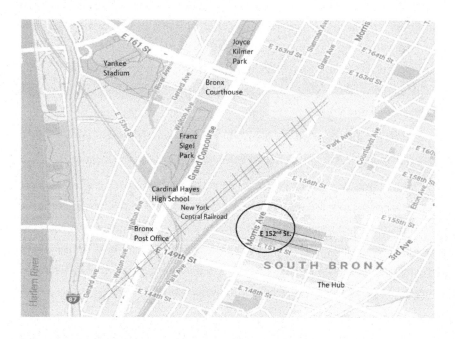

https://www.google.com/maps/place/The+Bronx,+NY/@40.8516388,-73.8584455,14z/data=!4m5!3m4!1s0x89c-28b553a697cb1:0x556e43a78ff15c77!8m2!3d40.8447819!4d-73.8648268

INTRODUCTION

2017

On a cooler than usual evening for August, my 49-year-old son, Michael and I travelled from my home in northern Westchester County to Yankee Stadium in the Bronx to watch our beloved team play a game against the Boston Red Sox. The Stadium is located on 163rd Street, just off Jerome Avenue. I suggested we go early and have dinner at Yolanda's Restaurant on 149th Street. After we parked the car near the Stadium, we walked up 161st Street to the Grand Concourse, one of the truly beautiful boulevards in New York City, and along Franz Sigel Park. This is a walk I had done many times as a youth. After we passed Cardinal Hayes High School and the Bronx Central Post Office, we turned east on 149th Street. Yolanda's has been in the same location between Morris and Courtlandt Avenues for more than sixty years and is owned by Neil Calisi, whose parents owned it before him. My connection to Yolanda's is personal. Neil and I were in the same class all through elementary school, and we graduated eighth grade together from Our Lady of Pity (OLP) on 151st Street.

Yolanda's has changed very little since it opened. Red-and-white checkered tablecloths on wooden tables and the menu just pure, genuine Italian food. The same aroma comes from the kitchen even today as it did in the 1950s. I closed my eyes for a couple of seconds and was transported back in time. The freshly made pizza pie was served very hot with homemade marinara sauce, mozzarella cheese, and partially burnt parts on the underside. The first bite was incredibly delicious even as the super-heated cheese would singe the roof of your mouth. I told Michael that my two older brothers and I would come here and share a six-slice pizza pie that cost 65 cents.

Michael asked incredulously, "How could an entire pizza only cost 65 cents?"

I told him, "That was the going rate. Some of the other restaurants were charging as much as 75 cents."

"How much for a slice?"

I said, "Michael, there was no such thing as selling pizza by the slice. There were several pizzerias on Morris Avenue between 148th and153rd Streets, and none of them sold pizza by the slice. You went in, sat at a table or booth, ordered a meal, which might be a pizza, and enjoyed the company of your family or friends just as you and I are doing now. A pizza pie wasn't something that hung around on a large metal tray waiting for someone to order a slice."

Michael looked at me with disbelief in his eyes. It was obvious he had trouble relating to the pizzerias of my old neighborhood.

I then explained that the custom of selling and serving pizza by the slice eventually did come to our neighborhood years later.

After a dinner that included fried calamari, fresh-made fettuccini, veal parmigiana, and glasses of red wine, Michael and I walked up Morris Avenue from 149th to 152nd Street. On Morris Avenue, I told him about the delis, pastry shops, butchers, and pharmacies that existed there once upon a time, which were now all gone. I showed him where Colasacco's Sandwich Shop was. It had the reputation for making the best Italian heroes in the Bronx. The only store still there from the 1950s was Judy's Florist, which is owned by the Mazzella family and had been there since the end of World War II.

My family lived at 294 East 152nd Street for three generations. Except for mail, we only used street numbers such as 152nd or 151 Street without the "East". Among our friends and neighbors on Morris Avenue, we referred to where we lived by the house number. So, we lived at 294. My grandparents bought the three-story house in 1917 just after World War I. My mother and her two brothers were born in the early 1900s and lived there throughout much of their adult lives. A third brother died as an infant. My brothers and I were born there also and delivered by a midwife. Now, most of what was 152nd Street, including 294, are gone and covered over by a sports complex that's part of Alfred E. Smith High

School. Back in the 1950s when I lived there, it was Bronx Vocational High School or BV for short.

BV was an all-boys high school and was by far the largest structure in our neighborhood, five stories of tan-rusty brick that took up half the space on 151st and 152nd streets between Morris and Courtlandt Avenues. It had a small parking lot, side yards and spaces, and a large school yard on its east side. The entire BV complex was surrounded by a black wrought-iron fence, six feet high with twelve-inch spikes all along the top. BV was the inspiration for a famous book by Evan Hunter, who was briefly a teacher there. Hunter went on to have a successful career as an author although he wrote under a few pseudonyms.

Blackboard Jungle sold over 5 million copies and was about an all-boys high school where young men learned a trade but were just as likely to drop out in order to go to work to earn a living for themselves and their families. Many of the students in the book are depicted as juvenile delinquents, and there are several bloody scenes in the book involving students and teachers and among students themselves. Sales of the book took off in 1955 when a movie based on the book was released, starring Glenn Ford, Sidney Poiter, Vic Morrow and Anne Francis. The soundtrack for the movie was *Rock Around the Clock* by Bill Haley and the Comets, one of the pioneering rock and roll bands of the 1950s. The reverberating beat of "one, two, three o'clock, four o'clock ROCK – five, six, seven o'clock, eight o'clock ROCK…" was the undisputed theme song for the early years of rock and roll. Turner Classic Movies listed the soundtrack of *Blackboard Jungle* on its list of the Top 15 Most Influential Movie Soundtracks of all time and said that the movie brought Hollywood into the rock and roll era.

Evan Hunter's original name was Salvatore Lombino. Supposedly, he took his pen name from two schools he attended, Evander Childs High School on Gun Hill Road in the North Bronx and Hunter College on the East Side of Manhattan. Many crime fiction enthusiasts would know him as Ed McBain who wrote a series of novels about the 87th Police Precinct. He also wrote the original screenplay for the Alfred Hitchcock thriller, *The Birds*.

Michael, who was raised in Westchester County in a small middle-class community, had some difficulty relating to a school like BV even though I tried to explain it as part of the feel and context of the place and period of my youth.

We walked to my old grammar school, Our Lady of Pity, which was two-stories high, its windows now cemented over. The church by the same name had also been closed for years and was recently deconsecrated, paving the way for the sale of the land to developers.

Michael wanted to know more about my friends, the school, and family members. He had also heard some of my friends who visited us at our house in Westchester County talk about fights and violence. There were indeed fights and violence back in the 1950s, as depicted in Evan Hunter's book. Blacks, Italians, Irish, Poles, and Puerto Ricans all had their own enclaves or turfs with well-understood boundaries, generally leading to a peaceful co-existence. But I could not deny that I saw a certain amount of violence growing up, including seeing a childhood buddy shot and killed no more than twenty feet away from me.

Michael asked more questions, "Where did you play with your friends? What was your school like? Why did you move away from here?"

Each succeeding question sent my mind further on its journey back into my youth. My childhood friends and I played a lot of sports in the BV schoolyard, had nuns for teachers, and developed close friendships that lasted throughout most of our youth and in some cases, beyond. The last question that Michael had asked was by far the most complex. Moving away wasn't only a physical moving away but the transformation of a way of life that had existed in an old ethnic enclave. It was also a transformation of values as the comfort of the insular neighborhood gave way to a more diverse city and world. I had a lot to share with him. It would be a good father–son talk or maybe book.

CHAPTER ONE

1951: 294 East 152nd Street

I was four years old in 1951 and my earliest memories are of my mornings in
our apartment in 294. My mother and grandmother were devout Catholics,
as were many Italian women of their generations. Our Lady of Pity had five
masses every morning, one every half hour between 6:30 and 9:00 a.m. And
every morning, my grandmother went to the 6:30 and 7:00 a.m. masses, came
home and took care of me while my mother went to the 8:00 and 8:30 a.m.
masses. My grandmother didn't speak English and I didn't speak Italian, but she
understood my every want and need. She brought me pieces of Italian bread
from the previous night's supper, put olive oil on it, and gave it to me for breakfast.
I remember a unique smell or essence about her that reflected the foods she
cooked in a little room off the coal furnace area in the basement. There was
incredible peace in our apartment when just the two of us were there. I would
play on the floor in the kitchen or the spare room with little toys that my father
or uncles had bought me. No words were exchanged between us, just looks and
nods of love and caring. She had a way of tilting her head back and raising her
chin to indicate that all was well. This ritual went on every morning from as far
back as I can remember and until I started kindergarten at age five. My grandmother's name was Pasqualina, but she was "Big Momma" to my brothers and
me. She didn't like being called "grandma," so "Big Momma" it was, even though
she was only about five feet, two inches tall. Every day, she spent hours cleaning
and sweeping the hallways in her house, chopping wood, and tending to the coal
furnace that heated all the apartments. But her favorite activity was embroidering
altar cloths with intricate patterns and religious symbols for our church, which

had one large main altar and three side altars. My mother told me it took Big Momma years to finish embroidering an altar cloth for the main altar. I kissed Big Momma every time I saw her, but I never spoke a word and neither did she to me.

Big Momma's house had three stories plus a basement. My mother, father, two brothers, and I lived on the top floor. My Uncle Tony and his wife, Aunt Jean, lived on the second floor. My Uncle Johnny and his wife, Aunt Zina, lived on the ground floor. I never heard anyone ever refer to my uncle as John. It was always Johnny. I never knew my grandfather who died in 1942. Big Momma slept in a room in my Uncle Johnny's apartment but chose to spend most of her time in a little one-room area in the basement that included a refrigerator, a table, and a stove. Big Momma's room in the basement was the warmest place in the house because it was right next to the five-foot high coal furnace that heated the entire building. Up until the year before she died in 1960, she shoveled the coal into the furnace to make sure all was warm for her family. My family was everybody who lived at 294. I was welcome in any apartment. Doors to the three apartments and the basement were typically kept open all day long, so I was free to roam in and out.

The basement was the most interesting place in 294. In addition to the furnace room with the adjacent coal bins and Big Momma's room, there were several dimly lit rooms including my Uncle Johnny's workshop. He painted, sculpted, and had other artistic hobbies like bronzing baby shoes for friends and relatives. I liked going down to the basement especially on winter nights to watch him work. My Uncle Johnny never went past third grade and was one of the tough guys in the neighborhood in the 1930s. To survive the Great Depression, both my uncles worked for the mob in the Bronx, ran numbers, and did petty larceny. They were both arrested in 1942 and told by the police they could go either to prison or into the army. They chose the latter and served in the infantry. With the 1st Army, they took part in the Allied invasions in North Africa, Italy, and Normandy. My Uncle Johnny would tell me stories about North Africa and Italy but rarely mentioned Normandy. He did tell me once that the D-Day invasion was the only time he really thought he would get killed in the war.

Our apartment on the third floor of 294 had five rooms. You entered through the kitchen, which was taken up mostly by a table where we had our meals. To the right was the doorway to the living room that in turn led to two bedrooms. To the left was our one bathroom that housed a commode and nothing else. When you used the bathroom, you came out and washed your hands in the kitchen sink. Lined up on the far wall of the kitchen were a pantry closet, a stove, the sink, and a bathtub. The bathtub had a metal cover that could be lifted and attached with hooks to a wooden cabinet above it. The bathtub stood on twelve-inch legs; so as a small child, I would step on a small stool to climb into the tub. More than once, I slipped on the wet edge and landed in the water.

The bathtub and its cover served multiple purposes. Most of the time, the cover was down, and the tub was blanketed from top to bottom with a linen tablecloth. On top of the tablecloth was a wooden board and long rolling pin used to make pasta and to knead dough for cakes and pastries. When Big Momma cooked in our apartment usually around the holidays, mouth-watering aromas came from the top of the bathtub. Big Momma cooked from scratch. She made everything with flour, herbs, fresh vegetables, and meats. Not a single item was from a can. Since our refrigerator didn't have a freezer, we didn't even know what frozen foods were. Big Momma would move back and forth between the bathtub cover and stove cooking and creating her masterpieces. If my brothers and I were lucky, she would give us a taste of freshly made struffoli, zeppoli, or whatever cake or bread she was making. She would only give us a small taste and would serve the rest after dinner. After a meal, the cover served as a place to dry the dishes, which were washed in the sink. The bathtub also served as the place where my mother washed clothes three days a week (Monday, Wednesday, and Friday) on a scrub board using brown lye soap. My father, brothers, and I took turns taking baths once a week on Saturday afternoon and night. I have no idea when my mother, who was spotlessly clean, took her bath. I presume it was whenever she was sure that my brothers and me were out of the apartment or possibly sound asleep. I cannot imagine a more horrifying situation for my mother than to be caught naked in the bathtub in front of one of her sons.

Also, on the left side of the bathroom was a spare room that housed four wooden clothes closets, a three-drawer bureau, a locked green cabinet that my father used to store documents, and Big Momma's foot-pedal Singer sewing machine. Next to the green cabinet, there were always cartons of glassware, brass plaques, women's clothes, and other merchandise that came from my father's warehouse. He sold these to friends of my mother, who lived in the neighborhood. In the center of this clutter, there was an open space on the wooden floor three feet wide and eight feet long, just enough for me to play in. I spent a good deal of my toddler years on that floor, imagining all sorts of settings for my toy cowboys, knights, and soldiers. At Christmas, my brother Donald would set up his Lionel trains on the floor. He had two sets of trains along with houses, stations, and greenery. It would take him all day on a Saturday to get the two sets up and running, and not crashing into one another. Donald was always the chief engineer and wore a stripped grey and blue hat, just as real engineers did. Peter and I would man the track switches to make sure the trains didn't collide. The timing for this had to be perfect. Donald would give Peter and me the "go-ahead" to flip the track switches that would direct one locomotive away from the other locomotive. Invariably, either Peter or I were late, and a collision would occur. I think Peter was late purposefully. Regardless, Donald never lost his patience and would re-arrange the trains on the tracks and test the transformer connection, and the trains were off and running again until the next crash. We did this for hours on end.

Our living room had a sofa, two stuffed chairs, a dark mahogany table, and a black and white television. The TV had six channels (2, 4, 5, 7, 9, and 11). We all had our favorite shows. My father loved Jackie Gleason because *The Honeymooners* reminded him of where he grew up in Brooklyn. My brothers loved the late-night comedians like Steve Allen and later Jack Paar. My mother didn't watch much television but enjoyed *The Goldbergs* because it was about a homemaker living in the Bronx. I liked the westerns, but I never just watched television. I was always playing with something else on the floor. The large mahogany table in the living room was very important because it opened up when we had a large gathering for dinner, which was every holiday including Thanksgiving, Christmas Eve, Christmas Day, New Year's Eve, New Year's Day, Mother's Day, and Easter. That was when Big Momma and my mother cooked for all the relatives, which generally numbered fifteen or sixteen people, half of whom ate their meal in the kitchen and half on the table in the living room. Our Christmases at 294 were the most special for me since in our family, someone always dressed up as Santa Claus on Christmas Eve. My grandfather did it, my Uncle Tony did it, and later my brother Donald played the jolly elf, giving us all sorts of gifts. Me being the youngest in the entire house and my brothers getting older, I was showered with lots of toys.

My mother and father's bedroom was separated from the living room by a large set of French doors. Inside their bedroom were a large bed, a tall chest of drawers, and a dresser with a mirror, all made of a fancy carved dark wood. My brothers and I slept in a smaller, not as fancy bedroom, which had a double bed for my brother Peter and me, and single day bed for my other brother, Donald. The little remaining wall space contained a bureau, and a small dresser on top of which my mother kept an altar with more than a dozen statues of Jesus, the Blessed Mother and her favorite saints. In the center of her altar was a votive candle that was always lit. This votive candle was a real candle with a real flame, and my mother would have considered it bad luck if the candle ever went out. It sat in a red glass holder that had a metal cap with little holes in it, so at night, there was always a modest light show on the ceiling of our bedroom as the flame flickered and swayed casting shadows and abstract images above us. The only open floor space in this room was about eighteen inches wide and six feet long. Every morning, our room was the scene of a mini demolition derby as my brothers and I woke up, searched for clothes, fell over each other getting ready for the day. Even this was not as bad as waiting to use the one bathroom and the one sink in the kitchen. It was imperative to get in the bathroom before my brother Donald, who took forever and liked to read entire comic books while sitting on the commode or, as my mother called it, the "terlit."

At this time of my life, one of my great accomplishments was learning to slide down the big bannisters from the third floor to the first floor. My mother was always yelling at me, "And don't slide down the bannisters. You're going to break your neck." This went on every time I left our apartment. I always slid down the bannister, and as I got older, I became expert enough to not have to hold on and I could slide sitting down instead of on my belly. My greatest accomplishment was when I could lift myself up and jump just as I got to the bottom of the stairs to avoid slamming into the four-inch ball on top of the post.

There was one thing that made 294 one of the most special places on the block. We had a backyard that was as wide as the entire house and stretched all the way to the backs of the tenement houses that fronted 151st Street. Just outside the house was a concrete patio with a two-foot wall topped with smooth slate slabs perfect for sitting. The left and back sides of the patio was surrounded by hedges that kept the sitting areas cool in the summer. Two woodsheds on the right side of the patio contained kindling for the coal furnace. Big Momma had a lifelong friend named Bartolomé (Bartholomew) who worked at the Bronx Terminal Market, kept our sheds filled with kindling, and used our yard on occasion to sell various types of produce in open crates. I liked it especially when Bartolomé used the yard to sell Christmas trees in December. The fire in a barrel in the center of the patio and the smell of the pine trees were signs that the holidays and Santa Claus were coming. Beyond the patio was a grassy area, kept neat by my Uncle Johnny. A large three-story oak tree was in the center of the yard and its trunk provided a place to attach clotheslines, which were needed because no one had a clothes dryer. Big Momma and other adults in the family were generous with our yard and were welcoming in letting their friends who lived in the five-story buildings that completely surrounded our house to enjoy it, and especially the patio as a place to chat. My father had also built a decent size "shack" at the back of the yard that had electricity, a linoleum floor, chairs, and two large tables. Sometimes, my brothers' friends used it to hang out or as a place to play cards or board games. And sometimes, my brothers, I, and our friends would sleep in it during the hottest nights in the summer. It didn't have heat, so it wasn't used much in the winter. My father would board up the sides of the shack with shutters in late fall, and in the spring he took them down. Our backyard served many purposes, most important of which was a place for me to play.

At this time of my life, I had a couple of friends to play with regularly. One was Lena, who was my mother's best friend's daughter. Lena and her family lived next door in 300, one of the five-story apartment buildings on 152nd Street. Our mothers would sit and talk on the patio, while Lena and I played in the grass area or in the shack. We made up games, usually based on TV characters. She was nice looking, and I liked her. Lena and I had a feeling that our mothers hoped that we would play together for the rest of our lives. For Lena, I was just another brother. She had two brothers, Johnny Boy, who was a very good friend of my older brothers, and Joey V, who was in between my brother Peter and me in age. Because of all these connections, we spent a lot of time in each other's homes.

My other friend was Ben-Ben. He was the son of the building superintendent at 300. He lived in an apartment on a low floor right next to our yard; one day, I asked him to come play with me, and that started a regular thing between us. Whenever I was playing by myself, Ben-Ben would come to the window and I would wave to him to come into the yard. We usually ended up in some type of chase game and although Ben-Ben was faster than I was, I was taller and a bit stronger. Our chases usually resulted in us wrestling each other to the ground. This was great because I could hardly do this kind of stuff with Lena. It was a lot of fun playing with Ben-Ben. My mother would sometimes look at me strangely, as if she wanted to say something, when I came upstairs to our apartment after I finished playing with Ben-Ben. But the words never came out of her mouth. This was unusual because my mother loved to talk. What I didn't understand was that he was "black" and his father, Bill, mother, Rita, and older sister, Geralyn, were the only black family on 152nd Street. They moved away about two years later, and I never saw Ben-Ben again.

CHAPTER TWO

La Familia

My grandparents on my mother's side, Donato and Pasqualina, came to this country in the 1890s from the same small village between Naples and Benevento. As was typical of immigrant couples and families back then, my grandfather came first to see if he could find work. He stayed in an apartment on 151st Street between Morris and Park Avenues with a paisano from his village. He was able to find work soon enough to send for Pasqualina. The only problem was that they hadn't been married, and Pasqualina would not leave her village unless she was married. In fact, she was adamant about not leaving. So, in order to save a few dollars, my grandfather suggested that they get married by proxy and asked a cousin to stand in for him at the ceremony. Pasqualina was very skeptical about this arrangement and needed assurances from her village priest that a proxy marriage was indeed a legitimate marriage. Pasqualina was eventually convinced after a lengthy negotiation by mail since neither my grandfather nor grandmother had a telephone, and so the couple got married by proxy. Pasqualina left her village and made the trip to her new home in the Bronx, never to return. When she arrived, they rented an apartment in the same building on 151st Street, where Donato had been staying with his friend. My grandfather did odd jobs and Big Momma, as she came to be called, sewed. They had four children, starting in 1909 when my mother, Philomena, was born. One child, the first John, died as an infant. Two more sons, Anthony and John, were subsequently born in 1913 and 1916. By 1917, their apartment was getting crowded, so they scraped together enough money to buy what my mother called a "shanty" at 294 East 152nd Street between Morris and Courtlandt Avenues. My mother said it was brown with wooden siding, outhouses, and a dilapidated porch in the entrance. It wasn't really what we think of as a shanty today since it did have the same three floors and apartments that I grew up in. By doing a lot of the work themselves, they tore down the porch and put up a beautiful white-speckled brick front entrance on the house. They also made a small three-story addition on the back so that each apartment had flush toilets. A new three-step marble stoop and interior entrance hall combined with the new brick front gave the building an attractive look unique for the block. Big Momma and my mother scrubbed that stoop and entrance spotless. Every day, my grandfather worked on and off at construction jobs, while Big Momma and my mother, who was still a young girl, took in sewing to supplement the family income. In 1921, my grandfather got a steady job as a "parkie," taking care of Crotona Park on 174th Street and Crotona Avenue. Big Momma lived on to play significant role in my upbringing. In the early years of my life, she was a quiet, calming influence who only cared about God and her family.

My paternal grandfather, Pietro, was a tailor and his wife, Maria, took care of the home. They both came to the United States from a village in Calabria, Italy. My father, Amadeo, was born near Ebbets Field in Brooklyn in 1909. He had three brothers and a sister. His brother, Amelio, died under questionable circumstances at the age of twenty-six in a local precinct jail, where he had been for "harassing" a former girlfriend. The cause of death was listed as a heart attack. My father's family never believed the police report of Amelio's death. As a result, my father and his brothers and sister distrusted the police for the rest of their lives. In fact, the police were the only group of people I ever heard my father disparage. His older brother, Ralph, married and settled in Hempstead, Long Island, in the 1920s, where he started an ice delivery business. My father's younger brother, James, became a "parkie" and his sister, Lena, was a seamstress. Neither of them married, and they lived together on Atlantic Avenue in Brooklyn for most of their adult lives.

My father never finished high school, but he could read well, write, and do arithmetic. As far back as I could remember, he read two newspapers every day, the *Daily News* and the *Daily Mirror*. During his early life, he did many jobs including working in a pool hall, being a clown for Macy's Thanksgiving Day Parade, and briefly for the New York City Transportation Department. The Great

Depression scarred him emotionally, and he was unable to find work for long periods at a time and eventually went to work in the warehouses on the docks on Manhattan's West Side. He used to say that he saw himself in the movie, *On the Waterfront*, which starred Marlon Brando, Lee. J. Cobb, Karl Malden, Eva Marie Saint, and Rod Steiger. He met my mother at a dance hall in Manhattan in 1933. They married in 1934 and lived on New Lots Avenue in Brooklyn. In 1935, just before my brother Donald was born, they moved to 294 and lived with my grandmother. My father was a bit too old to be drafted during World War II and had a bad back much of his adult life. By the 1950s, he was a manager in one of the waterfront warehouses. He was happy to have steady work, but he was always worried that he could be laid off at any time. He was very frugal and did not part easily with his money. He generally came home each night exhausted from work. My mother always had a home-cooked meal waiting for him. He loved linguini, fettuccini, or any long thin pasta. He had elegance in eating his pasta with a fork and spoon. He used the fork to twirl a small amount onto the spoon and ended up with a perfectly round mouth-size of pasta. It was a slow and deliberate method for enjoying his meal. He was respected enough on 152nd Street that he was able to build a side business doing income tax returns for neighbors for $2.00 apiece. He also mysteriously came home on a regular basis with a box or two of goods from his warehouse and sold the contents to friends and neighbors. When I questioned my mother about where dad got the boxes, she would say, "Don't ask!"

My father was a diehard Dodgers fan and was crushed when they left Brooklyn in 1957. He cursed the owner, Walter O'Malley, for the rest of his life. Mention O'Malley's name and my father went into tantrums. We were one of the first families on 152nd Street to have a television and our friends came over to watch programs. My father got entangled in comedic situations like trying to fix the television antenna located on the roof. As I mentioned earlier, our three-story house was completely surrounded by five-story apartment buildings so the delicate reception we had was constantly in peril. Whenever there was a bad storm, my father would have to go up on the roof to realign the antenna. One of us would go to a window and someone else would be in the living room yelling, which channels were coming in clearly. My father could always get the antenna set so that either the low channels (2, 4, and 5) could be viewed clearly or the high channels (7, 9, and 11), but rarely together. It was a frail balancing act requiring delicate moves and turns of fractions of inches to get it just right. My brothers, especially Donald, thought this was all hilarious every time we had to re-align the antenna, but my father always came back into our apartment red-faced and pissed.

My mother, Philomena, was an attractive young woman from what I saw in photographs that were kept in a family album. Black wavy hair, fine facial features and a slim body. She had to leave the newly built Our Lady of Pity (OLP) School because of discipline problems and never went to high school. My Uncle Tony told me that my mother use to answer the nuns back in OLP, for which she would get a slap in the face or a rap on her knuckles. My mother ended up graduating Pubic School 31. In her teens, she, as did a few of her friends at the time, worked in the sweatshops doing piecework sewing and getting a few cents for each "piece" completed. She used to say that she felt guilty if she got up from her sewing machine to go to the bathroom. She was also a bit of a spitfire and would quickly engage you in an argument if provoked. In fact, the only person my Uncle Johnny, who was considered a tough guy on Morris Avenue, would back down from was his sister. Giving birth to three children and taking care of our apartment as well as the entire 294 building with my grandmother took its toll on her. But like Big Momma, she was completely devoted to the Catholic religion and her family. In addition to saying fifteen rosaries and going to two Masses daily, she observed every single religious holiday and custom. She had a special devotion, as did many Italian women, to St. Anthony of Padua. Every year on his name day, June 13th, my mother always participated in a small procession and bought loaves of St. Anthony bread for the family.

My older brothers Donald and Peter were as different as two people could be. Donald was outgoing and the life of a party. He loved music, especially Fats Domino and the 1950's doo-wop groups. As a child, he had rheumatic fever and spent a year in a hospital. Rheumatic fever was not easily cured in the 1940s, and as a result of his illness, his joints were underdeveloped. He was a big person, with very small feet and hands, which made it difficult for him to walk and run. This never stopped him from playing sports, which he did with a relish, even though he could never be as good as he would have liked. He was certainly smart and was the first in our family to go to college, going at night to Fordham University and graduating with a bachelor's degree in accounting. I could not have asked for a better older brother. Besides being a lot of fun at home, he took me every place he went especially after 1958 when he graduated college, and my father bought him a brand-new Oldsmobile as a gift. He was twelve years older than I was and in many ways, was my second father since our dad was so exhausted from working at his job in the warehouse that he did not have the energy to do things with us at night. Donald had a cadre of very close friends who knew each other since grammar school. Augie, Skippy, Hook, and Dino were in our house all the time, especially Augie, who continued to come by every morning and have coffee before he and my brother went to work on the subway.

Peter was my middle brother. He was born during World War II when my uncles were away, and the entire country was in a state of upheaval and concern. He was basically a quiet guy but what we would call a "scooch" (slang for Italian scocciatore, meaning pest or a pain in the ass). Being the younger brother, I was the brunt of most of his teasing. We always got into fights and he always won. He was the smartest of the three of us but besides provoking me, one of his great loves was going to the movies on Saturdays, and depending on the movie, he would sometimes take me with him. Our favorite theater was the RKO Royal in the Bronx Hub, where we would sit in the first row of the balcony. We had to keep very quiet because there were lady ushers dressed in gray skirts, white blouses, and maroon jackets, who would come over with a flashlight and ask you to leave for more than one noisy offense. The Royal, as did most theaters in the Bronx in the 1950s, showed a minimum of two movies plus extras, which were comedy shorts, serials, or cartoons. You could stay in the theater as long as you wanted and could even watch a movie a second time if you wished. Peter and I did this many times, especially if a movie had a thrilling scene. I still remember the Nautilus crew battling with a giant squid in Walt Disney's classic *20,000 Leagues under the Sea* based on the Jules Verne's novel. The Royal sadly closed in 1965.

Just like Donald, Peter had a group of friends who were among the best athletes to come out of the South Bronx. Joey, Bobby, Billie, Fritzi, Lefty, Michael, and Jimmy could all play sports. They could run fast, had great coordination and knew the little things you need to know about winning. Peter too was a good athlete especially in softball. He could hit the ball well and always batted clean up on his team, the Eagles. He followed in Donald's footsteps, went to Fordham at night, and graduated with a bachelor's degree in accounting. He did not get a car from my father when he graduated.

My uncles (Tony and Johnny), and aunts (Jean and Zina), also lived in 294 and in every way, were our family. They were caring, loving people who showed great affection for my brothers and me. My uncles were well respected in the neighborhood and, as I said earlier, were involved with the mob and belonged to a group call the Frog Hollow Boys that had a tough reputation, and was mentioned in the *Billy Bathgate* book and movie about the life of the hoodlum, Dutch Schultz. They were also friendly enough with mobsters such as Vincent Coll who my mother said came to our house frequently. My mother liked to tell us a story about my Uncle Johnny who was running numbers before the war. One day, the police chased him right into our house and rather than get caught red-handed with the roll of the day's numbers, stuck them in my brother Donald's diaper. He may have lost that day's take. My mother never said. When both my uncles went off to World War II, Big Momma pledged to God that if they came home alive, she would never eat meat again. They came home, and meat never touched her lips for the rest of her life. More importantly, when my uncles returned from the war, they were better men, went straight, and never picked up their lives with the mob again. When I was growing up, the mob had lost its class, mystique, and, most of all, its respect. The guys still involved with running numbers and taking bets were looked upon at best as anachronisms and, at worst, assholes.

My Uncle Johnny and Aunt Zina had one son, Donald, who was five years younger than I was. Aunt Zina was a beautiful Sicilian woman from a family of musicians who lived in 300, the building next door to ours. Like my mother, she worked in the sweatshops, sewing and doing piecework. She was also an incredible cook, who regularly shared her dinner leftovers with us. She would bang on the steam pipe that ran throughout the three apartments to let us know, and either my brother Peter or I would go downstairs to fetch the dish of goodies. My aunt's breaded veal cutlets were to die for. My Uncle Tony and Aunt Jean did not have any children and treated my brothers and me as if we were theirs, especially at Christmas or on birthdays. They splurged, giving my brothers and me the toys and other gifts that would have belonged to their own.

CHAPTER THREE

1952: East 152nd Street

In 1952, I started kindergarten at OLP. Each day started with a one-block walk to school with my brother Peter, who was in fifth grade. Peter was very smart and skipped third grade, which was a rarity in our school. At that time, my brother Donald, who was twelve years older than I was, was already attending high school. The church and school were built by Italian immigrants at the turn of the twentieth century and occupied four buildings on the south side of 151st Street. Besides the church, there was a lower school for grades K-5 and a rectory whose ground floor served as the upper school for Grades 6–8. A convent for the nuns who taught in OLP was just up the street from the lower school separated by Vic and Connie's Fountain Shop, where you could get an egg cream for five cents. The church had a four-story bell tower on the left and a squared-off center facade made entirely of a dark yellow brick. Between the church and the lower school was a small yard where we assembled for classes. At the back of this yard stood a grey slate and stone grotto about twenty feet high, containing a statue of the Blessed Mother behind a plate of clear glass. A small spring beneath the statue sent a continual flow of water into a six-foot wide well that was two feet deep. I knew this for a fact because I fell into to it several times while playing around the grotto with friends.

Behind the grotto was a larger school yard for play and recess. The larger schoolyard was generally a buzz of activity, with children playing games in the morning before school started, at lunch time, and after school. It wasn't big enough for sports such as softball or stickball, but it was fine for games like roundup tag. Teams usually were made up of one class versus another class, where one team of students chases and catches members of the other team and puts them in a "pen." Students in the pen could be freed only if one of their own who had not yet been caught was able to penetrate the defenses of the other team and "free all" the caught kids in the pen. It sounds a bit complicated, but we understood the rules and played it enthusiastically. The best games were when one grade played against an older grade.

In July and August when school was closed, the school custodian would rig up water sprinklers on one of the walls in the school yard and we would run under the sprinklers to cool off. This was safer than playing in the streets and running through the open fire hydrants or "johnny pumps," but the hydrants were a lot more fun mainly because the pressure was so much stronger. The older kids would take an empty beer or soda can, remove the top and bottom, hold it under the open hydrant. This made a huge arc of water that reached all the way across the street. Of course, opening a hydrant was against the law, and if the police came to shut off the hydrant, all of us would run away into alleys and hallways until they left. Before the police left, they would shut off the hydrant. Fifteen or twenty minutes later, we turned the hydrant back on again. On the very hottest of days, this would happen three or four times and sometimes go on well into the night.

My kindergarten teacher's name was Sister Mary Karen and she belonged to the Franciscan (St. Francis of Assisi) Order of Nuns. She smiled a lot and was nice enough but could give you a withering stare if you misbehaved. Kindergarten was mostly organized play, but I was also introduced to the letters of the alphabet and numbers. There were no tests or homework. We learned simple prayers and were read stories from the Bible. We spent a lot of time making stuff from construction paper or thin cardboard and coloring with our Crayola crayons that came in a green and yellow very thin cardboard box and cost ten cents for eight colors. We had recess and if the weather was okay, we would go out to the small schoolyard and play games. There were about sixty children in my class and we only attended in the morning. There was another afternoon kindergarten with the same number of children. It was unusual to have two separate kindergarten sessions, but we were the first of the baby boomers to attend OLP. I liked Sister Mary Karen and enjoyed being part of well-behaved group of toddlers who always listened and obeyed her. But mostly, I liked returning to my home and backyard on 152nd Street at the end of the school day.

Our block, 152nd Street, was different from 151st Street, where the school was located. 152nd Street had BV and houses of different sizes, shapes, and colors. Actually, our block between Morris and Courtlandt Avenues was two communities. Starting at Morris Avenue Vincent's Butcher Shop on one corner and the Step-In Tavern on the other corner. Next to Vincent's was a small two-story apartment house followed by 278, the largest tenement on the block. Then came a small three-family house with stables in the back, where they kept horses used by the push-carters, who were peddlers who went through the neighborhood selling mostly food stuffs such fruits, vegetables, fish, and breads. There were smaller carts pushed by hand and the larger ones pulled by the horses. That September in 1952, there was a huge fire in the stables, and all the horses died. My brother Donald took me to see the sanitation workers remove the dead animals. It was a terrible sight to see, blood streaming from their nostrils and charred burn marks on their bodies. The fire ended the horse-drawn push-cart business in our neighborhood to be replaced soon by open trucks. Next came 288, another very large, five-story apartment building. Many of my friends lived in this building. On the ground floor was Santo's Delicatessen and Umberto's shoe repair shop. Then came two small houses, Mrs. Ricci's orange-brick home, which was two stories high, and then our house, with its white-speckled brick front. Another apartment building, 300, followed our house and then came BV.

On the other side of the street, next to the Step-In Tavern, was a small beige-colored apartment house with three families, followed by a parking lot for the growing number of cars on the street. My family didn't own a car at this time and wouldn't until 1958. After the parking lot, was the "Old Man's Stoop," which led into an unoccupied brown two-story house. The Old Man's Stoop was the subject of all sorts of stories because no one ever lived there during my time and there never were any lights on in it. Creepy as it was, it also had this wonderful two-story stoop that was ideal for hanging out on. Since no one lived in the house, we neighborhood kids were never bothered by anyone telling us to move along. Next came three three-story houses (one white, one brown with red trim, and one all brown). On the ground floor of the middle house was Fannie Red's Delicatessen. It was called Fannie Red's because the woman who owned and ran it was Fannie and she had a head of flaming red hair. Fannie and my mother were friends from childhood and went to grammar school together, so we always would buy our cold cuts and other foodstuffs from Fannie. On the ground floor of the brown house was a vacant storefront that hadn't been occupied for years. Next came four four-story brownstones that were as attractive and well-kept as any in the finest sections of Manhattan. The Pesces and the Russos, who were very close to our family especially Big Momma and my mother, lived there with several other families. Above the brownstones was another parking lot owned by Mr. Zanghelli. This parking lot on one side and BV directly across the street marked the invisible border of our (or lower) 152nd Street community. Beyond BV and the parking lot was the upper 152nd Street community with a variety of apartments and smaller private homes on both sides of the street.

The most important place on this block was BV's schoolyard, which extended the entire length of the space between 151st and 152nd Streets. This schoolyard was the community's playground. There were no swings or seesaws, but two basketball nets and a long cement playing field ideal for softball, touch football, stickball, and games such as tag, ringolevio, and at night, hide and go seek. Every day and in every season, as long as it wasn't raining, there were five or six games or other activities going on in this schoolyard, all organized by the kids and people in the neighborhood. Even as a five-year old, I was being taught to play team sports thanks to my brother Peter's friends. They taught us the basics as well as subtleties of the game. In softball, move men on base along, hit the cut-off man, and playing good defense were emphasized. In fact, a good play in the field was prized as much as if you made a big hit. Little did Joey, Bobby, Billy, and others know that they were changing lives, but they were. All I know is that I was trying as hell to hustle and play well and was scared to death that one of the older guys was going to yell at me for screwing up.

In the wintertime, when the custodians for BV would shovel snow into big piles against the east wall of the schoolyard, we could play king of the hill and have snowball fights. The schoolyard provided a space for us to play that was not the street itself. 152nd Street was so narrow that only one car could fit driving up, and with cars parked on each side, it was not a very good place to play games like stickball. The upper part of the street did have a very smooth tar surface though and was perfect for roller skating and riding bicycles.

Professional sports, especially baseball, were very much part of the culture on 152nd Street as well. The men in the neighborhood always were talking who had the better teams and players. The New York Giants, Brooklyn Dodgers, and of course, the New York Yankees were all in New York City then and the rivalries were intense and loud. My brothers were completely devoted Yankee fans. Having been born and raised in Brooklyn, my father was passionate about the Dodgers. As a child, I could not understand how my father could root for a team that did so much losing when the Yankees were a few blocks away on 161st Street, winning the World Series throughout the 1950s. Between 1949 and 1962, the Yankees won nine world championships. Players like Joe DiMaggio, Mickey Mantle, Yogi Berra, Elston Howard, and Whitey Ford were practically on our doorstep and the list kept going on.

The first ballgame my father took me to was at the Polo Grounds, to see a double-header between the Giants and Dodgers. The noise the fans made for these two teams made was ear-splitting. That day, each team won a game, but I never went to another Dodger or Giant game in my life because both teams moved to California in 1957. The Yankees were my team and the stadium was a short walk away. Growing up, my friends and I would go to a Yankee game every few weeks. Bleacher seats back then cost 75 cents (about the same price as a freshly made pizza pie) and the grandstands $1.25. We all loved baseball but because BV schoolyard's cement surface was not conducive to the game, we became avid softball players. From April through September, there were always softball games going on in the schoolyard regularly. On Saturday and Sunday mornings, the older boys and men some of whom were in their twenties and thirties, would play as well. People from the neighborhood, both young and old, gathered to watch these games. Betting on the games was not uncommon.

CHAPTER FOUR

1953: Morris Avenue

In 1953, I was in real school, the first grade. Lessons every day in reading, writing, arithmetic, art, music, and of course, religion. One of our books, the blue and white Baltimore Catechism would be a staple throughout the rest of my grammar school. The cover never changed but the book kept getting thicker and thicker with more stuff to learn. Every edition started with the same questions:

> "Who made us?"
> Answer: "God made us."
> "Who is God?"
> Answer: "God is the Supreme Being who made all things...."
> "Where is God?"
> Answer: "God is everywhere."

Every day for homework, we had to memorize the answers to these catechism questions. Of course, we also had to memorize our prayers—*Our Father, Hail Mary, Glory Be to the Father...*, and *The Apostle's Creed*. My indoctrination into Roman Catholicism started early and stayed with me forever.

In addition to religion, our basic tasks in first grade were to learn the alphabet, how to spell simple words, and how to add and subtract simple numbers. I did not find any of this particularly difficult, but I was never careful in how I formed the letters of the alphabet. My lines were not straight; they were a bit squiggly. The same was true for numbers. So, while I knew what to do, my homework and class assignments were not pretty. Also, I was not good at coloring. I held the crayons too tightly and would almost gouge the paper and rarely stayed in the lines of the shapes and figures. It would take me a couple of years to learn to color properly and to appreciate a neat and pretty presentation.

The only time during my school life at OLP that I didn't have a nun was in first grade. At first, I loved Miss Cassidy because she was pretty, and I could see her reddish-brown hair. Then I really came to love her because she decided to tutor me so I could get rid of my awful stutter. I couldn't start a sentence with the letter "I" or say a word that began with a "W". "What" took at least nine or ten tries starting with "Wha…Wha…Wha…Wha…." And those letters weren't all the troublemakers. My brother Peter was merciless and made fun of me all the time. As a result, I was a very quiet little kid and never raised my hand in class, a behavior that stayed with me through most of my school years, even into high school. Miss Cassidy's decision to spend her lunch hours having me say tongue twisters, very slowly at first, and then faster and faster. My first tongue twister was

P-P-Peter P-P-Piper p-p-picked a p-p-peck of p-p-peppers.
A p-p-peck of p-p-peppers P-P--Peter P-P-Piper p-p-picked.
If P-P-Peter P-P-Piper p-p-picked a p-p-peck of p-p-peppers.
Then where are the p-p-peppers that P-P-Peter P-P-Piper p-p-picked.

We spent about two months together during lunch hours, working on my speech problem, and eventually, my stutter went away. I was able to say Peter Piper and other tongue twisters like everyone else. God bless Miss Cassidy for the time and care she took in her work and for the extra effort she put in for me. She changed my life.

I started the school year walking back and forth with my brother Peter, but I soon was doing it on my own. There was one street to cross, 151st Street. It had a traffic light and so it was easy to learn to "cross at the green." This opened up possibilities for me. I would explore a bit on my own, especially on Morris Avenue. Unlike on my block, cars went in both directions on Morris Avenue and it had two wide lanes. Large trucks could go up and down it with ease. Between 148th Street and 153rd Street, Morris Avenue was lined with bars, pharmacies, Italian delis, sandwich shops, pastry stores, butchers, vegetable stands, fish stores, and hardware stores. My favorites were the ones that had aromas. The delis that had dried cod fish (baccala) in the entrances, the bread and fish stores, the pastry shops, the coffee store that ground fresh beans, and the dairy stores (latticini) where they made fresh cheese (formaggio). I used to walk down sections of the avenue with my eyes closed and try to figure out where I was strictly by the smells. My favorite store was Almanti's Pastry Shop where the smells from freshly baked cakes, pastries, and cookies were incredible.

Before I started school, my mother took me on a walk on Morris Avenue everyday so she could buy fresh food for the dinner. She bought meat at the butcher, a vegetable or two, a fresh loaf of Italian bread, and occasionally, a dessert at Almanti's. My mother prided herself on baking; mostly, she made her own cakes and pies. Big Momma also baked and made Italian cakes. My mother knew all the storeowners. Many were older and friends of Big Momma who would give me a sample of their offerings such as an Italian cookie, a slice of fresh mozzarella that was still soaking in water, or a piece of fruit. Almanti's sold homemade Italian ices, but only in the summertime. Five cents for a small cup or one scoop; ten cents for a large cup or two scoops. There were only three flavors—lemon, chocolate, and spumoni. I always asked my mother to buy me a five-cent scoop of the lemon ice. She almost always did. At night, Morris Avenue was filled with lots of lights and bright signs especially at the entrances to the bars, taverns, and restaurants. There were three or four social clubs, places where the older men hung out, drank coffee, played cards, and drank harder stuff at night. The Hollows Club had once belonged to the Frog Hollow Boys and was the place where what was left of the South Bronx mob hung out. They gambled, took bets on horses, and ran numbers. The daily number would be called in there in the late afternoon, and every once in while you could hear a shout of joy reach the street when someone hit the number. The Hollows Club lingered on from a bygone, pre-World War II culture steeped in illegal activities and occasionally, in violence.

San Silverio

A spectacular display occurred once a year on Morris Avenue. It was in the feast of San Silverio, the patron saint of the people who lived on the island of Ponza off the west coast of Italy. The feast happened in June and lasted for about eight days depending on the day of the week that San Silverio's feast day, June 20th, occurred. About two weeks before the beginning of the feast, workers would start securing forty-foot high green and red poles on each side of Morris Avenue from 149th Street to 153rd Street. Then cables were attached across Morris Avenue from one pole to the other. I liked watching the workers string and test the large, multicolored lights across the cables. The lights were turned on a few days before the feast, building the anticipation to its start. Canvas-covered booths and wooden stands were assembled on the curbs along the length of Morris Avenue. The booths and stands sold Italian foods and souvenirs. Some offered simple games to win prizes like stuffed animals and dolls. On the afternoon before the feast began, trucks with rides on them arrived and parked between 150th and 151st Streets. The last bit of construction for the feast was a thirty-foot high stage built on the corner of 151st Street where the bands and singers performed. On the Saturday nights of the feast, arias from Italian opera and traditional Italian songs were sung until after midnight. Big crowds gathered around the stage and traffic had to be detoured around Morris Avenue from 149th to 153rd Streets. At the same time as the San Silverio Feast, OLP Church would have a bazaar. You might think that the events conflicted, but they didn't because the neighborhood was large, and the bazaar specialized in games of chance otherwise known as gambling, which were set up to raise money for the church. It was a modest operation and was held in the OLP schoolyard behind the grotto.

The feast was a bargain. Just about any ride, attraction, or food cost ten cents. You could buy three sweet Italian dough balls (zeppoli) for ten cents. A small Italian sausage sandwich cost ten cents. One turn on any of the rides cost ten cents. You would get to throw three darts at a backboard with different fruit shapes on it for ten cents. If you hit three of the same shape, you won a doll. You could toss three ping-pong balls onto a platform of bowls that had goldfish in them. If the ball landed in a bowl, you won the goldfish. One year, one of the vendors would make an artificial scar on any part of your body for a dime. I had to have one. I wanted it just above my eyelid, down the side of my face and curved under my lip. When I went home, and my mother saw my face with the scar, she held her chest and almost fainted. The feast also seemed to make all the grown-ups more generous. It was like Christmas in June. My mother, who never gave me more than ten cents a day, would give me a quarter to go to the feast. So did my father and uncles. My Uncle Johnny would take me with him to the feast. We walked the feast from 153rd to 149th Streets and buy this or try that, but we always ended up at the OLP bazaar betting dimes and quarters on the games of chance. My favorite was the big dice wheel where you bet on a number from one to six. My uncle would let me pick the number. I almost always picked "one." If the wheel stopped on your number, you won. Simple and straightforward. A religious procession through the streets took place on the Sunday afternoon after June 20th. It had brass bands, statues with money pinned to ribbons, banners, priests, and altar boys and lasted about two hours and signaled the end of the feast and the bazaar.

The San Silverio feast signaled the end of the school year and the beginning of a two-month summer vacation. At OLP, we went to school on the Monday after the feast, received our report cards and, assuming we passed everything, said goodbye to our teachers. The grades on our report cards ranged from 65 to 100 with 70 being passing. My grades were in the high 70s. On the back of the report card were letter grades for behavior such as "respect others," "listens to the teachers". I got "Bs."

Summer vacation for my family generally meant hanging around in the neighborhood, but once a year in August, my father took my brothers and me to spend an all-day Saturday at Coney Island. My father loved the subways and prided himself on knowing how to get anywhere in New York City underground or on the El (elevated train). The subway ride to Coney Island was 75 minutes or more. We left around 10:00 a.m. and got home at midnight. Our other two vacation trips were by Port Authority bus to visit Uncle Pat's family in Lodi, New Jersey, or to visit my Uncle Ralph's family in Hempstead, Long Island, by taking the Long Island Railroad. I spent the rest of the summer messing around in the backyard, playing softball, stickball, and other games in the BV's schoolyard, and getting a soaking under the johnny pump. What a great life!

CHAPTER FIVE

1954: Joey V to the Rescue

In 1954, I started 2nd Grade at OLP. Sister Mary Vincent was my teacher. My brother Donald used to say to my brother Peter and me,

"Be careful if your nun has a man's name!

"They're always the ones who like to hit the hell out of you!"

Was he ever right! I could tell by the first few days of September that Sister Mary Vincent had a distinct dislike for boys. She looked at you as if she wanted to catch you doing something wrong.

She was the first teacher I had who would hit us regularly either with a ruler or her open hand. On the other hand, she was very organized, determined teacher and pushed us to do a lot of reading and writing.

One day, something very sad happened to one of the girls in my class. Sally was a pretty, very quiet girl but had trouble keeping up with the daily work. When Sister Mary Vincent would call on her, she always had difficulty answering the questions. One afternoon early in October, Mother Superior (Mother Mary Phillip) visited our class. Whenever Mother Mary Phillip came into our classroom, we knew to stand up, make a bow, and say, "Good morning (or afternoon) Mother Mary Phillip!"

And God help us if our bow downs were not in unison. Mother Mary Phillip always pointed two fingers at you whenever she spoke to make sure you were listening because she was invariably delivering an instruction or order of one type or another. On this day, she motioned Sister Mary Vincent outside the classroom door and two of them spoke in low tones for about ten minutes. When they returned, Mother Superior spoke a few words with Sally, took her hand, and led her outside of class. Sally never came back. There were rumors among Sally's friends in the class about what had happened, but no one knew for sure. Days later, one of Sally's brothers told a couple of us that Mother Superior and Sister Mary Vincent thought it best that Sally leave our school and go to P.S. 31, a public school on the Grand Concourse. Since Sally lived on the upper end of 152nd Street above BV, we would see her occasionally, but rarely did she play or hang out with the girls in our class ever again. For some reason, I have never forgotten Sally and the day she mysteriously left school. As I grew older, I suspected that a bit of cruelty on the part of our principal and teacher had played into their decision not to help her but just sort of cast her off at such a young age. But such was the way that our school, and many other parochial schools, operated. They were parish, neighborhood schools where any Catholic child would be welcome to attend, but very little help was offered if you needed special attention. I had somehow escaped being cast aside, thanks to the dedication of Miss Cassidy in 1st Grade.

In late April of the school year, another event occurred that jaded my view of OLP and the nuns. My mother bought me a rather loud red and white zip-up jacket that she made me wear to school every day. One day after class ended, we were lined up in groups of two by two to leave the building. Louie, one of my classmates told me how ugly my jacket was. I told him that his jacket was ugly too. In a very orderly way, we walked side by side until we were outside the building. After the line broke on 151st Street, Louie and I continued gibing until I pulled his jacket over his head, gave him a shove, and he fell on the ground. Louie and I were trading punches when Louie's Cousin Larry, who was a little older, joined the fray and started beating up on me. Now I was on the ground with Louie and Larry on top punching and kicking me. I covered up as best I could and not really getting hurt when all of sudden, someone pulled Larry off me and gave him a punch in the face. Joey V, my friend Lena's brother, had thrown a punch that hit Larry square in the nose. It started to bleed profusely. Larry must have taken his jacket off earlier because he was wearing the OLP standard white dress shirt with his blue OLP tie, and blood from his nose was dripping all over his shirt and tie and it looked pretty bad. As soon as Larry ran home, I hit Louie in the head, kicked him in the ass, and he went running home too. Joey V looked at me and asked, "Why did you pick a fight with two guys at once?"

"I only picked a fight with Louie and then Larry jumped in," I replied.

Joey V laughed, gave me a shove in the head, and walked away.

The next morning, I noticed Louie was sporting a couple of Band-Aids on his face and he had a few small bruises. Louie and Larry's mothers showed up outside our classroom with Mother Superior. We all stood, bowed and said, "Good Morning Mother Mary Phillip!"

Then Mother Mary Phillip and Sister Mary Vincent left to have a chat outside the classroom. When Sister Mary Vincent came back in, she asked me to come to the front of the class. Without saying a word, she started to slap me in the face over and over again until she grabbed me by the hair and banged my head against the blackboard. I went back to my seat crying and hating Sister Mary Vincent, Mother Superior, and the entire school. When I got home at the end of the day, my mother saw a little lump on my head and asked me how I got it. I told her the whole story. She told me I probably deserved it and that the nuns at OLP were never wrong. I couldn't wait for the second grade to end that year. Dark blue and black are the only color jackets I would wear for the rest of my life.

The school year ended with all of us second graders receiving the sacraments of Penance, Holy Communion, and Confirmation. We spent days memorizing the prayers for each of the sacraments and practiced a procession around the church and up to the altar, where we received Holy Communion on one Saturday and Confirmation on the next. All the boys were dressed in blue suits and the girls, in white dresses and veils. It was quite a show for our parents and relatives. Skippy, my brother Donald's good friend, served as my godfather. As a gift, he bought me my first wristwatch, which I cherished all my life.

Before we could receive Holy Communion and Confirmation, we had to go to confession (sacrament of Penance) and confess our sins to a priest. This was a new experience that could be pleasant or not depending upon who was the priest hearing your confession. If the priest knew you or, as in my case, knew my mother, it was terrible. Even though the confessional was poorly lit, the priest could see who you were and would lecture you about sin and then give you a penance, which was to say some prayers upon leaving the confessional. The more sins the longer the penance. I especially hated it when the priest would say, "What would your mother think?" Going to confession every week was mandatory. Every Saturday, my mother would remind my brothers and me to go. Fortunately, my brother Peter told me always to go to Father Alexander who had been a missionary for thirty years in Asia and contracted a disease, which made it difficult for him to speak. He also had a problem hearing. Peter told me, "No matter what sins you confess, he gives the same penance—three *Hail Marys*—and never asks any questions." Actually, Peter's secret was well known. If you went to confession at the scheduled time on Saturday afternoon, there would be priests available in all four confessionals, but you could easily tell where to find Father Alexander. The other three priests would have one or two people waiting outside the confessional to receive absolution for their sins, but Father Alexander had about fifteen people on his line. As a seven-year-old, my sins typically were "I lied twice. I disobeyed my mother three times. I cursed ten times." Occasionally, I would also confess fighting with somebody. Regardless of what I confessed, Father Alexander always would say "For your penance, say three *Hail Marys* and make an act of contrition." The latter I was required to say before leaving the confessional.

"O my God, I am heartily sorry for having offended you, and I detest all my sins because of Your just punishments, but most of all because they offend You, my God, who are all-good and deserving of all my love. I firmly resolve, with the help of Your grace, to sin no more and to avoid the near occasion of sin. Amen."

After that, my sins were erased, and I was free to sin for another week.

When I got my report card at end of second grade, I had 70s in all my academic subjects and "Cs" and a couple of "Ds" for behavior.

That summer, my Uncle Tony bought a big, shiny black Chevrolet. It was the first car that anyone in 294 ever had owned. My brothers and I thought it was awesome. On the first Saturday night after he brought home his car, my uncle and Aunt Jean took my brothers and me to the rides at Rye Playland in Westchester County. We had never been there, but it was something like Coney Island. On top of the rides, the whole experience of driving someplace at night was a big deal. A couple of weeks later, my mother told me one morning, "Uncle Tony and Aunt Jean want to take you to Orchard Beach."

"What is an Orchard Beach?" I asked.

"It's a place to go swimming and play in the sand," she answered me.

I was dubious about this: "I don't know how to swim."

"Uncle Tony will teach you" she replied.

"What am I supposed to wear?" I asked.

"A bathing suit, what do you think?" she asked.

I knew something was up. "But I don't have a bathing suit!" I said.

"You have short pants," mother said.

"I hate short pants, and I won't wear them," I cried.

I did hate short pants and I hadn't worn the couple of pairs I had in years. My mother found a pair of my old short pants but thank God they didn't fit, and I couldn't zipper them up. I thought I was out of having to go to the beach. Instead she said, "Let's go to Alexander's [Department Store] and I'll buy you a bathing suit."

We went to Alexander's and she buys me this ugly yellow and green-striped bathing suit. My mother had an affinity for buying me terrible looking clothes. I don't think she paid more than fifty cents for it. But at least it fit.

That Saturday, I put on my ugly bathing suit and went to Orchard Beach with my uncle and aunt and I must admit: I loved it! Orchard Beach is a pretty bay that Robert Moses built on Long Island Sound in the Northeast Bronx. There were no waves and you could walk out for quite a bit before getting into deep water. My uncle had me swimming within an hour. Uncle Tony, Aunt Jean, and I sat on a blanket in the sand. We had hotdogs and soda for lunch and ice cream afterward. I thought this was heaven. We did this several more times that summer, and I got the feeling that I was the child that my uncle and aunt never had, and they thought it was heaven too.

CHAPTER SIX

1955: Friends

The new school year started well enough with our third-grade teacher, Sister Mary Genoveffa. We called her Sister Mary Genevieve because Genoveffa was hard to pronounce. She turned out to be a gem of a teacher. She was a bit older than my previous teachers were although it was hard to tell exactly as all the Franciscan nuns wore wimples that hid their hair completely. We used to have dumb discussions guessing what the various nuns' hair looked like—everything from being shaved and crew cuts to long tresses. Sister Mary Genevieve's face was slightly wrinkled, but I think it was her demeanor more than anything else that gave her an aura of aged wisdom. She was very calm and reassuring in everything we did. Most important, she never hit anyone. She also promised that if we were good in class from Monday through Thursday, we could have a party on Friday afternoons. This worked wonderfully and we had a party every Friday. To pay for the party, we were to bring a quarter to class on Thursday afternoon. This would buy us each a hotdog, bag of potato chips, and soda. I had to negotiate the quarter with my mother since she only gave me ten cents a day allowance. When I told her about the party, she decided I could use ten cents from my Thursday allowance, ten cents from Friday, and she would give me another nickel to make up the twenty-five cents. This was quite a deal since getting money out of my mother was never easy.

Up until second grade, my allowance was a nickel a day, which I would spend mostly on candy. When I reached third grade, my mother upped my allowance to a dime a day. During the fifteen-minute recesses in the mornings and afternoons, our teachers would sell cookies for a penny a piece and milk for a nickel. I never bought the milk but would buy a cookie if it was something I liked. I loved Fig Newtons. If I didn't spend my allowance in school, I would buy penny or nickel candy in Santo's or Fannie Red's delicatessen. Occasionally, my father and uncles would give me change, which I saved in a sealed brownish-yellow glass jar that had a slot on top for coins. I kept it on the bottom shelf of the white kitchen cabinet where my mother stored canned goods and other packaged foods. One day, I went to the cabinet to put a few pennies in my jar and there was no jar. I was pretty sure that my brother Peter took it.

I asked my mother if she knew what happened to my jar.

"I dropped a can on it and it broke," my mother said.

"Well, where is my money?" I asked.

"I bought you a new pair of shoes with it," she said and went into the spare room and came out holding a pair of ugly brown shoes with buckles.

"How could you do this? They have buckles and look like girl's shoes," I yelled.

She just looked at me with her head up in the air and didn't say a word. After all, she was my mother, and besides, she could do anything she wanted in her house. From that day on, I hardly saved any money and if I did, I hid it in different places and wouldn't tell anyone where it was, especially my mother.

As I said, Sister Mary Genevieve was a good teacher who cared and was sensitive to us eight-year-olds. On the first day of class, I had noticed that the yellow and black strip above the blackboard, which always displayed the letters of the alphabet, had changed. Instead of A, B, C, D… there was *A, B, C, D*…. Some of the letters were similar but some were very different with curves and loops such as *F, G,* and *L.* As it turned out, the major task for the fall semester was to learn to write in cursive, or as it was sometimes called, script. Sister Genevieve, who was very patient, worked with each of us individually to make sure we formed our letters correctly. I took to it right away and developed good penmanship. The big challenge, however, was to come in the spring when we would learn to write with a fountain pen. Ballpoint pens were not allowed in OLP, so Sister Mary Genevieve asked us each to bring a dollar to pay for a new fountain pen and a bottle of Waterman's *Washable Blue Ink.* When I came home from school that afternoon, I told my mother, "Mom, I need a dollar to buy a pen and a bottle of ink."

Looking at me with her head turned slightly to the side, she asked, "Why a dollar?"

"That's was what Sister Mary Genevieve said they cost," I replied.

My mother could never refuse any request from a nun, but I could understand her skepticism. Until then, I had never asked her for more than a quarter for anything. She made me swear to her that I needed it for a pen and ink before she gave it to me. And the next day, I bought my pen and ink from Sister Mary Genevieve.

Before we learned to write with a fountain pen, we had to learn how to fill it with ink. My pen was black with a silver-colored metal top that screwed off so you could put it on top of the pen as you wrote. It was very similar to the one that Sister Mary Genevieve used. To fill the pen with ink, you took off the metal top and then you unscrewed a little cap that gave you access to the narrow clear rubber ink holder. The ink holder had a metal pincer that looked like a miniature tweezer. When you put the point of the pen in the jar of ink, you pressed the pincer to cause a vacuum allowing the ink to flow up to the ink holder. There was a lot that could go wrong with the inkbottle and pen in our little fingers. You could put the tip of the pen too far into the bottle and the ink would get on the rest of the pen and drip off when you pulled it out of the bottle, or you could squeeze the pincer too hard or too long and the ink would overflow on its own. For the first couple of weeks, more than a few times a day, someone would have to run to the bathroom to get water to clean desks, books, or clothes. What a debacle! Almost all the boys had at least one ink mishap. The girls, for some reason, were more adept at filling their pens. My major disaster occurred when I caught the tip of my pen on the top of the open bottle of ink and it fell over. Most of the ink spilled on my desk and flowed down into my lap. The bottom of my shirt and the top of my pants were soaked with ink. When I got home, my mother had a fit that lasted until the washable part of the ink proved valuable. In the end, and thanks to Sister Mary Genevieve's patience, we survived learning how to use a fountain pen.

We had one other teacher in the third grade, Mrs. Gershon, who taught us music. She was part-time and came once a week to our school and taught our class for about 45 minutes. She was very enthusiastic about music and we learned, in the limited time we had, about notes, scales, and instruments but always saved the last five or ten minutes for singing. OLP had a portable organ, which the older boys would move from classroom to classroom as Mrs. Gershon made her rounds. Mrs. Gershon would play the organ with great gusto and lead us in the singing frequently by waving one of her hands for us to raise or lower our voices. The girls loved this part of the lesson, but we boys would be struggling not to laugh under our singing. Part of the problem was Mrs. Gerson's choice of songs. One of her favorites was *Barnacle Bill the Sailor*, which has a clean version and an X-rated version. The clean version went like this:

The girls would sing:

"Who's that knocking at my door?
Who's that knocking at my door?
Who's that knocking at my door?
Cried the fair young maiden."

Then the boys would reply:

"It's only me from over the sea
Said Barnacle Bill the Sailor
I'm all dressed up like a Christmas tree
Said Barnacle Bill the Sailor."

The dirty version of this song that made its way down to us even in the third grade went as follows:

Who's that knocking on my door? (sung three times)
Cried the fair young maiden
Well...open the door you little whore.
Said Barnacle Bill the Sailor (sung two times)
Shall we go to the dance? (sung three times)
Said the fair young maiden.
"Well...to hell with the dance and down with your pants."
Said Barnacle Bill the Sailor (sung two times).

A couple of the guys, not me of course, would sing the dirty version in a low voice that only the boys could hear. Mrs. Gershon couldn't hear the lines, but she could see us laughing and assumed we were just loving the song as she played the organ and waved her hand around with extra enthusiasm. Mrs. Gershon was very dedicated to her profession; it was too bad we only had her once a week.

In third grade, I came to realize that I would always be in the same grade and the same class with the same kids that had I started kindergarten with. We would be together Monday through Friday for ten months each year until we graduated from eighth grade. Chris, Joey Fuzz, Mickey, P.J., Dominick, Nino, Johnny, and I became buddies. We went to school; we played together and would hang out with each other well into our teenage years. But that year, something important happened. A new boy moved in next door to me in 300. He lived on the third floor and his apartment overlooked my backyard. His name was Giuseppe. When he told me he was from Italy, I asked him how he knew English. He explained that before coming to the United States, he lived for two years in Canada, where it was easier to get permission to come into the country. He became my best friend.

Giuseppe was a couple of years older than I was, but he ended up in the same class as I was in because the practice in OLP was to start all recent immigrants two years behind so they could learn English. Giuseppe could speak English, was smart, and had great social skills, but he was put two grades back anyway. In OLP, rules were rules and rarely were they broken even if it made more sense. Giuseppe and I spent almost every day (and night in the summers) of our lives from third through eighth grade together. We played games and sports, and dated girls together later in our teenage years. We never once had an argument or seriously disagreed with one another, and developed a bond that never was broken.

Then, there was J.R. He was my mother's friend's son and lived in 288. J.R. was one of the best athletes in our neighborhood. In softball, he could play shortstop as well as anybody and always got the clutch hit in a game. I played second base and later third base. I could hit okay but not great. Several older friends of my brother Peter coached us. His friend Joey, especially, spent a lot of time with us showing us the basics and some of the nuances of softball. These guys not only taught us how to play well, they also knew that sports were a way to keep us from other less desirable activities. In sum, they took great interest in us and kept us from getting into trouble. We used to play in the BV schoolyard and in the Yankee Stadium parking lot if the Yankees weren't playing that day. If the Yankees were home, we had to leave two hours before the game. The Yankee Stadium parking lot was a full block square with foul lines and bases painted on the smooth tar surface just for the use of the neighborhood kids. In the wintertime, the Yankee operations people put out several chain-linked goals so we could play hockey on roller skates.

One day J.R. was playing shortstop and I was playing third base on a Sunday morning, and our game was running late. We were in the field and J.R. says to me, "Look who's hanging on the fence watching us play ball"

I turned around and there was the catcher, Elston Howard with the pitcher, Ralph Terry, of the New York Yankees, no more than fifteen feet away watching us play softball. Once I saw them all I could think about was that if the ball was hit to me I had to make the play. They stayed watching us for about twenty minutes. I never had a ball hit to me while they were there, but it felt like an honor just to have them watch us. In addition to playing sports together, J.R. and I hung out especially when our parents got together.

Joey V was a different kind of friend. He hung out with an older crowd further up on Morris Avenue. He didn't play sports as much as the rest of us even though he was athletic. We always had "hellos" and "hiyas" for each other and he kidded me a lot in a fun sort of way. Our families were close, but I actually played more with his sister, Lena, than I did with him, but I could tell he liked me as if I was his younger brother or cousin. Several times he invited me to his grandfather's apartment in 300 where he had set up an electric train set complete with miniature houses, stations, and trees. And of course, there was the time when he saved me from Louie and Larry. Too bad, he wasn't around the next morning when Sister Mary Vincent beat the crap out of me.

By the time school ended in June, I could write in cursive with a fountain pen and sing dirty songs, and I understood the meaning of friendship. Quite a year! Most of the academic grades on my report card were in the 80s and my behavior grades were in the "Bs". My best grades so far in OLP.

CHAPTER SEVEN

1956: The Hub, The Grand Concourse, and City Entertainment

By 1956, big changes were happening on 152nd Street. 278, the largest apartment building on the block, was being rented to Puerto Ricans. Until then, 152nd Street was inhabited almost entirely by Italians. The Italians and Puerto Ricans lived most of the time in harmony, respecting each other's space but rarely integrated socially in any way.

Meanwhile, life went on within the confines of OLP. My fourth-grade teacher was Sister Mary Harold. We nicknamed her Sister Mary Horror. She must have occupied the cell next to Sister Mary Vincent in the convent. From the first day of class, I knew she didn't like me. She had this red face, as if she was always mad at something, and she wore thick wire glasses that gave her blue eyes a piercing stare. For me, it was escalated into a glare. It seemed I was targeted by Sister Mary Harold and couldn't do anything right. It was about this time that I realized that I had a hearing problem. I had trouble hearing anything Sister Mary Harold was saying, or anybody else for that matter. Sister Mary Harold was not much of a hitter although she would take a swing at one of the boys, including me, occasionally. Mostly, she gave out writing assignments starting with "I shall not..." and fill in the blank. Her standard punishments were twenty-five or fifty lines to be done as homework and due the next day. If you did something especially bad, it was one hundred lines. I was getting these twenty-five times punishments at least once or twice a week for not listening, not doing this, or not doing that.

It got to the point where I couldn't hear, and I didn't care. One afternoon just as school was let out, my friend Dominick and I broke out of our two-by-two line, and I decided to cut across the street but didn't see a car coming. When the driver had to jam on his brakes, the screech could be heard all up and down 151st Street. Sister Mary Harold came hurtling towards us, took hold of Dominick and me and dragged us back to our classroom. Following a sermon about our behavior, our punishment was to write 250 times: "I shall be more respectful of the rules of Our Lady Pity and not cut out of lines when leaving the school." It was a Friday, so I had a weekend to write the punishment. My brothers helped me, but my mother was really pissed.

The following week, I got into a shoving match with a kid from the other 4th Grade. Sister Mary Harold found out and made me stay after school. After yelling and screaming at me about my behavior for a while, she left the room and came back with Mother Superior. When they entered, I stood up, bowed and said, "Good afternoon, Mother Mary Phillip."

They had already decided on my punishment; they were sending me back to kindergarten for two weeks. It was embarrassing being in a class with a bunch of five-year-olds to say the least. My brothers teased me mercilessly during my stay in kindergarten. My mother was in a fit the whole time. Thank God, no one ever told my father. When I returned to 4th grade, I had to sit with the girls for the rest of the school year.

Sometime after the New Year, my mother figured out that maybe there was something going on with me that was causing my constant battles with Sister Mary Harold. She took me to see a Doctor Nigro, an ear specialist in Manhattan, to check out my hearing. He diagnosed blockages in my hearing canals that went deep into my middle ear. To clear them out, he put a small hose up my nose and started sucking air through it with a syphon. He had a bedpan underneath my chin and suddenly all kinds of disgusting green and yellow stuff was coming out of my nose. It felt like he blew my brains out, but I could hear again. Dr. Nigro told my mother that my tonsils and adenoids were causing the infections and mucous buildups that brought on my hearing problems and that they should be removed.

My operation was scheduled for the following month at the New York Eye and Ear Hospital. My mother and I took the Lexington Avenue Express subway to New York Eye and Ear located on 13th and 14th Streets in Lower Manhattan. The hospital was originally founded in 1820, and I was assigned a room in the old wing. Many people now know what it looks like since it was famously used in the movie, *The Godfather*, when Mafia Don Vito Corleone was in a hospital after being shot, and his son, Michael Corleone, protects him against gunmen who are trying to kill him.

There were three other patients in my room. An older man, Walter, in his 50s, who just had an eye operation, had a huge patch covering the right side of his face. There was a younger fellow, Freddie, who was in a car accident and hit his face on the dashboard; this was before seatbelts. He fractured his nose and cheekbones and had bandages covering much of the upper part of his face. The third fellow was Lenny who was about thirty years old and just had his tonsils taken out. He was crying and making all types of painful sounds. I looked at my mother and pleaded with my eyes. Did I really have to go through with this? Apart from my brother, Donald, no one in our family had ever been to a hospital. Even my mother had given birth to the three of us in our apartment at 294, attended by Big Momma and a midwife. But there was no stopping having my tonsils and adenoids being removed. I didn't sleep the first night in the hospital because of Lenny's moaning and groaning. The next day, I had the operation and when I came out of the anesthesia, it felt like I had razor blades in my throat. Every time I would swallow, I wanted to scream from the pain. I stayed in the hospital for five days to recover. Freddie was a comfort and would sit by me and make mostly a one-sided conversation because it hurt when I spoke. Walter was mostly quiet, although at night he would yell at Lenny to take the pain like a man and keep quiet. It was impossible for me to sleep because of the pain in my throat and Lenny. The only food I could eat was ice cream and Jello. After leaving the hospital, I had to stay at home another seven days and couldn't go to school. I missed more than two weeks of school during the fourth grade because of the tonsillectomy and was way behind in my work. Sister Mary Harold didn't bother with me much after I returned maybe she felt sorry for me.

On my report card that year, I did poorly. I got 70s in the academic subjects and "Cs" and a couple of "Ds" for behavior. Between the time I missed for my tonsils, the two weeks I spent in kindergarten, and the fact that I couldn't hear for much of the year, I was not surprised. My mother on the other hand, was quite upset with me and told me that I should be more like Donald and Peter. Donald was her favorite and could do no wrong. Peter was the smartest and aced every test he ever took.

Despite the trials at OLP caused somewhat by my hearing problem, my world continued to expand. During this year, I learned to walk to The Hub by myself. The Hub was located four blocks from my house; it started on 149th Street and extended to 157th Street along Third Avenue. The center of The Hub was a broad intersection where Third Avenue, Melrose Avenue, and 149th Street all met. The Third Avenue elevated train operated then from 149th Street to Gun Hill Road in the North Bronx. The Third Avenue "El," as it was known, used to operate throughout the eastside of Manhattan also, but the Manhattan portion was discontinued, and the tracks torn down in 1955. The Lexington Avenue and 7th Avenue IRT subway lines also had a major stop at 149th Street, and bus routes crisscrossed the intersection and avenues. It was like a mini Times Square with billboard signs and lights. In the intersection, there were three movie theaters: the RKO Royal that I mentioned earlier, Loews National, and Bronx. Up on 156th Street and Third Avenue, there was another movie theater, the Victory. Stores were either in the large intersection or along Third Avenue under the elevated train. There were major department stores including Alexanders and Hearns; three five and dime stores: Woolworth, McCrory, and Greens; and several national chain stores like Florsheim's and Flagg Brothers (men's shoes), Davega (sporting goods), and Bonds Clothes. I also went with my mother to The Hub as she shopped for whatever she needed. My treat at the end of a shopping trip was a mello-roll ice cream. You bought a cone for two cents, which was round on the bottom and square on top and a cylinder-shaped roll of ice cream that cost five cents. The ice cream came in a paper-covered strip that you had to peel off carefully before dropping it into the cone. The ice cream was very smooth and creamy, and it melted quickly. I always ended up with half of it on my face.

I liked going to The Hub whether it was with my mother, just walking with friends, or by myself. It was a colorful and wonderful chance to look at the window displays, mannequins, and merchandize. That year, I also started going to the movies there with my friends. On Saturday mornings, you could spend all day in a theater, watching two and sometimes three feature-length films, a serial, and ten cartoons, all for 15 to 25 cents.

As a toddler, my father had taken me on walks on Sunday mornings across a small bridge over the New York Central railroad yards on 153rd Street. He rarely said anything, but I liked holding his hand, crossing streets, and walking over the bridge and beyond. We would stop on the bridge and watch the trains go underneath us. There was also a major railroad maintenance facility underneath, which stretched to 149th Street South and 154th Street North. Black railroad ties, replacement rails, train wheels, and parts were stored in piles in the yard. The facility was a beehive of activity on Sundays because New York Central needed to do repairs on the weekend so as not to disrupt weekday train schedules. I loved to watch the specialized equipment. There were trains with cranes on them, flat cars to transport repair materials, and the big work locomotives that moved slowly and made a chugging noise. My father got a kick out of how I enjoyed watching the same scene every Sunday. I think he enjoyed the trains too. He told me several times how he almost got a job as a conductor on the subway. He regretted that he never got that job.

We frequently would continue walking over the bridge to the Grand Concourse. The Grand Concourse is one of the most beautiful boulevards in New York City, especially the section between 138th Street and 167th Street. It is wider than Park Avenue in Manhattan and in addition to beautiful apartment buildings with front courtyards; there were parks and a few interesting-looking public buildings. The Grand Concourse was designed in the 1890s and patterned after the Champs-Elysees in Paris. It opened to traffic in 1909. It was 180 feet across and had three roadways separated by two tree-lined lane dividers that in total could accommodate six lanes of cars. When completed, it extended all the way from 138th Street to 215th Street and Van Cortlandt Park. On 144th Street and the Concourse was P.S. 31, a magnificent three-story school built in the 1890s in the Gothic style and referred to as The Castle. My mother had attended P.S. 31 as a child. On 149th Street was the four-story Bronx Central Post Office that was built in the 1930s. Today, it's listed on the National Register of Historic Places and is a New York City Landmark. It has a large terrace with beautiful, life-sized sculptures by Henry Kreis and Charles Rudy, and an interior lined with murals entitled collectively as *Resources of America* and created by Ben Shahn and Bernarda Bryson Shahn in 1938. The sculptures and murals were funded by the federal government as part of the New Deal. Cardinal Hayes High School on 152nd Street, which was next to the post office, was built in a curved Art Deco Style and opened in 1941. Across from Hayes was the entrance to Franz Sigel Park named for a Civil War Union General. It extends to 158th Street as Thomas Wolfe described it in his bestseller, *Bonfire of the Vanities*:

> "On the 158th Street side the courthouse overlooked Franz Sigel Park, which from a sixth-floor window was a beautiful swath of English-style landscaping, a romance of trees, bushes, grass, and rock outcroppings that stretched down the south side of the hill."

As Wolfe noted, Franz Sigel Park ends on the south side of the Bronx County Courthouse, a nine-story structure built in the early 1930s of white limestone and marble. Looking up the hill from Jerome Avenue especially at night, when it was lit up, it reminded people of the Parthenon in Athens. And just north of the Court House is Joyce Kilmer Park, a smaller version of Franz Sigel Park. All these wonderful places would sometimes be included in my Sunday morning walks with my father.

As I grew older, a stretch of 161st Street from Jerome Avenue to Courtlandt Avenue was a place to go for a night walk with friends especially after a Yankee game. Back then, Yankee Stadium was on River Avenue and bordered 161st Street and Jerome Avenue. Walking west on 161st was the Earl, a small movie theater with a fifty cents admission that was a bit pricier than the movie houses in The Hub. Across the street from the Earl was Addie Vallins, possibly the best ice cream parlor in the Bronx. To impress a date, a movie at the Earl followed by an ice cream soda at Addie Vallins would normally do it. On the northeast corner of 161st Street and the Concourse was the Concourse Plaza Hotel. It housed Yankee players who lived out of town as well as players from the visiting teams during the baseball season. I was never an autograph hound, but some of my friends were, and all you had to do was hang outside the Concourse Plaza and just wait for Mickey Mantle, Billy Martin, Bill Skowron, or many of the other Yankee stars. Further down on 161st Street near Courtlandt Avenue were the Courtlandt Steakhouse and Alex & Henry's Italian Restaurant, both fine places to eat and frequented by the ball players. Alex & Henry's Restaurant eventually expanded to be one of the major catering houses in the Bronx, a popular place to have a wedding or some other major social event.

A very special place in the Bronx undoubtedly is the Bronx Zoo. It opened in 1899 and is the biggest metropolitan zoo in the United States, comprising 265 acres of parklands and habitats This wonder was a short subway ride away from 152nd Street, and although it had an international reputation and was a major stop for tourists, it was our zoo. Admission was free except on Tuesdays when it cost ten cents to see its entire collection of animals from every part of the globe. We would never go to the zoo on a Tuesday because of the admission price. So normally, a full day cost us thirty cents for the roundtrip subway ride. My father, Uncle Tony and Uncle Johnny took us there regularly. When I got a little older, my friends and I would just take the subway by ourselves to the zoo. Because of its size, we would hang out the whole day walking from one enclosure to another or from one animal house to another. In the 1950s, many of the animals were in cages so it was possible to get quite close to them. We would play this game to see how long we could keep eye contact with an animal. It especially was best with the big cats who would stare at you forever as if ready to pounce.

Finally, for kids growing up in the Bronx in the 1950s and 1960s were trips to Manhattan especially to the movie houses on Times Square that featured first-run movies that were not available any place else in the city. *The Ten Commandments, Lawrence of Arabia,* and *Dr. Zhivago* had exclusive runs in major Manhattan movie houses. In 1956, I remember my brother, Donald taking me to Radio City Music Hall to see a movie version of *The Lone Ranger* starring Clayton Moore. For many of us who faithfully watched the TV series, Mr. Moore was the one and only true masked man. While waiting for the movie to begin, the organist at Radio City kept playing the *William Tell Overture*, which was the Lone Ranger's TV theme song, and after the showing, Mr. Moore, dressed in character, made a personal appearance. Donald even took me to several rock and roll shows emceed by Alan Freed. These were followed by a dinner in a restaurant, which was special because as a family we rarely ate out.

As I got older, my friends and I picked up where Donald left off and we would take the train to Manhattan to see movies or go to Madison Square Garden to see the Knicks or the Rangers. The Garden was located in those days on

Eighth Avenue and 50th Street. Back then, by showing a school ID card, admission was only fifty cents.

There was so much to do on any given day or night in my universe, the furthest boundaries of which could be reached by subway.

CHAPTER EIGHT

1957: Altar Boys

In February of my year in the fifth grade, my brother Donald had a telephone installed in our apartment. This was the first telephone in 294, and since my uncles and aunts didn't have telephones in their apartments, they came upstairs to use our phone whenever they needed. This was a major change in the way we communicated with anyone who didn't live within walking distance, especially members of our extended family. Prior to the telephone installation, my mother would begin by writing a letter to a relative like someone in my father's family who lived in Brooklyn, Long Island, or New Jersey. In the letter, my mother would say she would call them on a specific day and time and if it was okay, they should write back to her. If it was okay, she would go to Fannie Red's Deli and place the call on a pay phone on the agreed upon day and time. If there was an emergency of some sort, our relatives knew to call Fannie Red's pay phone number. Thus did our families keep in touch, plan our holidays, and communicate any big events.

Sister Mary Christina was my fifth-grade teacher. She was about 4 feet, 10 inches tall, had a deep, deep voice, and could be pretty funny when she wanted to be. She had the map of Ireland on her face that beamed her good nature. She had one little quirk—she liked to hit the boys on the backside with a ruler. To her credit, she was an equal opportunity whacker and rarely hit one boy but instead would hit several of us at a time. Sometimes, all the boys in the class would have to line up, bend over her desk, and get a couple of whacks on the ass. There was one exception and that was my friend Nino. He was by far the biggest kid in the class and one of the nicest. He had a good heart but unfortunately looked like the head of a gang since in addition to his size he started shaving at the age of nine. He would get into trouble along with the rest of us, but he never was the cause of the problem. Sister Mary Christina, however, always believed he was the instigator and a terrible influence on the rest of us. So, while we would get in line for a paddling and we each received a couple of whacks, when it was Nino's turn, it was not unusual for Sister Mary Christina to dish out twice as many whacks, and on any part of his body, including his head. A couple of times, she even got a bigger ruler when it came Nino's turn. Given Sister Mary Christina's short stature and Nino's size, she never actually hurt him. Most of us thought it was a kind of funny scene watching this little nun hitting such a big guy. I couldn't look at my friend, Giuseppe because if I did, the two of us would just start laughing. Regardless of the "whacking on the ass" flaw in her character, Sister Mary Christina was a good teacher and I learned a lot. I especially liked the way she drew illustrations on the blackboard. She had a great talent for explaining things through pictures, sketches, and diagrams. Back then, you took the good with the bad—or else.

Sister Mary Christina was also in charge of the church altar boys. She would recruit the boys from her class by contacting their mothers. When God in the person of Sister Christina, called, my mother was ecstatic. This was a request she couldn't refuse, so I agreed to be an altar boy along with Giuseppe, Chris, Johnny, and several other friends in my class. Since an altar boy assists the priest during mass and other rites such as funerals, weddings, baptisms, and benedictions, learning a small amount of the church liturgy was required. The rituals themselves might have been easy enough to learn except for the fact that that all the prayers were said in Latin, which meant we had to memorize prayers in this "dead" language. And there we were in fifth grade, still learning English. This task took several months of practice during lunch time and after school. We were given a small manual to use in memorizing the prayers. Below are the opening prayers (first few minutes) of a mass. The priest (P) and the altar boy (A) only said the Latin. The English translation was included in hopes we might understand what was going on.

Priest (P): In nomine Patris, et Filii, et Spiritus Sancti. Amen.

P: In the Name of the Father, and of the Son, and of the Holy Spirit. Amen.

P: Introibo ad altare Dei.

P: I will go to the altar of God.

Altar Boy(A): Ad Deum qui laetificat juventutem meam.

A: To God, Who gives joy to my youth.

P: Judica me, Deus, et discerne causam meam de gente non sancta: ab homine iniquo et doloso erue me.

P: Do me justice, O God, and fight my fight against an unholy people, rescue me from the wicked and deceitful man.

A: Quia tu es, Deus, fortitudo mea: quare me repulisti, et quare tristis incedo, dum affligit me inimicus?

A: For Thou, O God, art my strength, why hast Thou forsaken me? And why do I go about in sadness, while the enemy afflicts me?

P: Gloria Patri, et Filio, et Spiritui Sancto.

P: Glory be to the Father, and to the Son, and to the Holy Spirit.

A: Sicut erat in principio, et nunc, et semper: et in saecula saeculorum. Amen.

A: As it was in the beginning is now, and ever shall be, world without end. Amen.

The opening prayers concluded with the priest and the altar boys reciting the Apostle's Creed together.

Confiteor Deo omnipotenti, beatae Mariae semper Virgini, beato Michaeli Archangelo, beato Joanni Baptistae, sanctis Apostolis Petro et Paulo, omnibus Sanctis, et vobis, fratres, quia peccavi nimis cogitatione verbo, et opere: mea culpa, mea culpa, mea maxima culpa. Ideo precor beatam Mariam semper Virginem, beatum Michaelem Archangelum, beatum Joannem Baptistam, sanctos Apostolos Petrum et Paulum, omnes Sanctos, et vos fratres, orare pro me ad Dominum Deum Nostrum.

I confess to Almighty God, to Blessed Mary ever Virgin, to Blessed Michael the Archangel, to Blessed John the Baptist, to the Holy Apostles Peter and Paul, to all the angels and saints, and to you, brethren, that I have sinned exceedingly in thought, word, deed: (here he strikes his breast three times) through my fault, through my fault, through my most grievous fault, and I ask Blessed Mary ever Virgin, Blessed

Michael the Archangel, Blessed John the Baptist, the Holy Apostles Peter and Paul, all the Angels and you, brethren, to pray to the Lord our God for me.

Throughout the mass there are several of these prayer sequences, some of which were complicated and some of which changed depending upon the type of mass or ritual. After several months of lessons and memorization, my friends and I survived the Latin initiation. We were supposed to say these prayers loud enough so the entire congregation could hear. Of course, only the priest understood what we were saying. It was easy to make mistakes. I made one during my first funeral mass with Father Ernest, the pastor of OLP, officiating. The deceased was in a casket in front of the altar and the grieving family and friends in the first few pews. The entire funeral ritual was sacred and sorrowful.

At the end of a regular mass, the priest utters the last prayers:

P: Ite, Missa est.

P: Go, the Mass is ended.

A: Deo gratias.

A: Thanks be to God.

However, at the end of a funeral mass the priest says:

"Requiescat in pace," which translates to "May he (or she) rest in peace."

The altar boy's response for this is supposed to be **"Amen"** or "So be it."

During this my first funeral, the following exchange took place. I forgot the change here and in response to Father Ernest's solemn

"Requiescat in pace" at the end of the mass, I said in a nice loud voice **"Deo Gratias,"** which translates into "Thanks be to God."

After the mass, Father Ernest took me aside and explained in a stern voice that saying "Deo gratias" at the end of a funeral was akin to saying thank God that the person died. I never made that mistake again, but there were would be other mistakes that just sort of happened on the altar.

In the evenings at OLP, there were benediction services that lasted about twenty minutes. These were mostly attended by the women of the parish like my grandmother and my mother. Each evening was devoted to a saint or religious figure such as Saint Francis, Saint Anthony, or the Blessed Mother. Hymns such as the *Tantum Ergo Sacramentum* (*Down in Adoration Falling*) and *O Salutaris* (*O Saving Victim*) were sung regularly, and with a great deal of enthusiasm and little understanding by the congregation. Each woman in the church was trying to sing louder than the one next to her. But on Wednesday evenings, the benediction was said in English, and it ended with a very devout hymn, *Goodnight Sweet Jesus*. I was serving this benediction with a new altar boy, Paul, who was getting his on-the-job training with me. Before the service, I explained to him that just before this hymn, he was to go inside the sacristy and in a certain sequence, start shutting off all of the lights in the church so that when the priest and congregation start singing *Goodnight, Sweet Jesus*, the lights would gradually go out and by the end of the hymn, only the candles would remain lit on the altar. It was a very touching end to the benediction. I went over the sequence of shutting the lights with Paul several times and he seemed to understand it. When the right moment came during the benediction, I motioned him to go inside the sacristy and begin shutting off the lights in the church while I started blessing the altar with incense. Everything started well enough but somehow Paul got confused, and he started putting some lights back on and shutting them off again so that it became a kind of light show with everybody in church wondering what was going on as they soldiered on singing good night to Jesus. Paul finally got all the lights out a few minutes after everyone finished singing. At the end of the benediction, Father Luke gave us a brief talking down and hit us on the head with the knots of poverty, chastity, and obedience that were tied on his cincture. Paul went on to be fine altar boy and later became an electrician for a New York television station.

One of the most solemn rites in the Roman Catholic Church is conducted during Holy Thursday Night Mass that commemorates the Last Supper of Christ. There are various blessings, including the washing of the feet of twelve men who represent the Apostles. Holy Thursday is also one of the longest services at OLP and typically would take two or more hours. Part of every traditional mass is the moving of the missal from one side of the altar to the other side. When the mass begins, the missal sits on the right side of the altar for the first reading. Then, just before the reading of the gospel, an altar boy moves the missal to the left side of the altar. At OLP, the daily missal was about three inches thick and sat on a light wooden bookstand. But for special solemn high masses where there were usually three priests and anywhere from four to six altar boys, the regular missal was replaced by a very elaborate one that was about seven inches thick and rested on a beautifully carved bronze bookstand. The thicker missal together with the bronze bookstand was significantly heavier and an altar boy had to be very careful not to let the missal and bronze stand tip because one could easily lose one's grip and fall. On one such Holy Thursday, during the solemn high mass with the church packed, one of the altar boys, Dino, who was somewhat thin, had the responsibility for moving the missal. Giuseppe, Jamey, Chris, and I were the other altar boys. At the appointed signal, which was a hand gesture from the priest celebrating the mass, Dino goes up the five stairs of the right side of the main altar, picks up the missal and proceeds down the steps. We could see that the missal and stand were shaking a bit, but Dino made it down the steps. Next, he had to come to the front of the altar and genuflect before proceeding up the steps on the left side of the altar to place the missal. Dino duly genuflected but never made it back up, sending the missal and the bronze bookstand crashing onto the lower part of the altar. Giuseppe, Jamey, and I immediately rushed over, helped him up, and got him going to the steps on the left side of the altar. Dino went up three steps and down he went again. This time, one of the priests, Father Emanuel helped him, took the missal and stand up the rest of the way and put it on the altar. This was bad enough but when Dino came down the steps, he gave Giuseppe, Jamey, and me this dopey look and whispered, "That fuckin missal weighs a ton." We started laughing. It took about ten minutes for us to regain our composure, but I couldn't look at Giuseppe because he was desperately trying to get me to laugh again. We all got a good talking to by Father Ernest and then again by Sister Mary Christina. The fact of the matter was that "that fuckin missal" was too heavy.

Besides getting in a good laugh now and then, there were other benefits to being an altar boy. For instance, if there was a funeral at 10:00 a.m. during the week, several of my friends and I would volunteer to serve it because we could get out of class. On weekends, we would offer to serve weddings and baptisms on Saturday or Sunday afternoons because the people would give us tips, usually one or two dollars for a service. We were supposed to give the tip money to Sister Mary Christina, but we generally pocketed about fifty percent of whatever we made and gave the other fifty percent to Sister Mary Christina. Onetime,

Manny, who was about thirty-five years old and still an altar boy squealed on us that we did not give her the full amount that we received from the tips. Normally a transgression such as this would result in some serious punishment, but to our surprise, Sister Mary Christina didn't get overly upset with us. She made us promise that we would always give her all our tips in the future and then let the whole episode drop. Manny, it seems, had plenty of other social problems. He was unmarried, lived with his mother, and was gay. In a 1950s Italian neighborhood, there was little tolerance for homosexuality and Manny was a social outcast. Maybe Sister was ahead of the curve or maybe not. I still am not sure.

In early March, Sister Mary Christina asked several of the altar boys including me if we could stay after class for a few minutes.

"Would any of you consider singing in the choir?"

The fact is that OLP had a fine choir, with two organists and about thirty singers. They sang masses, hymns, and carols in English, Italian, and Latin, but they were all females—older women and younger girls. There never had been any males in the choir as far back as any of us could remember. Sister Mary Christina explained, "Several of the other sisters and Father Charles thought it might be a good idea to include some male voices in the choir."

We were dumbfounded. The thought of a male singing in the choir never occurred to us. I looked over at Giuseppe and he shrugged as if to say, "Where did this come from?" But because we liked Sister Mary Christina, we decided to give it a try. She was delighted and told us Father Charles would get in touch with us. Father scheduled us for a meeting in the church balcony where the choir sang. There were eight of us there and Father explained, "I have this idea that having some male voices for the Easter Holy Week services in April would be a nice addition. I have several hymns in mind that you all have heard and probably know."

He was being very nice. Father sang the bars of several of the Easter hymns. Then he gave us a sheet with the music and words to *Christ the Lord is Risen Today*. I understood the words but knew nothing about the notes or music.

"Let's all sing it together as I play the melody on the organ," he suggested.

Most of us couldn't sing well and we surely didn't know anything about singing together. Within seconds, I was singing one line while Giuseppe was singing another line. Some of the others weren't singing at all. It was just a mess. Father, however, was very patient and said in a hopeful tone, "That was very good for a first time. You will learn to sing together with practice."

After several more tries, we didn't get much better, so Father Charles sang the hymn by himself. He explained how the "Alleluias" went from high to low and to high notes again. He demonstrated what he meant. He sang a couple of more sections of the hymn again. I thought, "I think we're getting this down" as Father demonstrated yet one more time. And just as he hit the high note, one of his front teeth popped out and flew about eight feet across the balcony. Hysteria ensued. Giuseppe and I took one look at each. We wanted out of there and we weren't going to be singing anytime soon for fear of losing our teeth as well. Father Charles explained with a little lisp because of his missing a tooth, "I have a cap that loosened while I sang. That is enough for the day. I have to go to the dentist."

Giuseppe and I never went back. Several altar boys did go back, and they sang in the choir at one of the major Easter services. They were never asked to sing in the choir again.

In May, Donald graduated Fordham University. My father, mother, Peter, and I went to the ceremony. My father and mother could not be prouder. This was a big deal. Donald was the first in our entire family to graduate college. As a graduation gift, my father bought Donald a new 1958 Oldsmobile Super 88. We were all amazed, especially my mother who said, "That is the most money your father ever spent at one time in his entire life." The Super 88 was a big black car that looked more like a tank with chrome on it. My brother kept it clean and shiny. We could now visit our relatives and go places beyond the public transportation system. Donald liked going to beaches in New Jersey or on Long Island. Most of the time, he went with his friends, but he took me along especially if there weren't any girls going with him. That summer of 1958, Donald said he would treat Peter and me for the July 4th weekend and take us to Wildwood, a beach town in southern New Jersey. We would drive down early on Friday morning and come back on Sunday. I could take one friend with me and because his father always took me to places, I asked J.R. to come with us. This was something special because I never went on a vacation unless it was to visit a relative, either my Uncle Ralph on Long Island or my father's Uncle Pat in New Jersey. The trip to Wildwood was almost four hours. I had never been so far from home. I was fascinated by the scenery along the Garden State Parkway. Once there, we stayed at the Baywood Gardens Motel on the main street of Wildwood. This was my first time in a motel. The room had two big beds for the four of us. Donald and Peter slept on one bed and J.R. and I slept on the other. On Friday, we had dinner at the Wildwood Diner, which was right next door to the Baywood Gardens, and we went to see the fireworks display on the boardwalk. On Saturday during the day, Donald, J.R., and I went to the beach. My brother Peter hated the sand on the beach, so he stayed at the motel sitting by the pool and did crossword puzzles. On Saturday night, Donald and Peter went to a couple of nightclubs to hear rock and roll bands and groups like The Platters. J.R. and I went to the boardwalk and thought it was pretty cool to be out on our own in a strange place. My brother Donald gave us each a few dollars and we spent it all going on rides and eating junk food. After breakfast at the Wildwood Diner on Sunday morning, Donald drove us home. J.R. and I thought this was the greatest weekend and we talked about it constantly all summer long. Sleeping in a motel, seeing fireworks, eating at a diner, lazing on a beach, and going on rides. This was the life.

I had had a good year in fifth grade and my report card in June reflected it. I had gotten high 80s and one 90 in mathematics. I got all "Bs" in behavior. I was looking forward to sixth grade. But the whole summer was stretching out in front of me.

The summers of the mid-1950s were heady days in our neighborhood. With the success of the book and movie, *Blackboard Jungle*, we took a kind of warped pride in Evan Hunter's depiction of the tough and sometimes violent life on Morris Avenue. Bill Haley's *Rock Around the Clock,* and other rock and roll songs were blaring from the jukeboxes. Santo retired and his deli was now Jerry and Maria's Deli. One of the smart things they did was to put in a jukebox right at the entrance to their store. For ten cents a song or three for a quarter that juke box was playing all night long with rock and roll music. The summer nights on 152nd Street had a special character that had evolved over decades. It was very hot and humid in the apartment buildings on our block and the air just sat there.

Nobody had an air-conditioner. In the evenings, our fathers and other men played pinochle in front of Fannie Red's Deli, and after each round, they played boss and underboss for nip (six ounce) bottles of beer. They played cards until 11:00 pm or so and usually put on a little buzz. Rarely did anybody get drunk. My father was quite a good card player. He counted cards and was able to guess what the other players had in their hands. He also had a temper. If his partner blew a hand, he would start yelling. His favorite putdown was calling his red-faced partner a "muttonhead." After a while, none of the men wanted to play pinochle with him. It was just too embarrassing. My mother and her friends would gather on our three-step stoop. There wasn't enough room for everyone on the stoop, so my mother kept a bunch of fold-up chairs in the inside hallway of our house. The women, usually about fifteen or more, would talk until about the same time as the men finished playing cards.

Meanwhile, we kids were all over the place. Nighttime was the time for games like hide and go seek. Dark alleyways, the areas under some of the larger stoops, and dimly lit hallways were great places to hide. Games could have as many as twenty kids and a round would last fifteen to twenty minutes or more. We also played "Nevada's Lump." It got its name when Joey Nevada tripped one night playing roundup tag, fell on his head, and ended up with a two-inch lump on his forehead. Our games ended when our mothers called us in around bedtime. It was very hot in our apartment, especially in the small cramped bedroom that my brothers and I shared with the votive candle. My friends who lived in the five-story apartment buildings sometimes slept on their roofs where there were little breezes. On the worst nights, my mother usually would set up a small cot in the spare room and one of us would sleep in there. On weekends, we also slept in the shed that my father built in the backyard. My brothers would sometimes invite their friends to sleep in the shed with us. We slept in our clothes, or if it was really hot, slept in our underwear providing a free show for some of the ladies in the apartments. As with most fun things, the summer went by too quickly.

CHAPTER NINE

1958: Urban Renewal

Another school year begins, and I was in Sister Mary Agnes' sixth grade class. At first, she reminded me of Sister Mary Genoveffa, who I had in third grade. She was a little older, quieter, and had a very calm disposition. She rarely hit anyone and was enthusiastic in her teaching, so I came to like her a lot, and the way she taught clicked with me. She liked to test us on a daily basis and would give us ten-question quizzes on the previous day's lessons and homework. This was an important turning point in my education because I figured out that it was important to understand what the teacher wanted on a test. I was regularly getting 90s and even 100s on these quizzes, which I proudly brought home. This was a breakthrough and a major relief to my mother because compared to my brothers, Donald and Peter, both of whom did very well in school, she had thought she had a dunce on her hands and prayed for me regularly.

While my school year couldn't be going better, things in the neighborhood had started falling apart. That year, all of the owners of the buildings across the street from us on 152nd received notices from the City of New York that they would have to move to make way for an urban renewal project. All the houses between 152nd and 153rd Streets would be demolished, except for those fronting Morris and Courtlandt Avenues. People who lived in the condemned buildings, both owners and renters, were devastated. Three-generation families very much like ours had lived in the same houses for decades. Very good friends of Big Momma, my mother, my uncles, my brothers, and me all had to move. This included the Pesces, who owned the brownstone directly across from us. The owner, Mary, was one of Big Momma's best friends, and had come from the same village in Italy. Her daughter, Rose, and my mother went to church together on a regular basis. They also went to Woodlawn Cemetery on all the holidays to visit the graves of their loved ones. My mother visited the grave of her father and Rose that of her husband Anthony, who had died young of a heart attack. As a youngster, while Rose and my mother tended to the graves doing a little weeding and planting flowers, Rose's daughter Marie and I would play in this very beautiful cemetery, perhaps one of the most beautiful in New York City. The Pesces moved to the North Bronx. Mary, the grandmother, died three months after they moved. Big Momma also had a cousin, Filomena, who lived across the street. They were close and looked exactly like each other, except that her cousin was blind and lived with her daughter, my mother's cousin, Millie Russo. When they moved to Connecticut, the goodbye scenes were heartfelt, and they were playing out repeatedly as the days arrived for friends and relatives across the street to move.

The abandonment of the buildings proceeded quickly among the smaller private houses and brownstones so that by the start of the summer of 1959, most of the residents had moved. What an eerie feeling as we took in the abandoned buildings across the street from where we lived. Fannie Red's Deli was gone leaving just an empty shuttered storefront in its place. Some of the residents who rented in the larger apartment houses had trouble finding new places to live. This was especially true of the elderly on fixed incomes, the poorer tenants, and those who didn't speak English. Finding apartments in other parts of the city for a rent they could afford and used to pay on 152nd Street wasn't easy. Those of us who lived across the street feared that we would be next and that the destruction of the Morris Avenue community was part of a bigger plan on the part of politicians at City Hall. My father always believed that it was Mayor Robert Wagner's plan to raze all the old ethnic neighborhoods and replace them with public housing. This seemed to be the case in the South Bronx and in areas like Brownsville, Bushwick, Bedford-Stuyvesant, Harlem, and the Lower East Side. At the time, Robert Moses was the undisputed czar of public works in New York City and was instrumental in securing funding for a number of massive renewal projects, most of which meant displacing residents from their neighborhoods. Public housing from 138th Street to 148th Street on Morris Avenue and from 153rd Street to 161st Street had already been completed. Our small enclave between

148th Street and 153rd was all that remained, and its time had come. The Bronx did not have a Jane Jacobs.

Jane Jacobs had a keen eye for urban "communities." She understood that the old, mostly ethnic neighborhoods with their small stores and social clubs provided important lifelines for people to enjoy, share, and be with each other. Just like ours, two and three generations of families formed the fabric of these neighborhoods. Jane strongly objected to urban renewal projects that only focused on building housing and apartments without considering small commercial enterprises and community places to bind them. She thought neighborhoods should be improved incrementally and not gutted and completely rebuilt. Jacobs was met with vigorous opposition but was able to prevail in a few battles with architects and urban planners. Her battle with Robert Moses over his plan for the Lower Manhattan Expressway (LOMEX), which would connect the Manhattan and Williamsburg Bridges to the Holland Tunnel, was legendary. It would have eradicated SoHo, parts of Chinatown and Little Italy, but the plan was ultimately nixed in 1962 due to widespread disapproval from the public, led in part by Jane Jacobs.

The pastor of OLP, Father Ernest, saw a bleak future for our parish. With the loss of parts of 152nd and 153rd Streets to urban renewal, there was an immediate decline in attendance at the masses. Father Ernest organized a visit to City Hall and several grades including mine were present, to lend moral support. Father made an impassioned plea to Mayor Wagner and the other elected officials to please spare our neighborhood from any further urban renewal projects. The hearing took most of the morning, but in the end, did no good.

In addition to the fear that our side of 152nd Street would be next; it was depressing to see what was happening to the vacated buildings across the street. Junkmen came and parked their trucks next to the buildings during the day, and stripped all the copper pipes, metal, and any other building materials that might have some value. The constant din of their sledgehammers reminded all of us that the end was near for 152nd Street. At night, the abandoned buildings became firetraps. Years later, in October 1977, the infamous phrase "the Bronx is burning" was coined as a fire in an abandoned building was shown several times during a television broadcast of the Yankee-Dodger World Series. The phrase came to represent the nadir of what had once been a great borough and place to live. On Morris Avenue, the burning had already taken place in 1959 and 1960 as one building after another was torched. 152nd Street was burning.

1959 was a sad year for our family. My grandmother on my father's side died suddenly. She was the first person in our family who died in my lifetime. And that year, Big Momma began forgetting things and was diagnosed with advanced dementia. She could no longer remember how to cook and even had difficulty remembering who we were. One time, she chased me out of our backyard. My mother had tears in her eyes as she explained to me what was happening to Big Momma. They were so close and had been through a lot together. Although she never said it, my mother patterned her life after Big Momma.

At the end of the school year, I got mostly 90s on my report card for my academic subjects and mostly "As" for behavior.

CHAPTER TEN

1959: Not a Very Good Year

S ister Mary Magdalena was my seventh-grade teacher. She was an older nun
and similar in temperament to Sister Mary Agnes and Sister Mary Genoveffa.
However, there was one big plus for me. Sister Mary Magdalena had my brother
Donald in class when he was in the fifth grade. She loved Donald and assumed
I would be just like him. I was determined not to let her down. She liked me. I
liked her. I consistently got high grades on tests so at the end of the year, I got
90s and "As" on my report card. But aside from my improving academic perfor-
mance, 1959 was not a very good year.

A truly unfortunate incident took place on 152nd Street on Halloween.
Good-natured egg fights between the older guys and younger kids were a Halloween tradition in our neighborhood. We would buy cartons of eggs and fill
socks with flour and the egg fight would begin sometime around 7:30 p.m. My
brother Peter and I were right in the middle of the action. We were allowed to
stay out late because the next day was All Saints, a holy day in the Catholic cal-
endar, and we were off from school. There would be about 25 to 30 participants
running up and down 152nd Street and into the BV schoolyard, with groups
chasing each other, hitting all parts of the body with flour-filled socks and throwing eggs at each other. The trick was to keep moving and not to be caught because
if you were, you would be covered with eggs smacked on your head, in your
clothes, and worst of all in your pants. During the melee of the chases, it was not
unusual for one or two eggs to go astray and hit windows or cars, but never was
anything broken. On this particular Halloween, a wayward egg hit a Puerto Rican
man from 278 as he was walking down the street with three friends. The egg

struck him on the side of his head and broke on the shoulder of his jacket. He was about twenty years old, maybe older. He stopped, looked around and went to where the older guys were standing near a side entrance to BV and asked, "Who threw the egg?"

It could have been anyone. Nobody really knew. He asked again: "Who threw the egg?"

One of the older fellows, Joey, tried to explain that they we were having this Halloween egg fight and no one meant to hit him. He was having none of it and persisted in asking who threw the egg. With no answer forthcoming, you could tell by the glare in his eyes that he was getting madder and madder. The best thing he could have done was walk away and accept the fact that a bunch of us had accidentally involved him in a silly Halloween tradition, but he couldn't. Whether it was a macho thing, common among a lot of young men regardless of their ethnicity or something else, he couldn't gracefully extricate himself from the situation. After a couple of more minutes of arguing, he took out a knife. The biggest mistake he could have made. Caesare and Billie, two of my brother Peter's friends, without a second hesitation, both punched him in the face. Joey V was there too. He hit him again and he went down. His three buddies struggled with a few of my brother's other friends, but they were greatly outnumbered and after a few more punches ran away down to the safety of their building. The Puerto Rican who was on the ground, was being punched and kicked into a bloody mess. After the punching and kicking stopped, Caesare buttoned up the Puerto Rican's jacket and hung him up by the back of it on the black wrought-iron fence that encircled BV. The Halloween egg fight was over, and we all ran home. Later on, police cars could be seen in front of 278. I don't know who took the fellow from the fence and or what condition he was in but the next day, the police walked up and down 152nd Street asking questions. No one admitted knowing anything. The rest of that year and into the following spring and summer, the Italians and Puerto Ricans were tense with each other like the Sharks and the Jets in *West Side Story*, but nothing else came of it.

In January 1960, the City of New York sent letters to all the owners of buildings between 151st Street and 152nd Street that they had to move to accommodate the urban renewal project. People were devastated all over again even though they knew it was coming. My mother cried, as did many of the others who had spent their entire lives on 152nd Street. The letter indicated that the owners had a year to clear their buildings and move on.

On February 12th, 1960, Big Momma died. She was eighty years old and the dementia and other physical ailments had taken their toll. Maybe it wasn't such a terrible thing because I don't think she could have lived anyplace else. She was the first person on my mother's side of the family to pass on since my grandfather died in 1942. Our entire house was in mourning. I cried like everyone else in our family, even my father and uncles who I had never seen cry before.

In the 1950s, it was customary for Italians to have a wake for three days and burial on the fourth day. My mother and uncles met with Joe Casario to handle the funeral arrangements to be held in Ribustello's Funeral Home between 153rd Street and 154th Street on Morris Avenue. Unbeknownst to anyone, Big Momma had made arrangements with one of the nuns at Our Lady of Pity, Sister Mary Eusebia, to be buried in a Franciscan habit, an unheard-of occurrence. Sister Mary Eusebia was responsible for decorating the altars in OLP and had developed a close relationship with Big Momma over the years because of the wonderful work she did on the church's altar cloths. So Big Momma was laid out in the nun's brown habit of the Third Order of Saint Francis of Assisi, complete with cincture, a large crucifix, and rosary beads draped around her neck. She did not have on a wimple and it was striking to see that at eighty years of age, her hair was completely brown. Not a single gray strand. For three days, she laid in the coffin at Ribustello's, and there was a constant stream of people, mostly of the older generation, many of whom I had never seen before. The crying among the women was non-stop and was a terrible burden for my mother. All the priests and all the nuns from OLP came to her wake. On the day of her funeral, OLP Church was filled as three priests said a solemn high funeral mass. Big Momma was where she wanted to be. After the mass, the funeral procession proceeded down Morris Avenue and up 152nd Street. It was a funeral for Big Momma, for the neighborhood, and for our entire way of life. Pasqualina was buried later that day in Woodlawn Cemetery next to her husband, Donato.

CHAPTER ELEVEN

1960: Goodbye, Our Lady of Pity

I n spring of 1960, my mother and father had started to look for a new place for us to live along with just about everyone else left on 152nd Street. My Uncle Johnny and Aunt Zina had property in Mastic Beach, Long Island, and moved there. My Uncle Tony and Aunt Jean moved to the North Bronx. Many of my friends were moving too. J.R. moved to Gun Hill Road in the North Bronx. Giuseppe moved to the Belmont section of the Bronx near Fordham Road. Others moved to the Morris Park area of the Bronx. Several families, including Joey V's, only moved a couple of blocks away to Courtlandt or Melrose Avenues. My parents looked at houses in Queens and the Soundview section of the Bronx but settled on a small attached house on 234th Street and Baychester Avenue in the North Bronx. There was a small garage for my brother Donald's car and a basement, which my father promptly finished, complete with light brown paneling and a bar. There was a stoop that led to the main or first floor, which had a foyer, a living room, a dining room, an eat-in kitchen, and a small bathroom. Upstairs was a large master bedroom that my brothers would share. My mother and father took the second largest bedroom for themselves. And I ended up with the smallest bedroom, but it was all mine and I did not have to share it with anybody. I couldn't have been happier. My mother also set up her altar with a dozen or more statues and votive candles, but praise the lord, she put it on top of the dresser in my brothers' bedroom. But the real joy of the new house was that there was a bathroom upstairs with a bathtub and shower located in it. For the first time in our lives, we could take a shower. Not only could we all take showers, we also had the privacy of a locked door. I still was not sure when my mother took her baths in 294, but she must have been thrilled now not to have to be sneaking around in the middle of the night to take them. A backyard capped off our new home but compared to the yard at our house on 152nd Street, it was small, and we made little use of it.

Unfortunately, during the move to our new house, we lost all our Christmas decorations and Donald's train sets. A moving company took care of our furniture, but we had moved all our personal belongings ourselves by making several trips in Donald's car. The last belongings that we had to move were a few items in our small storeroom in the basement of 294. We moved on a Wednesday and intended to go back on Saturday to pick up these. When we went back on Saturday, someone had broken into the basement and our storeroom, and stole everything that was in there. Some of the decorations were in our family for decades and although Donald did not say much, I am sure he was bothered to have lost his trains.

One big decision that came with the move was whether I should finish grammar school at OLP or go to a school near to our new home. There were two Catholic schools and a public school nearby, but we decided that I could learn the IRT subway and take the train to OLP for one more year. It was the absolute right decision even though it added about two and a half hours of traveling to my daily routine. There was a fifteen-minute walk to the 233rd Street train station, although I sometimes took the bus especially in bad weather. The bus had an infrequent schedule so I was better off walking whenever I could. The train ride from the 233rd Street Station to 149th Street—Third Avenue was lengthy and had seventeen stops. Within two days, I had memorized the sequence of stations:

233rd Street
225th Street
219th Street
Gun Hill Road
Burke Avenue
Allerton Avenue
Pelham Parkway
Bronx Park East

177th Street—West Farms

174th Street

Freeman Street

Simpson Street

Intervale Avenue

Prospect Avenue

Jackson Avenue

149th Street—Third Avenue

Later in life, I would come to learn that each of these stops represented some small community in the Bronx, which had their own cultures and histories, just like my own did on 152nd Street.

My ninth and final year at OLP started in September 1960. Thank heavens I had Sister Mary Magdalena again for my teacher in eighth grade. It must have been Big Momma's blessing on me. I just picked up where I left off in seventh grade and was doing well. I understood everything Sister Mary Magdalena said and was acing my tests.

As a result of my daily commuting, I did what I saw most other people doing on the subway and read. The train trip to school took about forty minutes and it was perfect for reading a chapter or two of a novel. I became a lover of pocketbooks and always had one in my book bag and only cost fifteen cents. My mother was feeling sorry for me because I had to travel on the subway every day, so she got generous with allowance and gave me a dollar a day. This paid for lunch and any other little things I wanted. I could eat at the OLP lunchroom for free, but if I did not like what they were serving, I could buy a hero sandwich for twenty-five or thirty-five cents at Colasacco's on Morris Avenue. I did not have to pay for the subway because school children received free monthly passes to ride back and forth to school. I read James Fenimore Cooper's *Leatherstocking Tales.* I loved Natty Bumppo, better known as Hawkeye. *Mutiny on the Bounty* by Charles Nordhoff and James Norman Hall was another good one. I even read Nathaniel Hawthorne and Charles Dickens. I was getting a first-rate second education provided on the IRT subway line.

Commuting to the eighth grade meant that my time with my friends was pretty much restricted to school and maybe an hour or so afterwards before I had to head back home. Several of my friends had taken jobs after school, mostly in the stores along Morris Avenue, so I found myself more often than not going directly home after school. Eventually, I made some more acquaintances in the new neighborhood by playing sports. Public School 87 on Bussing Avenue, about two blocks from my new home, had a community recreation program every Tuesday, Thursday, and Friday night from September through June. I enjoyed going there to play basketball. One of the directors, Bob Milani, was a fine athlete and taught small groups of us the finer points of basketball. Thanks to his instruction and guidance, I developed a good understanding of team play, hit the open man, and how to play defense. I also developed a decent jump shot (shoot the ball in a high arc) and good rebounding techniques (don't stand directly under the basket). Basketball was definitely the "in" sport in this neighborhood. Two of the Catholic grammar schools, St. Frances of Rome and the Nativity, had teams for the sixth, seventh, and eighth graders, and played in a North Bronx Catholic Youth League. As it turned out, many of the boys, who also came to play at the recreation center, played on these teams. Mr. Milani organized full court basketball games, and I enjoyed them as much as any other aspect of living in the North Bronx.

As the eighth grade at OLP moved along without incident, a big decision had to be made about high school. I wanted to go to school in what we now called "the old neighborhood" and attend the all-boys Cardinal Hayes High School on the Grand Concourse, just as my brothers had. To go to a Catholic high school, you had to take a "diocesan test" and rank-order the schools that your scores would be sent to. Most boys at OLP would rank Cardinal Hayes as their first choice and most of the girls selected Cathedral High School, an all-girls school. As we neared the date for taking the test, my teacher, Sister Mary Magdalena thought I should be considering a new high school that was just opening up in the North Bronx. Cardinal Spellman, named after the Archbishop of New York, was to be a high-scholarship school. She thought I would not only get a good education but be challenged academically. My mother liked the idea too mainly because I could walk to the new high school, which was located only about six blocks from where I lived. I took the test and was accepted to all the schools I ranked, including Cardinal Hayes and Cardinal Spellman. With a lot of pushing on the part of my mother and Sister Mary Magdalena, I agreed to go to Cardinal

Spellman. I was worried I made a big mistake but as it turned out, many of the boys from OLP didn't choose to go to Cardinal Hayes High School that year. Because of moving to new homes, the boys scattered themselves to Catholic and public schools around the Bronx including St. Helena's, All Hallows, Grace Dodge, and Dewitt Clinton. None of the boys went to BV.

Sometime during eighth grade, my friends and I started to realize that the girls in the class were not just classmates who wore dark blue OLP uniforms but that they were becoming women. Several even had breasts that protruded a bit under their clothing. Two in particular, Gina and Lana, were developing nice sets of bosoms. Gina was standoffish but Lana seemed to like the attention she was getting. She even flirted a bit and kept her blouse open just enough to offer glimpses of flesh. Out of the blue, one day in late May, several of us were invited by one of the girls into her home after school. We always had a shortened school day on Tuesdays because of religious instruction, which was every Tuesday so Catholic kids in the public schools could come to OLP to learn their catechism and prepare for Holy Communion and Confirmation. Kathy invited Rita, Lana, and three boys (Frankie, Dominick, and me) in to have soda and snacks. There was no one else in the apartment. This was an unusual set-up and had never happened before, at least not with me. The closest I had ever gotten to Lana was at one of the OLP Friday night dances. These were fun, simple affairs with music playing and light refreshments run by Father Urban and several of the nuns who took turns chaperoning us. My friends and I would go to these and hang out with the girls in our class. We danced with the girls, but if it was a slow dance, the nuns made sure there was daylight between the boy and girl. The popular admonition among the nuns was "make room for the Holy Ghost," as they placed their hands between us. There was this one girl, Lynn, whom I liked, and I think she liked me. She was different from most of the other girls in our class. For one thing, she lived on Courtlandt Avenue not Morris Avenue, and for another, she was the only Irish girl in our class. She was a strawberry blond, which was a rarity in our neighborhood. We would dance with each other and make small talk. Her mother took her to the dances and would take her home, so there was never any alone time for us.

Now getting back to Kathy, it seems she really had an interest in, if not the hots for, Frankie. After an hour or so of soda drinking and talking, we started playing spin the bottle, a harmless game that resulted in the boys giving the girls kisses on their cheeks. I had never played this game before, but I was all in. The game took a more interesting turn when Kathy invited Frankie into her bedroom after one of the spins. Kathy came out after a few minutes and said, "Why don't we play this game in separate rooms?" I was sitting next to Lana, and Dominick was with Rita. Things were getting warmer in the apartment. I suggested to Lana that we go to another room in the apartment. I think it was Kathy's older sister's room. We left Dominick and Rita alone on the living room couch. Lana and I sat on Kathy's sister's bed, looking at each other and trying to figure out where this was going to go. I started thinking about Lana's breasts, which were filling out her blue OLP uniform. I kissed her on the cheek and then again and then on her lips, and she did not stop me. To the contrary, she seemed to like it. I decided this was my chance, so I felt her breast. She froze a bit but again didn't stop me. I continued to caress her, and we continued to kiss. At one point, I opened her blouse and touched her bare skin and I got to see her nipples. We continued to kiss and touch. My first-ever make-out session flew by and before we knew it, there was a knock on the door. It was about 4:30 pm and Kathy said her mother was coming home soon. Frankie, Dominick, and I left exchanging stories and decided it had been a great afternoon, "Isn't this great," Frankie said, "A bunch of OLP altar boys feeling up the girls in the afternoon while the public-school kids are getting their religious instruction." We laughed and true to my altar-boy training, I said, "Deo Gratias!"

Frankie and Kathy started going out together in June. After graduation, Lana and her family moved away from Morris Avenue and I never saw her again.

In June 1961, I graduated from Our Lady of Pity School. I had received a good education especially in the basics of reading and arithmetic. I had some good teachers and some not so good teachers, but the last four years were fine, and I did well. I had friends that made living in the South Bronx special. These were friends who spent the last nine years with me, just about every day of our lives. We kept no secrets and we knew all about each other. During the summer, after graduation, I traveled down to Morris Avenue once a week or so to see these guys, but things just kept changing. Some moved never to come back and others had jobs that kept them busy. Several of my friends would get together at night, but because of where I lived, it was difficult for me to hang out in the evenings.

There was general disruption going on in the neighborhood with houses being torn down, while those still standing abandoned. I was ready for a new experience at a new school in September 1961 or so I thought.

CHAPTER TWELVE

1961: Cardinal Spellman

In September 1961, Cardinal Spellman High School was still under construction. The gym and several ancillary areas saw workmen finishing walls and installing electric, plumbing, and other building systems. Academically, Cardinal Spellman was aiming to establish itself as the top academic Catholic High School in New York City. The students were a mix of Catholics from mostly Irish, Italian, Polish, German, Puerto Rican, and Black backgrounds, who lived in the Bronx and Southern Westchester. Competition was encouraged since report cards provided students with not only their grades but also their ranking within the entire cohort of about 250 students. My academic subjects in the first year were religion, World History I, English, Latin I, algebra, and general science. Mercifully, we didn't have to read or memorize questions in the Baltimore Catechism, and since the gym was still being constructed, we didn't have physical education. The boys were taught primarily by the Christian Teaching Brothers of John Baptist de la Salle. The girls, by the Sisters of Charity. There were also some priests and lay teachers. Spellman was a modified coeducational school that meant both boys and girls were admitted but the two sexes did not take classes together and were kept in separate building wings except for lunch and library. Even in these two spaces, the nuns kept a watchful eye to make sure there was no intermingling. The brothers didn't care. That first year, my teachers were all Christian Teaching Brothers, with the exception of one lay English teacher, Mr. Dean, who was friendly enough but had trouble keeping control of our class. He was also a bit disorganized and went off on tangents within five to ten minutes of most classes, talking to us about all kinds of things, many of which had nothing to do with English. But he did love Charles Dickens and we spent a good part of the first semester reading and analyzing *Great Expectations*. Since I was becoming a regular reader of novels, this suited me just fine.

To my surprise, I enjoyed studying Latin. My teacher, Brother Peter, was very good and knew how to present complex sentence structures that included multiple declensions and conjugations in a well-organized way. In Latin, the subject comes first, then object(s) and finally the verb. For simple sentences, this is not too complicated but for complex sentences with multiple subjects, verbs and objects, deciphering the relationships and meaning can be confounding. Learning Latin provided me with insights into the English language, for vocabulary as well as grammar. For the second semester, our major project was to translate *Jason and the Argonauts* from Latin to English. Each day, our homework was to translate a passage or two. Then work on it in class the next day. I took to the challenge right away and loved getting to that moment when the meaning of a passage started to emerge from the Latin morass. The story was a great tale full of adventure and mythical challenges and Latin was no longer the "dead" language of the Catholic mass to me. I was also enjoying my science class with Brother John. I had never had science in OLP. I don't think any of us Catholic school kids were ever exposed to science in grammar school probably too dangerous and maybe beyond the ken of the nuns. Our science class was in a laboratory, with lots of hands-on activities.

The Christian Teaching Brothers were generally no-nonsense, organized, solid teachers who knew their subjects. I would find this to be the case throughout my four years at Cardinal Spellman. For whatever reason, many of them liked to give short quizzes rather than long, extended tests. I did well on these, having seen the test-taking light in Sister Agnes' class in sixth grade.

It was in my first year at Spellman when my father asked me if I wanted to work for a few hours on a couple of afternoons a week at his warehouse in Manhattan. In the mid-1950s, my father had become a manager, and his company moved him off the docks on the Hudson River to a warehouse on Eleventh Avenue. The nature of his work had also changed because his company was getting less and less merchandize through overseas shipping and more from manufacturers in the United States. Instead of large heavy wooden crates and tea chests arriving by ship, merchandize was being delivered by trucks in smaller cardboard cartons. My father's warehouse was a middleman operation, with large lots of cartons coming from American manufacturers that the warehouse shipped in smaller lots to department stores in the eastern half of the country. Both my brothers were working in Manhattan then, and Donald was driving the three of them to work in the mornings. So, I accepted my father's offer and worked off the books whenever he needed some additional help. He would give me ten dollars every time I came down to his warehouse. He somehow charged this to his company. After work, we all met at the warehouse and drove home together. At about this time, Bob Milani also asked me if I wanted to help him coach the sixth, seventh, and eighth graders for the Nativity Church school basketball team. The Nativity school was about a ten-minute walk from my house. I accepted. Bob did all the coaching and I worked with individual players. But despite my very full life attending Cardinal Spellman, working some afternoons with my father and doing volunteer coaching, something seemed wrong. I was missing my friends in the old neighborhood.

CHAPTER THIRTEEN

1962: Piecework and Schoolwork

During the summer of 1962, I essentially spent several days a week working with my father. It was boring work, but I made a few dollars and that allowed me a little financial independence. I was introduced to doing piecework that had been the bane of my mother and aunt's lives when they worked doing sewing in the 1920s in the sweatshops of the Bronx and Lower Manhattan. In my case, I was packaging merchandize in self-mailers. The company my father worked for had landed a lucrative contract with Sears & Roebuck, at the time one of the largest department stores in the country. It also had a big mail-order catalogue operation. To get the account, my father's company agreed to send all the merchandise in individual cartons that could easily be mailed by Sears & Roebuck to its customers ordering from the catalogue. So, if my father's company had an order to ship 100 brass plaques or glass figurines, they had to be wrapped individually or sometimes in sets, put in a small carton, taped, and stamped with a Sears & Roebuck inventory number. Someone had to package, tape, and stamp each of these. My father and I negotiated a rate of three cents per individually wrapped carton and one cent for stamping and shipping. I figured I could make $15 to $20 per day, so I did it. I would go in a couple of days a week and make enough money to do almost anything I wanted. I eventually negotiated different rates depending upon the type of merchandise. For instance, if I had to package more than one piece or a set of pieces into one larger individual carton, the rate was five or six cents per carton.

The most lucrative rate I got was for assembling bibles with brass or silver-plated covers, wrapping them into a decorative gift package, and putting them each into an individual carton. When my father approached me with the offer to do this job, I did a trial run and I thought I could do about 10–12 an hour, so we entered into a negotiation.

"OK, Dad, How about 30 cents per bible?"

"I have to ask one of the higher-ups," he said.

The next day he told me, "They'll pay only pay 22 cents a bible."

"Let's ask for 25 cents a bible," I said.

He came back later and said, "It's a deal."

I added, "Plus a penny for stamping and shipping each package."

He just looked at me with that stare and said some curse word in Italian under his breath that I didn't understand. In any case, after a little practice, I was assembling and packaging twelve bibles per hour at 26 cents per bible, which came to a little more than $3.00 per hour or $21.00 for a seven-hour day. Sometimes, I would work longer or only take a half-hour lunch and make closer to $30.00 for the day. Pretty good money for a fifteen-year old.

In September, I was happy when my sophomore year started. I had six subjects—religion, English, World History II, geometry, biology, and Latin II. I had Brother Peter again for Latin, and we spent the entire year translating Caesar's *Gallic Wars*. I liked it just as much as *Jason and the Argonauts*. Brother Basil, for English, had us read literature. I was fine with it and enjoyed learning how to analyze plot, character, and conflict. He gave me a new way of thinking about the novels I had learned to love on the subway. Brother Bernard had a Ph.D. in biology, and in addition to teaching us the basics, he would talk about research and opened new worlds to us. I had Father Collins for religion. He was very modern in his approach and we discussed social movements and civil rights issues, a big departure for this boy from 152nd Street.

The school year proceeded well, and I was kept busy with my school subjects, working, and in the winter, helping Bob Milani coach basketball again. In the spring, I joined the track team, mainly because I did not have to go to a team practice every afternoon. I was given a workout schedule that I could fit it into my own schedule, sometimes practicing in the early mornings and sometimes in the afternoon. I mainly ran relays and did shotput at meets. I did okay.

Occasionally on a Friday night or Saturday, I would go down to Morris Avenue to see my friends. The logistics of hanging out were difficult since guys were coming from all over the place, so we hung out in a deli on 154th Street or at a small pizza place on 150th Street, where they sold a slice for 15 cents. The idea of selling pizza by the slice had finally come to our neighborhood. A lot of our conversation revolved around what we were doing in school, sports, and girls. Most of us were working at part-time menial jobs to make a few dollars, so there were stories from work. A group of girls, most of whom went to OLP, started hanging out with us too, and several of my friends started dating the girls and were going "steady." I didn't.

On June 23, 1963, I got a call from my friend Jamey from OLP. He lived on 150th Street between Morris and Park Avenues. That block was still intact and hadn't been affected yet by urban renewal. He went to Grace Dodge High School and after school worked in a butcher shop on Morris Avenue. We had not seen each other in a while and after exchanging catch-up talk as to what we were doing, he came to the point.

"Several guys were talking about starting a club," he said.

"What kind of a club?" I asked.

"A social club."

I laughed and said, "Those are for the old guys!"

"No, no; listen, I spoke to Salvo and Dino, and there's a storefront vacant on Morris Avenue between 152nd and 153rd that's looking for a tenant. We need about 15–16 guys to make it work. We'd have to pay rent and fix the place up."

I asked, "How many guys have you got?"

"Ten for sure, mostly the guys who still live around here. I'm calling a few other guys who live further away," he said.

Without hesitating another minute, I said, "Count me in."

CHAPTER FOURTEEN

Summer 1963: Club 19

In July 1963, we had our new club that was called Club 19 because we had nineteen members. Most everybody that Jamey contacted wanted to be a member. In addition to those of us who attended OLP, six guys from 148th Street and Morris Avenue had started to hang out with us and joined the club. They all had attended St. Rita's School on College Avenue just off 145th Street and Morris Avenue. We all quickly became good, close friends who would do anything for each other.

Club 19 was situated in an ideal location midway between 152nd and 153rd Streets, on the east side of Morris Avenue. The club had two rooms. The front room with minor alterations would be the public place where we could have parties and other gatherings. The back room was for members and would be used for meetings and card playing. There was also one bathroom with a sink and a second sink in the back room. The walls and ceiling had old-fashioned tin covering which needed a good paint job. All in all, it was not in bad shape but needed sprucing up.

To join the club, each member had to pay twenty dollars upfront and monthly dues would be five dollars. The upfront money would be used for some renovations, buy furniture, and to establish a fund for repairs and emergencies. The monthly dues would cover exactly the rent, which was $100 per month. It was anticipated that we could generate additional income by putting in a juke box, charging admission to parties, and having raffles. Jamey was elected president of the Club 19 and Salvo elected treasurer. They did an excellent job of organizing everything.

The members spent the entire summer cleaning and painting the interior. We also put in softer lighting with the assistance of Nino's father who was a contractor. For the front room, we bought some attractive tables and chairs, a television, and a pool table. For the back room, we bought a table for playing cards, some chairs, and a sofa, which became the place to make out with a girl. Our hormones were in high gear, and increasingly, we were talking about picking up girls and doing this and doing that with the opposite gender. Several guys and girls from OLP also became main squeezes for each other. Later in the evenings and at night, you had to make sure to knock on the door to the backroom to avoid interrupting any romancing.

The club solved a lot of logistical problems for those of us who had to travel from other parts of the Bronx. We had a place to hang our clothes, to put our book bags, and to sit down to have something to eat. A couple of us even slept on the couch when it was too late to go home, or we had a bit too much to drink. Also, the discomfort of hanging out on a corner or in a deli was gone. This was our place and we could enjoy its comforts as we wished. We took turns cleaning it and set up crews who had responsibility for mopping and sweeping floors on a regular basis. For me, it was a godsend, and not only did I have a place that was a home away from home, but also had my friends again after a couple of years of living on Baychester Avenue. I would go down every Friday night, Saturday, and Sunday and spend much of my time at the club. I would even stop by after work occasionally during the week if I knew guys were going to be there.

CHAPTER FIFTEEN

1963: Working Papers

In July 1963, things were going along well. My friends and I were busy fixing up Club 19 on Morris Avenue. School was out and I was making a few dollars doing mostly piecework at my father's warehouse. My father came home from work one night and called me into the living room. I had not gone to work that day because there wasn't anything for me to do.

He said to me, "I was visited by an inspector from the Department of Labor and he was told there was a minor working here. I explained to him that you were my son and came in occasionally to help out. The inspector told me that because there was machinery in the warehouse, if you were to continue working, you had to get working papers from the Department of Health."

"Okay, Dad; I will go get working papers in the next day or so," I said.

We had no idea how the inspector found out about me. My father presumed someone in the warehouse must have said something about me working there. I looked up information on the New York Department of Labor in the Cardinal Spellman library and sure enough, if you were under eighteen and working in an environment with any type of "heavy or otherwise dangerous equipment," you had to have working papers. My father's warehouse had hydraulic equipment and carts for moving crates and cartons. There was also wiring and taping machines with sharp blades for sealing cartons. I looked into how to apply for working papers and found out I could go to the New York City Department of Health on 170th Street and Fulton Avenue, a short bus ride from Morris Avenue. The next day, I decided I would stop at the club, see what was going on, and then take a bus to the Department of Health. My friend P.J. said he would take a ride and keep me company. P.J. and I had been in OLP together. He was now going to Cardinal Hayes. He was a good friend but could fly off the handle easily. We walked up to Melrose Avenue and took the bus. It was a short twenty-minute ride. The Department of Health was a monstrous brick building that dominated the entire area, which was hard to do because there were other large apartment buildings and low-income housing projects in and around it.

P.J. and I went in and asked the guard about where to go to get working papers, and he directed us to a room on the 3rd Floor. We went into a large waiting area and there are about twelve or more young guys waiting to be examined. Most of the guys in the room were black or Puerto Rican. I went to the main desk, wrote my name on a waiting list, and gave it to a receptionist, who asked me to take a seat. After about forty-five minutes, I was called and was told I would have an interview and a physical examination, which would take about thirty minutes. P.J. could not come in with me and had to stay in the waiting room. In the examining room, I filled out an application and some other paperwork attesting to my health and then sat for the interview. I answered questions about the nature of the work I would be doing. I then was directed to another room where I had the physical examination. All of this was very routine. After the exam, I returned to the interviewer who stamped and approved my working paper application. I went back to the waiting area to find P.J. in an argument with four black guys, about what I had no idea. All I knew was that it was heated and P.J. was saying to one of the black guys, "I will see you outside!" We all go outside in a small open space, bigger than an alley, behind the Department of Health. Before you knew it, P.J. and I are trading punches with four black guys, which became about ten black guys. We were getting our asses kicked but delivering hits also. All I could keep thinking was not to end up on the ground because that is when you can really get hurt. You can get kicked in the head or the ribs and have some real damage done to your body. Two guards from the Department of Health came to where we were fighting and broke us up, but P.J. wanted to continue fighting. He cursed several times at the guy who was in the room with him and said, "Let's do it just you and me and I'll break your fucking ass!"

This started the melee all over again, with the two guards in the middle of it. By now, there was a crowd of about twenty or thirty people looking at us, the black guys, and the security guards in a scrum of fists. P.J. and I were bleeding, but so were several of the black guys. The security guards finally got P.J. and me back into the Department of Health and out of harm's way. However, we could not get out of the building as a crowd of about one hundred people, all black, was outside, waiting for us. One of the security guards must have called the police because a squad car with red lights and siren blaring came and two officers came inside and escorted P.J. and me to their car. At first, I thought we were being arrested because they asked us all kinds of questions and were writing everything down in a black book. In the meantime, the crowd outside was getting bigger.

One of the officers asked, "Where do you live?"

P.J. boastfully told them, "Morris Avenue and 152nd Street."

"We will take you home," one of the officers said.

As the patrol car edged past the crowd very slowly, we had our windows up even though it was a hot and humid July day. P.J. began rolling down his window getting ready to say something to the crowd, but I pulled him away and rolled his window up.

When we got within a few blocks from the club, I asked the officers, "Just drop us off here and we can walk the rest of the way."

I did not think it would be good for all of Morris Avenue seeing P.J. and me getting out of police squad car.

P.J. and I washed up in the club and bandaged our faces.

When I got home that night, my mother asked, "What happened to your face?"

"Nothing. Just a little scrap," I replied.

My father also asked me, "What happened?"

I told him, "I went for working papers at the Department of Health."

Later I told my brothers what happened, and they laughed like crazy.

CHAPTER SIXTEEN

August 1963: The Melfords

The summer was coming to an end, and we were planning a small party to open the club for ourselves and closest friends. By now, girlfriends and other girls from OLP hung out with us in the club. We already had had some small get-togethers where we had pizza and beer. We were planning a bigger event with decorations and liquor. We were developing a taste for booze. The party was going to be on the Saturday of the Labor Day Weekend. As we were making plans for this, an emergency meeting of all members was called by Jamey and Salvo. This was unusual because we never had an emergency before. Guys who were doing repairs, painting, or buying something would get together and decide what to do. Jamey or Salvo usually attended and kept us on track and within budget. Jamey explained to us at this meeting:

"Mr. Zangelli, the landlord who owns the building, has a problem with the lease. He wasn't being a bastard or anything, but he said the club had no legal standing and that if there was an insurance or other type of problem, Club 19 was just a name on the window and had no charter with which to operate."

Salvo added, "I looked into incorporating Club 19, but we would need a lawyer and it might could cost a couple of hundred dollars. The landlord did not want us to operate any kind of public activity until this was resolved. And the kicker was that if we did not comply, he would ask us to leave."

Salvo felt the landlord was doing the right thing, but it put us in a bit of bind.

About a week later, another emergency meeting was called to bring us up to date on the charter and lease issue. It seemed that one of Fuzz's uncles was a member years ago of a club called the Melfords. His uncle happened to still have the charter even though the Melfords hadn't existed for decades. Salvo checked the charter and determined that it could still be used and had never been rescinded or terminated. Jamey asked Salvo, "Would we be okay with using the Melfords' charter and changing the name of the club? It would save us a chunk of money and we would get the landlord off our backs."

We knew nothing about the Melfords. Fuzz said his uncle mentioned, "The name was a combination of Melrose Avenue and Fordham Road and that it was mostly a softball team."

That seemed a bit crazy because although Melrose Avenue was just two blocks from Morris Avenue, Fordham Road was a good thirty blocks away up in the central Bronx. It was possible that the Melfords existed closer to Fordham Road at some point. Regardless, Jamey asked for vote and we were all for it.

We had a charter. The landlord was happy. We changed the name on the window. We had our little end of summer party for ourselves, girlfriends, and a few people who helped us get the club in shape. There was a great spirit in the air at the party, and you could tell that everyone was very happy with what we accomplished that summer. The 1960's Melfords had arrived on Morris Avenue.

CHAPTER SEVENTEEN

September 1963:
Back to Cardinal Spellman

With the end of summer, I was not looking forward to the beginning of school. For the past two months, I had re-established myself back on Morris Avenue, but I understood the value of my education and approached it as positively as I could. My subjects that year would be English, Latin, Spanish, American History I, religion, and advanced algebra. I was put in an advanced Latin class, which meant we covered two years of work in one year. For the first semester, we translated Cicero and *The Trial of Catiline*. In the second semester, we did Virgil's *Aeneid*. Both proved to be challenging because we were translating four or five pages of Latin every night. Cicero's work was a bit dry, but I thoroughly enjoyed Virgil's story that connected the founding of Rome with Homer's epic, *The Iliad*.

In mathematics, I had Brother James Paul again. I had him for freshman and sophomore mathematics also. He was a first-rate teacher and could be funny teaching algebra, geometry, or any other type of mathematics. I liked him and learned well.

I had a choice in my junior year of taking chemistry or another language. I decided to pass on another science subject, which was probably a mistake, but I enjoyed Latin enough that I wanted to study another language. Our Spanish teacher, Mr. Conte, was excellent and was very animated in his teaching, and brought life to his subject. He also knew a cousin of my father, who sang in the chorus of the Metropolitan Opera. I never met this cousin Nicolino, but my father used to speak of him. My father liked opera and would play it on the radio. His brother, my Uncle James, was an opera buff who would speak of his cousin who sang in the chorus. My Uncle James' was a parkie at the Madison Square Park on 23rd Street and Madison Avenue in Manhattan. We used to visit him there occasionally especially around Christmas to see the tree he put up and decorated. Like my father, my uncle never graduated high school, but he knew opera as well as anyone. He had a good friend who was an usher at the Met who would let him in free. My uncle said he would stand in the back, or if he saw a vacant seat, he would sit down in the second act. He attended about 15–20 performances a season and knew the work of every major composer, conductor, and singer.

I had Brother Albert for religion. He was very formal, rarely smiled, and always addressed us as "gentlemen." Every Monday morning in class, he assumed all of us had gone to mass on Sunday and he would start by asking, "Gentlemen, what was the lesson of yesterday's gospel?"

Several of the students answered, and for forty-five minutes, we discussed the previous day's gospel. If no one raised their hands to answer, Brother Albert called on someone. My brothers and I were not going to church on a regular basis at this time of our lives, much to my mother's chagrin. On one occasion when none of the students volunteered an answer to his Monday morning question, Brother Arnold called on me. Rather than say I didn't know and admit I hadn't gone to church, I made up something and said, "The gospel was the parable about the mustard seed, Brother."

This was just a stab in the dark on my part because I had no idea what the gospel was. Brother Albert bent his head, looked at me over his eyeglasses, and corrected me that was not the previous day's gospel. He told the class what the gospel was and proceeded with the lesson. The following Monday, Brother Albert didn't not ask the class what the gospel was but instead called on me directly and asked, "What was yesterday's gospel?"

I said, "The gospel was the parable about the mustard seed, Brother."

Again, he corrected me. This scenario went on for about three weeks, with me always answering, "It was the parable about the mustard seed." Brother Albert eventually gave up, but he took me aside to tell me about the importance of spirituality in our lives and that as good Catholics we should be going to church. To be honest, I did not like this class and didn't care much about what was going on in it. If my brothers went to mass on Sunday, I would go with them. If not, I did not go either.

I spent my weekends on Morris Avenue with the Melfords. The big local news on the avenue in 1963 was that construction would soon begin on 152nd and 153rd Streets between Morris and Courtlandt Avenues, on a new public elementary school. The school would be Public School 1 and would have outdoor playing facilities for basketball and handball, and a large area for softball and touch football. P.S. 1 and the play facilities would take up all the area on the north side of 152nd Street vacated in 1958. In January 1964, Our Lady of Pity Church announced that its school would be phased out and would not be accepting any new students. This made economic sense because the parish population had decreased to 25 percent of what it once was prior to the urban renewal projects. As a result, there just were not enough students to sustain the school. There was even concern about whether there were enough parishioners to keep the church open.

CHAPTER EIGHTEEN

October 1963: Halloween

My daily schedule changed somewhat from the last year. I was going to school and working several afternoons with my father whenever he was busy and needed me. My father told me that his company was squeezing everything they could out of the warehouse operation and weren't hiring anyone new. He genuinely appreciated me coming to work with him. I also was still running track at Cardinal Spellman and again would work out on my own schedule. The track coach was Brother Peter who I had for Latin in my freshman and sophomore years and he had no problem with it. I would no longer be volunteering my time to be an assistant basketball coach with Bob Milani. Bob was offered a position coaching basketball at one of the Catholic high schools in Westchester County, north of the Bronx and could no longer coach at the Nativity School. I must say that Bob had an influence on my life. In addition to improving my basketball skills, he was also a role model for giving back to the community. Unfortunately, we did not keep contact and I never saw him again. However, I did like to play basketball and I would play sometimes with my friends on Morris Avenue. I noticed and so did everyone else that I was getting taller. I grew about five inches in two years and was taller than everyone else in my family, including my two brothers. My basketball game benefitted a lot from my added height. In addition to having a decent jump shot, I could jump vertically from a still position and touch the rim of the basketball hoop. Ten years later, in the 1970s, I was contacted and would coach the same team at Nativity that Bob Milani coached.

In early October, Jamey and Salvo called a meeting for anyone who wanted to attend about having in Halloween party at the club. The tradition of having egg fights had ended after the incident in 1959. In addition to having a good time, the purpose was to raise money for the club's expenses.

Salvo explained, "We are not in dire straits, but we have pretty much run through most of the upfront money that we initially contributed. It would be good to rebuild our reserves." Salvo added: "We could have a band, sell tickets and drinks and make a few bucks for the club."

It meant us doing some work in terms of cleaning the place up, renting or buying some chairs and small tables, buying liquor, and hiring a band. Several questions were asked and suggestions made. We ended up deciding to sell tickets for $5.00 each. Members would be free, and non-members would have to pay. We hoped that we would have about fifty people come and pay the $250 to cover all our expenses. All the money we would make by selling drinks would be a profit. We encouraged costumes and masks and advertised we would give a prize to the best costume. Halloween or October 31st was on a Thursday and we decided to have the party on Saturday, November 2nd. Jamey raised one more very important issue: "We need to make sure there are no fights or other disruptions at the party. The last thing we need is someone getting hurt or having to call the police should something happen."

He asked for volunteers who would act as "keepers of the peace" and if necessary bouncers should something get out of hand. He emphasized that the members should not contribute to any problems that might arise. Several of the guys including myself volunteered.

Halloween arrived and the party was on. We had a crowd of about 70–80 people, including the members and their guests. Chris, who was a Melford, played drums for a three-piece rock band, and they were excellent. They also kept much of Morris Avenue awake passed midnight. Sal, one of the policemen, who walked the beat on Morris Avenue, stopped by a couple of times and had no problem with what we were doing. We assured him that there were no drugs going on in our club. Later in the evening, he suggested we tone down the band. We developed a very good relationship with Sal. Jamey was smart to give him a key to the club that he could use anytime he wanted. When Sal had the late-night beat, he used our club to sit a bit. We never had a problem with him nor him with us. He was born and raised on 150th Street and Morris Avenue and basically knew we were not causing any major problems.

The costumes turned out to be fun and about half the crowd came dressed up. There were vampires, witches, and ghouls. Nino, the biggest guy in our class at OLP, came as a caveman, wearing a leopard-skin outfit that just about covered his balls. He hadn't shaved in a while and looked the part. He won first prize (a twenty-dollar gift certificate) for best costume. We sold liquor and drinks (rum and coke, seven and seven) for fifty cents and small bottles of beer for thirty-five cents. There was one brief skirmish, which was promptly attended to by Jamey's volunteers, and no one was hurt.

I was happy to see Joey V at the party. I had not seen him in quite a while. He and his family moved to an apartment on 153rd Street off Courtlandt Avenue when we all had to move out of 152nd Street.

I asked him, "How is your sister, Lena, and brother, Johnny Boy?"

"Lena is at Cathedral High School and Johnny Boy is working with my father," he replied.

His father owned a small contracting business.

I asked him, "Where are you hanging?"

"With guys further up on Courtlandt Avenue and 155th Street," he said.

I did not know them and thought it strange that he drifted away from any of the 152nd Street guys with whom we both grew up. I asked him, "Are you still in school or working?"

"I graduated Grace Dodge High School in June and am working with my dad, but I am joining the Army in January," he said.

I told him, "I was at Cardinal Spellman High School and working part-time with my father also."

We talked some more and wished each other well. I told him that if he does go into the Army, we should try to get together before he leaves.

As the evening came to an end, it seemed everyone had a good time; our first Melford party was a success and the club made about $100.00.

CHAPTER NINETEEN

November 1963: Civil Rights

For American History I, I had Father Collins, a diocesan priest who I had last year for religion. He knew his history; however, he added something to this class, which was most important. He discussed current events and especially the Civil Rights Movement. At least once a week, sometimes more, an entire period would focus on social justice issues. On November 7th, he brought in a recording of Martin Luther King. Jr.'s *I Have a Dream* speech that was delivered three months before on August 28, 1963, at the Lincoln Memorial before several hundred thousand black and white civil rights protesters. It was not very long, but the words and passion of Martin Luther King, Jr. stirred something for me that wasn't there before. Father Collins played the speech in its entirety. You could feel the spirituality of King's message through the record player.

> *I am happy to join with you today in what will go down in history as the greatest demonstration for freedom in the history of our nation.*
>
> *Five score years ago, a great American, in whose symbolic shadow we stand today, signed the Emancipation Proclamation. This momentous decree came as a great beacon light of hope to millions of Negro slaves who had been seared in the flames of withering injustice. It came as a joyous daybreak to end the long night of their captivity.*
>
> *But one hundred years later, the Negro still is not free. One hundred years later, the life of the Negro is still sadly crippled by the manacles of segregation and the chains of discrimination. One hundred years later, the Negro lives on a lonely island of poverty in the midst of a vast ocean of material prosperity. One hundred years later, the Negro is still languishing in the*

corners of American society and finds himself an exile in his own land. So we have come here today to dramatize a shameful condition.

...

We must forever conduct our struggle on the high plane of dignity and discipline. We must not allow our creative protest to degenerate into physical violence. Again and again we must rise to the majestic heights of meeting physical force with soul force.

...

Let us not wallow in the valley of despair.

I say to you today, my friends, so even though we face the difficulties of today and tomorrow, I still have a dream. It is a dream deeply rooted in the American dream.

I have a dream that one day this nation will rise up and live out the true meaning of its creed: "We hold these truths to be self-evident: that all men are created equal."

I have a dream that one day on the red hills of Georgia the sons of former slaves and the sons of former slave owners will be able to sit down together at the table of brotherhood.

I have a dream that one day even the state of Mississippi, a state sweltering with the heat of injustice, sweltering with the heat of oppression, will be transformed into an oasis of freedom and justice.

I have a dream that my four little children will one day live in a nation where they will not be judged by the color of their skin but by the content of their character.

I have a dream today.

I have a dream that one day, down in Alabama, with its vicious racists, with its governor having his lips dripping with the words of interposition and nullification; one day right there in Alabama, little black boys and black girls will be able to join hands with little white boys and white girls as sisters and brothers.

I have a dream today.

I have a dream that one day every valley shall be exalted, every hill and mountain shall be made low, the rough places will be made plain, and the crooked places will be made straight, and the glory of the Lord shall be revealed, and all flesh shall see it together.

...

And if America is to be a great nation this must become true. So let freedom ring from the prodigious hilltops of New Hampshire. Let freedom ring from the mighty mountains of New York. Let freedom ring from the heightening Alleghenies of Pennsylvania!

Let freedom ring from the snowcapped Rockies of Colorado!

Let freedom ring from the curvaceous slopes of California!

But not only that; let freedom ring from Stone Mountain of Georgia!

Let freedom ring from Lookout Mountain of Tennessee!

Let freedom ring from every hill and molehill of Mississippi. From every mountainside, let freedom ring.

And when this happens, when we allow freedom to ring, when we let it ring from every village and every hamlet, from every state and every city, we will be able to speed up that day when all of God's children, black men and white men, Jews and Gentiles, Protestants and Catholics, will be able to join hands and sing in the words of the old Negro spiritual, "Free at last! free at last! thank God Almighty, we are free at last!" (Martin Luther King, Jr., August 28, 1963)

Father Collins asked us specifically about certain lines:

"How do you feel about the words:

...the life of the Negro is still sadly crippled by the manacles of segregation and the chains of discrimination...

...I have a dream that one day this nation will rise up and live out the true meaning of its creed: "We hold these truths to be self-evident: that all men are created equal."

...when this happens, when we allow freedom to ring, when we let it ring from every village and every hamlet, from every state and every city, we will be able to speed up that day when all of God's children, black men and white men, Jews and Gentiles, Protestants and Catholics, will be able to join hands and sing in the words of the old Negro spiritual, "Free at last! free at last! thank God Almighty, we are free at last!"

As I listened to these lines, I must say that they had an effect on me. I thought very little about the issue of race and the plight of blacks in our country in the past. My attitudes evolved from my family, my friends, and others in the neighborhood. No one in my immediate family (father, mother, and brothers) ever engaged in any racial talk. Our next-door neighbors on Baychester Avenue were black. My father worked with blacks in his warehouse. Some of my friends from Morris Avenue would make racial comments once in a while, but I did not let any of it sink in. However, hearing Martin Luther King's passion and reverence for the gravity of racial discrimination and bigotry touched me. Our class was mostly white and while several students offered comments, no one said anything particularly stirring. I think they were all like me. The Civil Rights Movement meant very little to us and that it was mostly a southern issue. Father Collins repeated this exercise with other portions of Martin Luther King, Jr's speech and the responses were similar. Father Collins concluded his lesson with references to God, Christianity, and social justice. I had heard this part of the lesson last year in religion but somehow now after the *I Have a Dream* recording, something was different. I found myself questioning my values and more so my lack of awareness of the society around me. I would come to realize that this was a most important juncture in my education.

A couple of weeks later on a Friday, we had a half-day because the faculty in our school had a meeting and we were dismissed at 12:00 noon. I decided I would do my track team workout and then go downtown to work at my father's warehouse. I was doing wind sprints around the 440-yard track on the north side of the Cardinal Spellman campus with a couple of other track team members when an older man yelled something to us from the sidewalk about the president. This part of the campus was surrounded by a chain link fence about six feet high, and there was a fifteen yard-grass buffer between the sidewalk and the track. The man repeated what he had said again, but we could not make it out.

After my workout, I was heading back to the lockers to take a shower and had to go through the large gym. When I got into the gym, there were about 50 or 60 students in various gym and sports uniforms listening to a broadcast over the public address system. Everything was dead silent; no one was saying anything. I could not make out who the person was who was doing the broadcast. It sounded like there were several different people reporting. I whispered to one of the students what was going on and she said that President Kennedy had been shot. My first thought was that this must be a joke, but it wasn't. I joined the group in the gym and stayed listening to the PA system. A short time later, someone was reporting that it was confirmed that President Kennedy was dead.

The world changed that day and was never the same. For me, it was another awakening of the larger society around me. I stayed home much of that weekend, watching President Kennedy's funeral, the shooting of Lee Harvey Oswald, and listening to Walter Cronkite. I grew up that weekend trying to figure how our president could be killed and who was behind the assassination. My favorite classes this school year would be with Father Collins. I wanted to know more about the world, our society, and me.

CHAPTER TWENTY

December 1963: Reading and Basketball

Father Collins stirred in me a need to question a bit more what I had automatically been told by the elders around me—that essentially we lived in the greatest country and greatest city in the world. America was invincible after defeating the Germans and Japanese in World War II. We belonged to the one true church. The pope was infallible. We had the New York Yankees, the greatest team in any sport of all time. It was at about this time that my reading habits changed. I always had a book with me that I read on the subway that was a constant part of my life. I spent hours either traveling to Manhattan to work or to be with my friends on Morris Avenue. But instead of reading boy's adventure novels, I moved to reading books that made me think about a lot of things. In *To Kill a Mockingbird,* Harper Lee had me thinking about a small town in Alabama and Atticus Finch, a lawyer who defended a wrongly accused black man. In *Fahrenheit 451*, Ray Bradbury, created a future American society that burned books and attempted to control what people read, see and hear. *The Ugly American* by Eugene Burdick and William Lederer depicted the utter failure of American diplomacy in Southeast Asia. Rather than paying attention to the lives of starving people at the hands of corrupt local officials, America sent pompous and bungling bureaucrats who lived their lives going from one cocktail party to another.

It was also at this time that my brother Peter asked me if I wanted to play basketball with some of his friends. They would be playing at a gym at Morris High School on 166th Street. One of my brother's friends had an uncle who was the custodian at the school and for about thirty dollars a session he would let us use the gym. This meant we each had to contribute a few dollars to play. This gave me something else to do in the winter and came at a good time because I enjoyed basketball and wasn't playing as much as I used to. It was also important to me because it was another clue to me that I was growing up. My brother's friends were always the "big guys"—older, taller, stronger, better fielders, and better hitters. Some of my brother's friends were top-notch athletes but in their teen years, they had to work or wanted to work to make a few dollars, so they didn't convert their talents to getting college scholarships. I saw my brother asking me to play with them as a compliment but also that I was growing up. I was as tall or taller than any of my brother's friends and I could play basketball as well as any of them. It was an awakening for me that I was no longer a little kid. I enjoyed these basketball games and sometimes we played against other pickup teams in the Bronx or in Harlem. Invariably, the teams we played against were predominantly black, but the basketball was a high caliber and we never once had a racial problem of any sort. We surely played hard and banged bodies a lot under the boards and got into a scuffle occasionally but nothing serious. I continued playing with Peter and his friends for several years afterwards.

It was about this time that Peter also bought a portable television for his bedroom. This changed the dynamic within our family a bit. Rather than watching television with my mother and father, my brothers and I more likely watched it in their bedroom. We were not a family that watched a good deal of television. Except for the Mets, my father usually fell asleep watching the tube particularly if it was a weekday and he was tired from his job. My mother could take it or leave it and usually said her rosaries while sitting in the living room and did not pay attention to what was on the screen. *The Goldbergs,* one of her favorite shows back when we lived on 152nd Street, was no longer being aired. Apart from sports, my brothers and I did not have favorite shows. However, watching a Yankee game or a late-night Jack Paar or Johnny Carson show was something we enjoyed. Not only did the three of us watch television together, we also talked more about anything that came into heads. Peter would lay in his daybed, Donald would prop himself in his bed, and I would sit on the floor between them. Our conversations were all over the place, but some were such that we probably would not have had them with my mother saying her rosaries next to us.

The holidays were soon upon us and we were looking forward to celebrating. Our family was somewhat smaller now and only my Uncle Tony and Aunt Jean would come over for Christmas Eve and Christmas. My mother still cooked most of the traditional foods. She took great pride in her homemade sauces and soups, but pasta was now bought in an A&P and not made fresh. My brother Donald got the idea that we should put lights outside our house, which some of the neighbors were doing also. I don't know how many strings of lights he bought but there were at least several dozen. We were trying to have a Christmas tree pattern for the lights, and we had trouble synchronizing the blinkers. Regardless, Donald loved our light creation, and Peter and I loved it because Donald was having so much fun putting it all together.

CHAPTER TWENTY-ONE

January 1964: Brother Thomas

The New Year started well for me. We had a small party on New Year's Eve at the Melford's club for just members and girlfriends. I did not have a regular girlfriend but the girls who hung out with us were always invited to our private parties. We had drinks, food, and played the jukebox. Since we leased the jukebox from a small company and split a percentage of the monthly take, we could open it and play songs for free, which we did on rare occasions such as our private parties. A party was a fun time and it served to strengthen our bonds as the Melfords. A couple of us who lived away from Morris Avenue stayed overnight and slept in the club.

It was the end of the Fall 1963 semester and I did well on my report card and had my highest ranking (12th) ever while at Cardinal Spellman. I had good grades in all my subjects except religion. My English teacher, Brother Thomas, was an exceptional teacher who was able to get us most interested in world literature, which was the focus of our course. We had a thick world literature reader that provided substantive excerpts of classical works almost all of which were written by European authors. We read parts of Dante's *Inferno*, Sir Thomas Malory's *Le Morte D'Arthur*, Victor Hugo's *Les Miserables,* Cervantes' *Don Quixote*, and a host of other notable authors of the Western Canon. We also studied several plays by Shakespeare and Chekov. Brother Thomas was adept at teaching the subject matter and had a fine way of teaching us about symbolism and figuring out what the author was saying. To see the text through the author's eyes. It wasn't enough to read words and sentences but to figure out meaning of the plots and subplots. He would discuss the characters in depth and about what they represented. For a term project, we had to select and analyze one of the authors from the world literature reader and read an entire work not just an excerpt. Brother laid out a set of objectives that guided us. This was the first "term" paper I had ever written. I had written lots of other smaller compositions and essays but never something of this length. Selecting the author proved a bit difficult and I ended up reading Chekhov's play *The Seagull*. Remembering Brother Thomas' emphasis on symbolism, I wrote my paper on how the seagull in the title represented a few of the characters and not just the tragic and ill-fated Trigorin. Brother Thomas liked it, made a lot of encouraging comments on my paper, and gave me an "A." I was very proud of this and felt good about the school, writing, and what I was learning.

About a week later and about two days before the start of the Spring semester, Brother Thomas announced in the class. "I am sorry to have to tell you that I will be leaving Cardinal Spellman High School and will not be your teacher next semester," he said. We were in shock for several reasons. First, we never had teachers for just one semester but for the entire year. Second and more important, we liked Brother Thomas a lot and was relating well to everything he was teaching. I raised my hand, which for me was a rarity, and asked him point blank, "Why are you leaving us?"

For about fifteen minutes, he explained that he was having doubts about the faith and his calling as a religious brother. The class was mesmerized about everything he was saying in his confession about Catholicism. He said that he was leaving for a three-month retreat, which was required before a brother gave up his vows. I felt terrible, and on the last day of class for the semester, we wished him the best of luck. I thought about him a lot after that especially what he said about Catholicism. I had my own doubts about the faith, which would continue on and off for much of my life. Brother Thomas' departure was another one of life's lessons that seemed to be piling up in my teen years. Brother Thomas' decision would also prove to be a harbinger for others in the religious life. In the late 1960s and 1970s, a number of priests, brothers, and sisters would leave the religious calling. My classmates and I presumed that he went on to be a fine English teacher at some other school, but we never saw him again.

What could not be worse was that Brother Thomas's replacement was Brother Crispus. He was a nice enough teacher, but for the spring semester, he was going to emphasize grammar, vocabulary, and the semester project was a debate. Gone were literature and reading fiction. I don't know if this was the planned curriculum for the year or Brother's emphasis. We were all pissed. For a semester project, we were to partner with one other student and Brother would assign us a topic, which we had to develop and debate with another pair of students. I could not have hated anything more, but such was the agony and ecstasy of high school and life in general. It lifts you up and knocks you down. My debate partner Lenny and I were given a religious issue—the infallibility of the pope. Throughout many of our discussions and practice sessions, I thought of the character Trigorin's suicide in *The Seagull*.

CHAPTER TWENTY-TWO

February 1964: Joey V Joins the Army

On Saturday, February 8th, there was a small party for Joey V who was going into the Army the following Monday. The party was held in one of the small private rooms at Alex and Henry's Restaurant on Courtlandt Avenue. The party was organized by his brother Johnny Boy. There were Joey V's family and a few of the 152nd Street people, most of whom had moved. I spoke to Joey V and his sister Lena.

As I was speaking to them, I thought about us having grown up in the post-World War II/1950s era when there was relative peace. The Korean War had ended in 1953 and while the Cold War with the Soviet Union had heated up, American soldiers were not actively engaged in any serious fighting. However, there were rumblings in Southeast Asia. We had been hearing from President Dwight D. Eisenhower about the "Domino Theory"—that if one country falls to communism in the area, they all will eventually fall, laying the rationale for American involvement. President Lyndon Johnson was not John F. Kennedy and there was a certain unease about him. Unrest had been escalating in Vietnam, and there had been a few guerilla raids on American military bases and several soldiers killed. The previous August, the United States lost confidence in South Vietnam President Ngo Dinh Diem and backed a military coup to replace him. This did not do much to stem the unrest. If anything, it emboldened the aggression of the North Vietnamese.

As my brothers and I said our goodbyes to Joey V, he seemed confident that all would be well. He was hoping to be assigned overseas, maybe in Germany.

Little did I know that over the next couple of years, I would be attending a lot of these parties as my friends joined or were drafted to serve our country.

At about this time, a new bar opened up across the street from our club diagonally on the corner of Morris Avenue and 152nd Street. Dave's Bar was possibly the first commercial establishment owned by a black person on Morris Avenue between 148th Street and 153rd Street. However, it made sense given that the housing projects between 153rd Street and 159th Street had attracted a large black population. There had always been a black population on Courtlandt Avenue, which went back several generations to the post-World War I period, but rarely would they be involved with those of us on Morris Avenue. The housing projects changed that. One Friday evening, I was in the club with P.J., and he asked if I wanted to go for a drink. We generally did not drink liquor in the club unless there was an occasion or party. We did drink beer, which we bought at a local deli. But if we wanted a hard drink, we would go to one or two bars on the Avenue that would serve us. Most of us were underage but we had doctored up draft cards, which back then served as appropriate ID to get a drink. We could not go to the Step-In Tavern, which was just about forty feet away from the club because too many people knew us and knew we were underage. P.J. said he had been to Dave's Bar across street and that they would serve us. When we entered Dave's, there was a long, dark-wood bar on the left that stretched to the back wall. There were tables and chairs on the right side. P.J., and I sat at the bar where two black barmaids, Dotty and Carla, served the customers. Dotty was blond, and a very attractive older woman. Carla was younger and drop-dead gorgeous. She gave P.J. a big "Hello" and asked him how he was doing. P.J. introduced me to Carla, who asked us what we were having. I asked for scotch and water and P.J. had a rum and coke. I quickly realized as I scanned the room that P.J. and I were the only white people in the place. There was an older black man sitting at the end of the bar near the wall and after we had gotten our drinks, came over to us and introduced himself as Dave, the owner of the place. He already knew P.J.'s name and welcomed me. We had a brief but good discussion, but I could tell that he was very happy that a couple of white guys, even though we were underage from the neighborhood, would have a drink in his bar. After a couple of drinks, P.J. and I left and headed back to the club. I told him, "Dave seemed like a real nice guy."

"Dave was really cool and liked the fact we would come into his bar for a drink," P.J. responded.

P.J. also could not stop talking about how pretty Carla was. He and I and some of the other guys would end up going to Dave's on a regular basis. Without a doubt, P.J.'s main interest in going there was Carla.

Another major development in February was that we decided to do a renovation of the club. It seemed the club had built up a little nest egg from dues and parties, and so we asked Nino's father to assist with a number of changes like lowering and sound proofing the ceiling, putting in wood paneling on the walls, building a new bar, and buying new drapes for the windows. Nino's father directed us on how to do the work although he took responsibility for the new electric and plumbing parts of the job. We also negotiated for a new jukebox that could hold twice as many records as the previous one. After these renovations, the interior of the club became one of the social gems on Morris Avenue.

CHAPTER TWENTY-THREE

March 1964: Uptown Girls

J amey, the president of our club, and Matts, one of our members, were in their last year at Grace Dodge High School. They were dating girls from that school. Jamey was pretty much going out with Ellen and I had met her at the club. Matts was just dating one of Ellen's friends, Annette, but they were not serious from what I could tell. Ellen and Annette had this other friend, Joy, with whom they would have liked to go on a group date. Jamey asked me if I would be interested in going on a triple with him and Matts. My first question was "What does she look like?"

"She is a fine-looking girl and we will all have a good time," Jamey assured me.

I was dubious because I had never been on a blind date, but Jamey was a good guy who would not bullshit me just to get me to go.

I said, "OK."

The date was for the following Saturday night. The plan was for Jamey, Matts, and I to pick the girls up at Ellen's apartment. Ellen lived with her parents just off the Grand Concourse on 166th Street and Grant Avenue. The three of us took the Courtlandt Avenue bus to the Grand Concourse and walked a couple of short blocks to Grant Avenue. While we were walking, there were six guys on a corner and as we walked by, one of them said, "What are you doing in our neighborhood?"

Without hesitating for a minute, Matts replied, "We have dates with some girls down the block."

One of the guys said, "Why are you coming here to date our girls? They must really be ugly."

I said in a put-down tone, "Do you have some problem or do just like saying stupid things?"

Jamey was now pulling on me to just walk away, which would have been the smart thing to do but now Matts was also getting into dishing back and forth. It was clear the there was no peaceful solution. I kept quiet for a bit and just waited to see who was going to throw the first punch. Sure enough, one of the six threw a punch at Matts and a free-for-all started with fists flying. I am not sure if either side was winning. Next to where we were trading blows, there was a small Con Edison street construction going on, with these wooden police horses cordoning off the work area. I don't know where Matts got the strength, but he turns around and picks up one of the wooden horses completely over his head and crashes it down square on the head of one of the other guys. The guy who got hit went down and out. He banged his head on the sidewalk and was bleeding pretty badly. His friends looked at him then looked at us. The fight in them was gone. They picked their friend up and hustled away.

We wiped ourselves with our handkerchiefs as best we could. We cleaned off the scrapes on our faces with our own spit, combed our hair, zippered up our jackets, and went to Ellen's apartment to pick up our dates. The girls looked at us and Jamey did all the explaining. We ended taking them to the Earl Theater to see *Kissin' Cousins*, an Elvis Presley film, which I did not really like but the girls seemed to enjoy. We went to Addie Vallins afterward for ice cream sundaes. It was a pleasant evening for March, so we took a walk-through Joyce Kilmer Park. We sat for a while on a bench and talked about all kinds of things. We each dropped the girls off at their apartments; the three of us decided to meet up again and headed back to Morris Avenue.

Joy, the girl I was with, said, "I had a very nice time and I hope we could do it again."

"I had a good time too and I would like to see you," I replied.

We kissed a bit and I said, "I will be in touch."

Although we could have taken a bus, we decided to walk along the Grand Concourse past Joyce Kilmer Park and Franz Sigel Park. It was during our walk that Jamey says to Matts and me, "Guys, I am seriously thinking of joining the Air Force after I graduate high school in June."

I could not believe what he said and asked him, "Why?"

He said, "I am not going to college and I don't want to be a butcher, so I think I need to get away from Morris Avenue."

He added, "I also need to learn some useful well-paying skill and my guidance counselor at Grace Dodge suggested the Air Force or Navy might be a good way to go."

Matts and I looked at each other, and I think we both felt a bit empty. Jamey was someone with whom we had spent so much of our lives and whom we liked a lot, and he was saying "I will probably be leaving you guys maybe for good." He started our club and was its leader from the beginning. I was concerned over Jamey's plans but understood why he was making his decision.

The rest of the walk back to Morris Avenue was quiet and sober. Jamey continued to date Ellen. I don't think Matts dated Annette much afterward. By the summer, he was going steady with one of the girls from Morris Avenue. I never did call Joy and we never saw each other again.

CHAPTER TWENTY-FOUR

April 1964: Softball

Easter was early this year on March 29th. I liked this holiday for several reasons. First, it was the sign that warmer weather was coming. Second, my
mother would bake Easter cakes and pies that she never did at any other time of
the year. Even when Big Momma was alive, they had this ability to make you
start thinking weeks in advance about what they would cook or bake for the
holidays. Their secret was that they made these foods but once a year. Homemade
fettuccini with aglio e olio sauce on Christmas Eve, struffoli and honey on
Christmas Day, fatty bread on the Sunday before Lent, and homemade lasagna
on Mother's Day. When we lived on 152nd Street, we rarely went out to eat, and
pretty much every dinner was at home so what we ate was what my mother and
Big Momma prepared. There was nothing to complain about though because
between the two of them, our meals were genuine, fresh-made hearty Italian
fare. My mother continued the tradition of cooking special foods once a year all
her life. On Easter, she would make sweet Easter bread that we would have with
butter or olive oil. This could be eaten anytime of the day or night for breakfast,
lunch, or dinner. The pizza rustica or meat pie was a deep-dish pie made with
sausage, prosciutto, soppressata, mozzarella, and provolone. The piecrust was
very thick and covered the pizza rustica top and bottom. A slice of this was a
meal unto itself. Well into her 70s, my mother would have people ask her to make
them a pizza rustica for Easter. The third reason I liked Easter was that it was
always a week and a half off from school. Among Catholics, Holy Thursday and
Good Friday are to be observed as much as Easter, and schools such as Our Lady
of Pity and Cardinal Spellman started a spring recess on the Wednesday of Easter

Week and continued through the second Monday after Easter, a good eleven days off.

It was in late April that my brother Peter mentioned that his friends and the guys we were playing basketball with would probably start winding it down and they were forming a softball team that would continue to play at Morris High School on Saturdays and/or Sundays and maybe one or two nights a week. He asked if I was interested in playing with them. I said I'd like to think about it. It just so happened that a couple of days later, a group of the Melfords decided also that we should form a softball team. It was an easy decision for me to play with the Melfords rather than my brother's friends. We would play at the Yankee Stadium parking lot. We decided to buy ourselves softball shirts to wear at our games, but we needed to meet to decide colors and emblems. I thought this would be a twenty-minute meeting, but it went on for two hours. The colors were easy, and the shirts were to be a light blue with black lettering, but in terms of an emblem, we were all over the place. The word "Melford" did not have some specific meaning. Various animals such as tigers, eagles, and bears, were suggested, all of which were turned down. It was Salvo who asked a good question, "Well, who are we and what do we like to do?"

Giuseppe and P.J. said almost in unison, "We like to drink!"

Everybody laughed, but Salvo came back with, "Suppose we have a picture of a bum on our shirts!"

And that is exactly what we did. P.J. sketched a couple of figures and we ended up agreeing on an unshaven bum with a ratty top hat on his head, a bottle of booze in one hand, and holding on for dear life to an old-fashioned lamppost with the other hand. There were a few softball teams in the South Bronx including several Puerto Rican teams with whom we ended up playing a lot of games. Softball turned out to be another way of breaking down our ethnic differences. I would not say we became friends, but if we met some place on the Avenue, we could now say "Hi" and chat a bit. It was not likely that we would have a fight or racial incident with them, and we never did.

At the end of April, we had another party. Our club was beginning to get a reputation as a place to go for a good time. Live music, fun guys and girls, and inexpensive drinks.

CHAPTER TWENTY-FIVE

May 1964: Dave

P.J., Giuseppe, Nino, and I were at Dave's Bar on a Friday night in May of 1964 at around ten o'clock. We were sitting in what had become our usual seats at the bar and by the door. Dave was in his regular seat at the very end of the bar, with his back on the wall. The jukebox was playing, and people were dancing. We were putting on a little buzz from the booze. P.J. was flirting with Carla and she was smiling up a storm for him. I'm sure that P.J. thought this would be the night that he would get it on with her. We were laughing and teasing P.J. about it, and it was turning into a fun Friday night. All of sudden, we heard BANG from the back of the bar where Dave was sitting. Dave grabbed his shoulder, and someone was waving a gun. P.J., Giuseppe, Nino, and I decided to get out of there as quickly as possible and ran right out the door. It just so happened that Sal the cop was on the beat. He was only about fifteen feet from the entrance to Dave's with his gun in his hand, telling us to halt. We yelled at him that there was a guy in there shooting up the place. As it turned out, Dave was hit in the shoulder, but not seriously. The guy who shot Dave had had too much to drink and went on some kind of liquor-induced madness. Squad cars arrived and the police took the gunman away. Later, Sal the cop, told us that Dave wasn't going to press charges but told the guy with the gun never to come back. Sal also said that when he saw us running out of the bar, he thought that we had robbed the place until he recognized us.

Back at the club, Giuseppe said, "We were lucky! We could have been shot!"

"You're not kidding." I said. "Do you realize we were almost shot by Sal? Suppose he didn't recognize us right away?"

P.J. was pissed. "This was going to be my night with Carla."

Giuseppe said, "Yeah. Sure."

We were pretty shaken up. I kept thinking about this episode for weeks afterward. None of my friends ever carried guns. In fact, I had never seen or heard one go off. Why did the guy in Dave's Bar even have a gun?

In June, about half of the Melfords would be graduating high school. With Jamey telling us that he was joining the Air Force, a lot of talk at the club had already started on who was going to do what after graduation. Several guys were thinking about going to local colleges, either full-time or part-time, and were finishing up admissions paperwork. St. Johns, Fordham and City College were on their radar. One of the guys, Sammy, was already notified that he would be receiving a football scholarship and would be leaving for South Dakota. At least two Melfords, Georgie and Matts, would be applying for New York City uniform service positions in the police and fire departments. Manhattan offered lots of opportunities for jobs on Wall Street, in banking and other financial services. Several of the guys were thinking about that. There was also more talk about Vietnam and that the draft was going to be accelerating in the next year or so. It was becoming clear that some of the Melfords would be gone for quite a while. With a four-year commitment to the Air Force, surely Jamey wouldn't be coming back anytime soon. Sammy was going off to college for at least four years. There was a realization among us that Bob Dylan was right:

Come gather 'round people
And admit that the waters
Around you have grown
And accept it that soon
You'll be drenched to the bone
If your time to you is worth saving
Then you better start swimmin' or you'll sink like a stone
For the times they are a-changin' (Bob Dylan, *The Times They Are A Changin'*, 1964)

The times indeed were a changing, but they hadn't changed yet. The poles and lights for San Silverio's Feast were going up and there would be time for fun, music, and dancin' in the streets at least for a few more months.

CHAPTER TWENTY-SIX

June 1964: Father Collins

In June 1964, my brother Peter was the second in our family to graduate college. He followed in my brother Donald's footsteps. He worked at Manufacturers Hanover Trust Company during the day, went to Fordham University at night, majored in accounting, and was well on his way to a fine career in banking. Peter received a graduation gift of one hundred dollars in cash from my father but no car. It could have been that Peter was already making a decent salary and maybe my father felt he could buy his own car. Anyway, Peter didn't have a driver's license and didn't seem to be in a hurry to get one. Our family was proud that we now had two college graduates who were doing quite well. It seemed like one or the other was getting a promotion every other month. Donald was already the chief financial officer for his company and Peter was in charge of all the tellers in his bank. And once he graduated, Peter was transferred to a major branch on the ground floor of the Empire State Building on 34th Street. According to Peter, this was a big promotion and would open up lots of opportunities for him.

The San Silverio Feast started on June 13th and would end on Sunday, June 21st, one day after the saint's feast day on June 20th. People from all over were walking up and down Morris Avenue taking in the usual sights, sounds, and aromas of our Italian street festival. The Melford Club was right in the middle of it. We didn't run a booth or sell anything, but there was music emanating from our jukebox, so young people especially noticed who we were and hung around inside and outside of the club. We were fans of rock and roll, Motown, and rhythm and blues. The Beatles and Rolling Stones were in full swing and the Animals had just recorded *The House of the Rising Sun*, which became one of the favorites among the Melfords. However, the music that was most popular in our club before, during, after the Feast, and forever would be the songs of the Temptations, the Four Tops, the Drifters, Smokey Robinson and the Miracles. Guys were constantly arguing over which group was the best. In any case, for the two weekends of the 1964 San Silverio Feast, young people were dancing outside on the sidewalks of Morris Avenue in front of the Melford Club.

At Cardinal Spellman High School, I was getting ready for final exams and the New York State Regents. These tests were a long tradition in New York. The New York State Regents had established rigorous standards and used these tests to determine student achievement in many high school courses. They were also used to determine the quality of a high school program. It was optional for high school students to take them although it was very difficult to be accepted to a college without having passed them and received a "Regents Diploma." At Cardinal Spellman, we had no choice. We all took the Regents Tests. A few of them, especially the Latin and mathematics Regents, had reputations for being difficult so our teachers had tutoring sessions on them after school and in the evenings. The Cardinal Spellman administration and faculty were determined that we do well on these tests. The tests were administered during the week of June 22nd. Most of us at Spellman passed all the tests and in some cases, we aced them. I got 80s and a couple of 90s on them.

Our last day of school would be Tuesday, June 30th, when we would receive our final report cards for the year, but on Monday, June 29th, we would go to our regular classes and basically say good-by to our teachers. When we went to Father Collins' class in American History I, he greeted each of us and told us we did well on our final exams. Most of our teachers talked about the past year or asked what we might be doing for the summer. Not Father Collins, who instead asked us, "Have any of you read or been following the death of Andrew Goodman?" Several students knew that he was one of the three young men killed in Mississippi the previous week, but no one knew enough to offer anything in the way of a reply. Father went on to explain in some detail who Andrew Goodman was and the tragedy of his murder. He told us, "Andrew Goodman was born and raised in Manhattan. He was Jewish. He lived with his parents and went to Queens College of the City University of New York. While he was there, he joined the Congress on Racial Equality (CORE) and volunteered to take part in its

Freedom Summer campaign in the South. He was sent to Meridian, Mississippi, and on June 21, 1964, with two of his friends, James Chaney and Michael Schwerner, went to visit the Mt. Zion Methodist Church, that had been bombed by the Ku Klux Klan. On the way back to the CORE office, Deputy Sheriff Cecil Price arrested the three of them. Later that evening, they were released from the Neshoba jail only to be stopped again on a rural road where a white mob shot them to death."

Andrew Goodman's death bothered Father Collins greatly. He was emotional and angry as he explained to us, on this our last meeting of the year with him, about racism, bigotry, and the cruelty of Goodman's death. We sat quiet, listening, and didn't know what to say. No one had ever spoken to us the way Father Collins did or about the things that he did. When the bell rang ending our class period, he said, "Gentlemen, have a good summer!"

For weeks afterward, I followed the Andrew Goodman story on news broadcasts and in the newspapers. Although I watched TV news programs if I was home, I really had never paid close attention to them. I started to read the newspapers on a regular basis. There was a world out there beyond Cardinal Spellman High School and beyond Morris Avenue. I needed to know more.

CHAPTER TWENTY-SEVEN

July 1964: Jersey Girls

I was reading the newspapers and following the civil rights struggle in 1964, when on July 2nd President Lyndon Johnson signed the Civil Rights Act that prohibited discrimination in public places, provided for the integration of schools and other public facilities, and made employment discrimination illegal. The newspapers were praising it as the most sweeping civil rights legislation of the century. The Civil Rights Act had been proposed by President John F. Kennedy but had faced vehement opposition and filibusters on the part of the southern elected officials. President Johnson rightfully took the credit for working with or intimidating members of the Congress to get it passed. The newspapers described him as a giant, bully, and dealmaker. When you were in the Oval Office, you knew it, like it or not.

In early July, Salvo came up with the idea that we should get light windbreaker jackets. The guys were enjoying their Melford softball shirts and wore them all the time. A meeting was held that I couldn't make because I was working late but I was all for the idea. The decision was made that the windbreakers should complement the softball shirts, which were light blue with black lettering and had the bum for the logo. The windbreakers would be black with light blue lettering and have the bum for the logo. They were ordered and even though it was July, the guys wore their windbreakers. Several of us wearing the same black jackets walking down the avenue made quite an impression.

With the end of school, Jamey thought it would be a good idea to have a small party at the club for invited guests. Since several of the Melfords had graduated high school, it seemed a celebration was in order. Many of the members brought girlfriends. I didn't have a girlfriend and didn't invite anybody. Nino invited his three cousins, Dana, Jane, and Lisa, who lived in Monmouth, New Jersey. They were pretty and nice, and struck up conversations with some of the guys, me included. A week after the party, Nino told a few of us that we were invited to a party at Dana, Jane, and Lisa's house in New Jersey on Saturday, July 18th. It sounded like a fun idea, but we had to figure out transportation and a place to stay. Nino said that his cousins had offered us to stay at their house if we didn't mind sleeping on couches and maybe on the floor. They also said that their parents would be gone for the weekend.

On Saturday night, Nino, Giuseppe, Matts, Fuzz, Jamey, Chris, and I met at the club at 6:30 p.m., took the subway to the Port Authority, and caught a 7:30 p.m. bus for Monmouth. We had all agreed to wear our Melford jackets. We looked cool walking to Nino's cousins' house, a several blocks' walk from the bus top. When we got there, in addition to Nino's three cousins, there were six or seven of their girlfriends there and two guys who were brothers and family friends. The house was big, and the party was in a rec room that opened to a yard with an above-ground swimming pool. Music was playing and there was a table with snack food. We brought six packs of beer and we got right into the party mood. The girls wanted to know all about the Melfords from New York City. We inflated our lives on Morris Avenue. We danced, ate, told Bronx stories, and generally had a good time. By midnight, girls and guys were pairing off and I ended talking with Theresa, a pretty, thin blonde girl. She was going into her senior year of high school like me, but it was obvious she had been doing a lot more thinking about graduation and beyond than I had. She hoped to go away to college and the farther the better.

I asked her, "Why?"

"Monmouth is way too confining. Everybody knows everyone else's business. I want to experience a big city."

"How about New York?"

"New York is too big and too close to home. I am looking at colleges west of the Mississippi. What are your plans?" she asked.

"I haven't thought enough about it but I might go to college at night like my two older brothers," I said. Then I told her how they went to Fordham University and majored in accounting and how proud my parents were that they were the first people in our family to go to college.

"My father went to Rutgers University and was an engineer," she said. "And my parents definitely wanted me to go to college full-time and live on a campus. I'm not sure yet what I want to major in but I'm leaning towards becoming a teacher. I think I'd like working with people and children," she went on.

I must say, I had never spoken to a girl as confident about what she wanted to do as Theresa. And I was enjoying our conversation immensely. We moved our talking out of the house and onto a bench on the patio. She let me put my arm around her and we got closer. I didn't know whether I wanted to talk to her or kiss her. I gave her a kiss and she responded warmly.

She said, "Let's go for a walk."

We walked three blocks and ended up in a small, dimly lit park where we sat on bench.

She told me, "This was where a lot of kids in the neighborhood come to make out."

I could see figures on other benches. I couldn't tell if any of them were Melfords. We kissed and touched a bit. Theresa surely had done this before, and she touched and allowed me to touch her as our lips explored each other's mouths. It was about two o'clock when she said she had to go home. We walked and talked some more, and I told her, "I had a great time with you."

"The same here," she said, and I walked her to her door, kissed her and said, "Goodbye!"

I made my way back to Dana, Jane, and Lisa's house. There were two couples in the rec room and two on the patio. Nino saw me and asked, "How did it go with Theresa?"

"I had a great evening," I told him.

He told me that Jamey and Matts were in the living room. I went in and they were both asleep—one on the couch and the other on a chair. I sat in the other chair and fell asleep. We all woke up about nine o'clock in the morning. We went out on the patio and exchanged stories. Everybody had had a fine time. Dana brought us coffee, rolls, and donuts. We ate, thanked Dana, Jane, and Lisa for their hospitality and for the great party, and then headed for the bus stop. On the bus ride back to the Port Authority, in between a couple of nod-offs, I kept thinking about Theresa and what she was saying about college, where she wanted to go and what she wanted to do. I got home about three o'clock in the afternoon, exhausted. Sleeping in a chair in the living room was better than sleeping on the floor, but it wasn't restful. For the next several months, Giuseppe, Chris, and Fuzz went out to Monmouth and dated the three sisters regularly. I went with them a couple of times and saw Theresa again. We always would end up talking about college. It was obvious that her parents were helping her as to what to do. In my home, Donald and Peter provided all my guidance and when it came to college, it always came down to Fordham at night, majoring in accounting.

CHAPTER TWENTY-EIGHT

August 1964:
Jamey Leaves for the Air Force

With the enactment of the Civil Rights Act in July, there was a sense that America was finally beginning to address its race issues. President Johnson was being given credit by civil rights leaders, including Martin Luther King, Jr. and Roy Wilkins, for the passage of the legislation. Johnson was up for re-election and the Democrats were feeling heady. At the end of August, President Johnson easily won the Democratic nomination for president over a challenge by Alabama Governor George Wallace who was an avowed segregationist. Next, Johnson would face Arizona Senator Barry Goldwater, who had voted against the Civil Rights Act, as the Republican standard-bearer. Goldwater also appeared willing to use nuclear weapons in Vietnam while Johnson favored limited involvement in what at the time was being referred to as a "conflict."

For the Melfords, the summer of 1964 continued to provide lots of things to do. The softball season was in full swing, and the team had a couple of games a week. I was playing third base and hitting fine. Most important, the team was winning more than it was losing, which generated a good deal of spirit and camaraderie among us. We played most of our games next to Yankee Stadium and after each game, we would go back to the club for beer and sandwiches. Sometimes, we would invite the other team back to the club.

We didn't have any large parties planned for the summer because we didn't have air-conditioning. There was some talk about going out to Long Beach on Long Island for a weekend just to get away from the heat and humidity. Finally,

Fuzz, Mickey, Chris, Giuseppe, and I decided to do it and made plans on spending the weekend of August 1st, 2nd, and 3rd in Long Beach. None of us had cars, so we would have to take the Long Island Railroad. We left on Friday late in the afternoon. I had never gone there so I just followed the other guys. We grabbed a bite at Penn Station while waiting for our train and then chugged off on a seventy-minute train ride to Long Beach. Long Beach turned out to be a bungalow community with lots of small houses and cottages that people used mainly in the summer. There were no motels in sight and just a few motley-looking boarding houses. When we left the South Bronx, the sky had been clear and the sun hot, but when we got to Long Beach, it was mostly cloudy. We made our way to the beach and found a spot near a jetty that we thought would work out for a place to sleep. The beach itself is one of the nicer beaches on the south shore of Long Island, with a good deal of beachfront, long rolling waves and tides that were not particularly high or low. The problem was that at about ten o'clock, it started to rain lightly and got steadier and never let up. While we had brought our windbreakers, we were getting wet and feeling the cold. Just off the beach, there was a small school with a play yard that had little six-foot wide houses based on nursery songs such as *Itsy-Bitsy Spider* and *Mary Had a Little Lamb*. We jumped the fence and went into the nursery rhyme houses. It was a miserable night, with little sleep and lots of complaining. By Saturday morning, the weather was partly cloudy. There was a great little restaurant and bar with music called The Beach House, which was literally on the beach and we spent the day in and around it. The weather was warm enough to go swimming. Around five o'clock, it started raining again, and the five of us decided to get a room in a boarding house rather than spend another night in the nursery rhyme houses. It was going to be a tight fit in one room, with guys having to sleep on the floor, but there was a bathroom and shower, and we could at least get cleaned up. That night we went to The Beach House at about 7:30 p.m. and got a table. By 8:30 p.m., the place was packed, the music was blaring, and people were dancing. *The Twist* by Chubby Checker and *Do You Love Me* by the Contours brought everyone onto the dance floor. There was a novelty song called *The Martian Hop* by The Ran-Dells, which for some reason, was obnoxiously popular at The Beach House. We danced with a lot of different girls, but nothing clicked for any of us, so at midnight, we headed back to the boarding house and slept well. On Sunday, it was raining again, and we headed back to the Bronx late in the morning. Not a great weekend but some fun just hanging together.

But while we were messing around in Long Beach, North Vietnamese patrol torpedo boats attacked one of our destroyers, the USS Maddox, in international waters in the Gulf of Tonkin. Within five days, on August 7th, 1964, the U.S. Congress passed the Gulf of Tonkin Resolution authorizing President Lyndon Johnson to take all necessary measures to repel any armed attack against the forces of the United States and to prevent further aggression. The Resolution also stipulated that no prior approval or oversight of military force would be required by Congress. Within a year, President Johnson prepared orders that would result in drafting tens of thousands of young men into the military each month to fight in Vietnam. The Gulf of Tonkin Resolution would be the subject of much debate in subsequent months and years as the United States escalated its involvement in Vietnam.

On Sunday, August 16th, it was still sweltering and about ten of the Melfords planned a day trip to Glen Island Park, a beach area on Westchester County side of Long Island Sound. We all would bring girlfriends or dates with us for our trip to the beach. Glen Island is not an easy place to get to from the South Bronx. We met early on Sunday morning at the club, and our caravan up to Westchester County got underway. On Sunday morning, the subways were pretty much empty, and we all got seats and chatted our way up the Bronx on the IRT subway line. I invited a girl named Cindy who hung out at the club. I did not know her very well, but it was easy to talk with her. We discussed school and our mutual friends, all very nice and light for a summer day. When we got off at the last stop of the subway at 241st Street and White Plains Road, we walked about seven blocks through Mt. Vernon to a large circle where we could then take a forty-minute bus ride to Glen Island. This time, the day at the beach was everything that we hoped for. The sun was warm, we swam in Long Island Sound, our dates brought lunches, and all was fine. At about four o'clock in the afternoon, we decided to pack up and make the trip back to Morris Avenue. We caught our bus and made our way back to Mt. Vernon, and then walked to the IRT train station on 241st Street. On the walk back, several of us straggled a bit and stopped at a drug store to buy ice cream cones. By the time we came out of the drugstore and continued walking to the train station, we could no longer see several of the guys and girls who were ahead of us. As we got closer to the station, we could see that P.J. and a couple of our guys were face to face with about six fellas discussing something and whatever was going on didn't look good. The other fellas looked Italian. P.J. was yelling at one guy, and the guy was yelling back. Neither one was giving any ground. It seemed that one of these guys said something to one of our girls and P.J. just couldn't take that from anyone. Before you knew it, punches were flying back and forth, and one of their guys took out a knife and was waving it at us. Just then, a police car pulled up. P.J. and a couple of the guys from 241st Street ran away. A second police car arrived on the scene and four policemen began rounding us up. We had to face a wall of an apartment building and put our hands up so they could search us. None of us had anything that was a problem, so after giving us a talking down, they left. The girls were all shaken up but were beyond happy that the cops let us go. The only problem was that no one knew where P.J. was. He took off as soon as the police came, and we had not seen him since. Giuseppe and I decided to walk the area to find P.J., but he was nowhere to be found. After a long time, we walked back to our friends and decided nothing could be done but take the train back to the South Bronx and hope that P.J. would meet us down there. Actually, P.J. had already taken a train back and was waiting for us at the 238th Street Station where the cops couldn't find him. He was fine. We were all fine and went back to the club.

Just before the Labor Day weekend in late August, we had a small going-away party for Jamey. He had joined the Air Force and would be gone for at least four years. The party was not a joyful event but a somber "wish you well" affair. It wasn't even a party. Jamey was not just another Melford but someone who was a good guy and a good friend. It wasn't an accident that he was the president of our club; it reflected how we all felt about him. At one point in the evening, Jamey repeated some of what he said back in June to me and Matts. He was joining because he wanted to get away from Morris Avenue. He saw no future here and the Air Force seemed like a good alternative. Our little get-together ended about 11:00 p.m., which was kind of early. After the hugs and good wishes, I headed home. I decided to take the Webster Avenue bus with Giuseppe. It added about fifteen minutes to my trip, but I wanted to talk to him about Jamey. We got on the bus and sat in the last seats in the back, which was where we always sat.

"When do you think we might see Jamey again?" I asked.

"I don't know." Giuseppe responded.

"I don't think we'll ever see him again," I said.

"Do you think something will happen to him, like get killed or something?" he asked back.

"No, I don't think anything tragic like that'll happen. I just don't think he wants to come back. He wants to just leave here," I told Giuseppe.

"When I get drafted," Giuseppe said, "I want to go into the paratroopers."

"Why?" I asked.

Giuseppe went into a long explanation about the excitement of jumping out of a plane and floating in the sky. He was looking forward to it while I was concerned for him.

Jamey went on to make a career in the Air Force, got married, and raised a family in Oklahoma. I never did see him again.

CHAPTER TWENTY-NINE

September 1964: New Semester

In September 1964, I was in my senior year at Cardinal Spellman High School. My courses were religion, English, American History II, Spanish II, economics, typing, and driver education, an easy schedule. I was happy to have Father Collins as my teacher again in American history and Mr. Conte again in Spanish. My other teachers all seemed fine also. Brother Justice for religion, Brother Linus for English, Mr. Kent for economics, and Brother Kenneth for typing. Mr. Conte also was my driver education teacher. I took driver education because I had this idea about buying a used car when I graduated in June to make my trips down to Morris Avenue easier on me. The subway ride and walk took an hour and fifteen minutes while a car ride would be 25–30 minutes. I also wouldn't be at the mercy of the late-night subway schedule. My mother would also appreciate it if I got home earlier. She generally had trouble sleeping but especially if one of her sons was not at home.

Father Collins welcomed us back on the first day of classes, and he didn't miss a beat from where we left off in June. But instead of discussing civil rights, he started discussing Vietnam. After he described the textbook we would be using and the general periods we would be covering ending in the present day, he asked, "Have any of you been following the developments in Vietnam?"

Most of the class raised their hands.

"Have any of you read about the Gulf of Tonkin Resolution that was passed in Congress in August?"

About seven or eight students including me raised our hands. He had made copies of Section I of the Resolution and passed it out to us:

Section 1

Whereas naval units of the Communist regime in Vietnam, in violation of the principles of the Charter of the United Nations and of international law, have deliberately and repeatedly attacked United States naval vessels lawfully present in international waters, and have thereby created a serious threat to international peace; and

Whereas these attacks are part of a deliberate and systematic campaign of aggression that the Communist regime in North Vietnam has been waging against its neighbors and the nations joined with them in the collective defense of their freedom; and

Whereas the United States is assisting the peoples of southeast Asia to protect their freedom and has no territorial, military or political ambitions in that area, but desires only that these peoples should be left in peace to work out their own destinies in their own way: Now, therefore, be it

Resolved by the Senate and House of Representatives of the United States of America in Congress assembled, That the Congress approves and supports the determination of the President, as Commander in Chief, to take all necessary measures to repel any armed attack against the forces of the United States and to prevent further aggression.

He said that it was likely that the United States would be going to war with North Vietnam in the coming months. And that the Resolution gave President Johnson full authority to make that decision.

"Why would we go to war with North Vietnam?" he asked.

Two students answered that the United States was going to help the South Vietnamese and to protect the world from Communism.

"Your responses are fine and the vast majority of the people in the country would agree with you."

He then went on to explain the domino theory of countries in Southeast Asia falling to communism.

"Does anyone else have another opinion as to why the United States should go to war with North Vietnam?"

Reluctantly, I ventured a half-hearted upward movement of my arm. Father Collins called on me.

"Father I don't know why we would go to war in Vietnam," I said. "The South Vietnamese government is corrupt and I don't know why we should be supporting it."

My answer was based on a couple of news items about the overthrow of President Diem in 1963 but mostly on the book *The Ugly American* that I had read a few months ago. Father Collins gave me a nod of approval. I felt a follow-up question coming from him but, thank God, the bell rang, and we got up from our seats and I headed to Spanish with Mr. Conte.

Mr. Conte was in rare form and eager to begin the new year. His enthusiasm for Spanish was good and bad. Good because he pushed us and bad because it meant a lot of work. One of the students started addressing him using the Spanish word "profesor," accent on the last syllable. Mr. Conte seemed to like it, so we all referred to him from then on as "Profesor Conte."

I took typing because my brother Donald thought it would be a good skill to have. Up until then, I always asked him to type my papers, which he did gladly, but he encouraged me to learn how to type in school. The class was held in a special room with about twenty typewriters, all of which had the letters and numbers missing on the keys. In the front of the class was a large graphic of the typewriter keyboard with keys labelled, which forced us to keep our heads up while typing. A good teaching ploy. Brother Kenneth was very well organized and clearly had a plan about what he was going to cover each day, but he would get very upset if we did not stop typing when he asked us. This went on almost every day. He would tell us to stop typing so he could explain something, but one or more students would continue tapping the keyboard just for a few seconds that always seemed like an eternity. Brother Kenneth would get red in the face with frustration as he waited for the typewriter clicking to end. If the clicking went on for too long, you could hear him saying under his breath "God damn it!"

Brother Justice, in religion, was modern in his approach and said that in addition to church teachings, he would also be discussing American social issues.

Brother Linus, in English, said we would be focusing on our writing and reading current literature.

Mr. Kent was okay, but I thought he was a bit boring, or maybe it was the subject matter. On the first day, he defined terms like GDP, inflation, trade, and balance of payments, which we would be studying during the year. He started lots of his classes with definitions.

The subject I was most interested in was driver education. It was a one-semester course, and we would be finished with it in January and be eligible to take the New York State Driver's License road test. The school had purchased a car with dual brake mechanisms so that Mr. Conte could stop the car when one of us was driving. We would need his quick firm foot many times especially in the early going.

CHAPTER THIRTY

October 1964: Thinking about College

As September rolled into October, I was working more than ever at my father's warehouse, going there three or four afternoons a week. I wanted to save money to buy the used car, and the more I worked the more I would have at the end of the school year in June. My brother Peter said that his friends were going to play basketball again over the winter and asked if I wanted to play with them. I said yes. All the seniors at Cardinal Spellman were informed that during the fall we had to attend required advisement sessions to help us consider colleges to which we might apply. These were held once a month. At the first group session, Brother Andrew, who was the boy's guidance counselor, talked about majors and how we should consider colleges that might be good fits for what we wanted to study. This was important for me. The only thing I knew about majors was the accounting program at Fordham University's night school. My mother and father assumed that I would be going there since Donald and Peter did, but I was not so sure. I made an appointment to meet with Brother Andrew, whom I had never seen before until the first advisement session. We met on a Tuesday afternoon. He had silver hair and talked in a low voice. He had a small packet of brochures to give me, which were from several New York colleges and about taking the Scholastic Aptitude Test (SAT). We sat down. He had my high school transcript in front of him.

"You have good grades and you can apply to a wide range of colleges. Have you thought about a major?" he asked.

"That's the problem," I replied. "I have two older brothers, and they went to Fordham University at night and graduated. They both majored in accounting. All I know about college is what they tell me. My family is assuming that I'll be going to Fordham at night also."

"How come your brothers went to night school?" Brother Andrew asked.

"My father didn't make that much money, and they were expected to pay their own tuition," I replied.

He said, "Fordham is a fine school if you are going to stay local and major in accounting. Are you sure you want to major in accounting?"

He then mentioned that several seniors at Cardinal Spellman were considering majoring in engineering and going to Manhattan College in Riverdale in the northwest Bronx. He said I had good math grades and might consider going there. Manhattan College was a Catholic College and was run by the Christian Teaching Brothers of Saint John Baptist de la Salle, the same order that taught here at Cardinal Spellman. He also mentioned that some of my classmates were thinking about becoming doctors, lawyers, or teachers.

I didn't want to tell him that I had doubts about going to a Catholic college, period. So I said, "I probably will be majoring in some area of business, but I'm not sure."

In fact, it was at this meeting with Brother Andrew that I began to be sure that I was not going to go to Fordham and major in accounting. I thanked him for his advice and told him I would come back to him once I sorted out what majors I was considering.

At the end of October, we had another Halloween Party at the club. We had the formula for throwing a party down and it was a grand success. People were coming from all over the Bronx and beyond to our parties. Nino's cousins, Dana, Jane, and Lisa came. I asked them how Theresa was. They said she was doing fine and wanted to come to the party, but her parents wouldn't let her. The party made more than a hundred dollars in profit and the Melfords were doing well.

CHAPTER THIRTY-ONE

November 1964: Melrose Avenue

On November 3rd, 1964, President Johnson was easily re-elected over Barry Goldwater who had been portrayed in the press as a conservative extremist. Johnson won a landslide victory and carried forty-four states. A couple of weeks later on a quiet Saturday evening at the club, I was with several guys, playing cards in the backroom. Frankie, one of the Melfords, came in around ten thirty. It was obvious that he was banged around a bit. His lip was split, he had bruises on his face, and there was some blood on his Melford windbreaker. We assumed he got into a fight and got the short end of it. He had been dating a girl from 156th Street and Melrose Avenue, which was a German and Polish neighborhood that had been spared from urban renewal.

"I've been going out with this girl, Kirsten. One of her brothers didn't like me and the fact that I come from Morris Avenue," he said.

This was just another way of saying that he did not like Italians.

"After I dropped Kirsten off at her apartment, her brother and some of his friends were on the corner and asked me what I was doing in their neighborhood. I just kept walking and ignored them, and the next thing I knew I was getting punched and kicked," he went on.

We had no reason to doubt him. Frankie was not a troublemaker. I couldn't think of a time he ever was involved in a fight. There were six of us in the club, so we decided we were going to 156th Street and Melrose Avenue to see if we could find the guys who beat up Frankie. Two of our guys who lived close by said they wanted to go home for a quick change of clothes since they had their Saturday night "best" clothes on. We then walked up to 156th Street. Giuseppe, Matts, P.J., Larry, Frankie, and I were walking two by two about twenty yards apart not to attract too much attention. Larry was walking with me. Of all the guys who belonged to the club, Larry had the least connection to the rest of us. He originally came from 163rd Street and Morris Avenue and had moved to 152nd Street between Morris and Park Avenues only two years prior. He was a little flaky but basically a good guy and joined the Melfords about six months before. As we were walking, the adrenalin was kicking in and I asked Larry, "Are you okay?'

"Yeah. I have my friend with me," he said.

I wasn't sure what he meant. Did he mean me or someone else?

"Who is your friend?"

He pulled out a small handgun and said, "This is my friend!"

"What the fuck are you going to do with that?" I exclaimed. "We're not looking to kill anyone. We're just going to let some wise asses know that they can't get away with beating up one of our guys. And make sure you don't even take it out of your pocket."

He looked at me half in disbelief and half-hurt but got my point.

When we got to the corner of 156th Street and Melrose, we didn't see anybody. There was a bar about halfway down the block, and there were a bunch of guys outside it. We went down there, and Frankie said that they were the guys who beat him up. We walked up to them and Giuseppe said, "We did not like the idea that you beat up one of our guys." And pointed to Frankie. At first, not a one of them said anything. Giuseppe repeated his comment. Two of them walked forward. It was turning into the classic confrontation, with Giuseppe and P.J. talking with two of the other guys. The rest of us were behind them. The guy Giuseppe was talking to was tall, about 6 foot three but thin. Giuseppe was noticeably shorter but could take care of himself. After some give and take, Giuseppe said, "I want to know the guys who punched out our guy Frankie here?" The tall thin fellow with a good deal of bravado said, "I did!" and looked down into Giuseppe's face. Without any hesitation, Giuseppe gave the guy an uppercut square in the jaw. He went down and the rest of us moved in. We started throwing punches at the other guys; whenever we could, we would give the guy who was down a couple of kicks mostly in the head. Pretty soon, it became clear they wanted no part of us, especially with their big talking leader on the ground being kicked mercilessly. Most of them ran away. We didn't follow.

P.J. said to the guy on the ground, "Don't fuck with the Melfords" and gave him one more kick in the gut. We walked back to Morris Avenue.

We went to the club and washed up, and then went to Dave's Bar across the street. Dave came over and P.J. told him what happened.

Dave said, "If you ever need any help with anything like that again, let me know. I have a couple of tough mother-fuckers who would be happy to lend a hand."

He gave us a round of drinks on the house. We thanked him. I'm glad that he didn't know that Larry had a gun in pocket. It was a night to remember.

The following week, I met with Brother Andrew about college. I had been speaking to my brothers and friends about college. I was beginning to narrow down my choices.

CHAPTER THIRTY-TWO

December 1964: College Application

December was the deadline for submitting applications for college, although most of the admissions offices also posted a late application deadline, which was usually around February 1st. My father assumed I was going to follow the exact same path as Donald and Peter. It worked for them and it would work for me. I had spoken with Donald and Peter about Fordham. Donald felt I should go to Fordham at night, major in accounting, and work during the day, just as he did. Peter had mixed feelings and said that it really was a grind working all day and going to school at night. He also thought accounting was "blah." My schoolmates at Cardinal Spellman High School were a mixed bag. Who was going away to college? Who was staying home? Who was going at night? Most of them were going to go full-time during the day and a lot of them would be going to Manhattan College. About four or five of the Melfords were applying to college; almost all of them would go to a local college. Mickey, Salvo, and Wally were interested in St. John's University in Queens. Georgie was already going to City College at night. Joey Fuzz was hoping to go to Hunter College full-time. Fuzz and I went all through grammar school together at Our Lady of Pity from kindergarten to the eighth grade. He was smart and very level-headed, and we knew each other well. I hadn't thought about Hunter College until speaking with him. I'd been considering Queens College and even went to see an admissions adviser there. It was a long subway ride followed by a long bus ride to get there from the Bronx. I liked the school and the campus but dismissed it for travel reasons. I had it in my head that I would be going part-time at night. I spoke to Georgie about City College, but the only reason he was going there was because he wanted to be a policeman, and it was one of the few schools in New York that had a program in criminal justice. Joey Fuzz said he was interested in Hunter's Bronx Campus and planned to take most of his courses there and not at the Main Campus on 68th Street in Manhattan. I decided to read up on it.

Hunter College was founded in 1870, originally as a women's college, for the preparation of teachers. It had since expanded its academic programs and students could major in education, nursing, the liberal arts, social work, and even accounting. I made an appointment to see an admissions adviser at the Bronx Campus. Mr. Jaekel was an enthusiastic recruiter for the college, and I enjoyed speaking with him. I had seen in one of the bulletins that generally an applicant had to have a 90 high school average from a New York City public high school to be admitted. My high school averages ranged from 87 to 89 for three years. I asked him about admissions requirements and told him what I had seen in the bulletin.

He said, "A 90 average is generally required if you attend a public high school. What high school do you attend?"

I told him, "Cardinal Spellman High School on Baychester Avenue."

"The admissions committee takes into consideration if an applicant attends a selective high school such as Spellman. They frequently admit students from these schools with lower than 90 averages. What is your average?" he said.

"About an 88," I said.

"You shouldn't have a problem being admitted. What courses have you taken?" he asked.

I went through all my courses. Four years of English, four years of social studies, three years of mathematics, three years of Latin, two years of Spanish, two years of science, and four years of religion.

"Have you taken the New York State Regent Exams?" he asked then.

"I took them for just about all of my courses except religion," I replied. "And passed them all."

Then he said, "I can't guarantee it, but you would likely be accepted here."

That was good news to me. I then asked him, "How much is the tuition?"

"Twelve dollars," he replied.

I quickly multiplied in my head 9 credits a semester times $12.00 if I went part-time and came up with $108.00 per semester and said, "I should be able to afford $108.00 a semester."

He asked, "How did you come up with $108.00?"

I told him, "I multiplied 9 credits times $12.00 a credit, which is $108.00."

"The total tuition for the semester is $12.00. It's not $12.00 per credit," he said.

"What?" I said in shock, and he repeated himself.

He then explained that everyone who was admitted to Hunter and the other four-year colleges at the City University such as CCNY, Queens, and Brooklyn all were tuition free. He told me to make sure I took the SATs because it was a university requirement and that the admissions committee would mainly look at my high school record to determine admissions. Mr. Jaekel had made my day.

After my meeting with Mr. Jaekel, I walked around the campus. It was very attractive and right next to the Jerome Avenue Reservoir, which looked like a big lake that bordered the entire west side of the college. There were six buildings on the campus, two modern and four old style Gothic type. One modern building was the library and the other, the Shuster Hall, housed administrative offices and classrooms. The Gothic Buildings (Gillet Hall, Davis Hall, the Student Union, and the gymnasium) were all three stories high and copies of each other. They were surrounded by tree-lined paths, and there was a big manicured grass commons in the center. The campus also had a baseball field, a softball field, a dozen red-clay tennis courts, and lots of open space. The area around Hunter was also attractive. In addition to the Jerome Avenue Reservoir, the college was surrounded by three large high schools: Walton High School, the Bronx High School of Science, and Dewitt Clinton High School. It would be very convenient for me to get to by subway, with a station on the IRT line only two blocks away. I was sold. Hunter College was the only college I would apply to. While I really wanted to go full-time during the day, I decided I would probably go at night. I figured I could take nine credits a semester and three over the summer and finish in six years.

In addition to cost and attractiveness, there was another reason for me to go to Hunter College. I had spent most of my life living with Italian Catholics and at Cardinal Spellman with Irish Catholics, Polish Catholics, and German Catholics. I was curious about other people who were not Catholics—blacks, Jews, Latinos, and WASPS. I had read about them but had little or no real interaction with them. I wanted more diversity in my life.

The next week, I met again with Brother Andrew and told him about my meeting with the admissions counselor at Hunter College and that I would likely apply there.

"That's fine. Are you going full-time or part-time?" he asked me.

"Part-time," I told him.

"Think about going full-time some more," he replied.

When I got home that night, I told my parents and brothers that I was planning on going to Hunter College. My brothers supported me, but my father and mother were upset. My mother couldn't understand why I wasn't going to a Catholic school. My father turned red and I could see his temper coming.

He yelled at me, "You should be going to Fordham and be like your brothers."

"I don't want to major in accounting, and I don't want to go to school with a lot of Catholics anymore," I retorted.

If I was younger or shorter, he would have given me a slap in the face or worse, but he knew it would be useless. I looked at him and he got my message.

CHAPTER THIRTY-THREE

Christmas 1964

The Christmas holidays were soon upon us. Peter and I helped Donald put the lights on the outside of our house. Donald bought six more strings of lights and they were going every which way. He saw the pattern of a beautiful star, but Peter and I kept looking at his creation sideways and upside down trying to see what he was seeing. In any case, Donald was happy, and Christmas was off to a good start.

As usual, my Uncle Tony and Aunt Jean came over for Christmas Eve, but so too did Donald's girlfriend Dottie. I had met her several times and she had already been to our house on other occasions. After dinner, we all exchanged gifts. Donald announced that he would be buying a new car and should have it in about one or two weeks. And then, Peter, who had been learning to drive with Donald and recently passed his driver's test, said he would be buying a new car too. They both were buying new Oldsmobiles. And then came the biggest surprise of all; Donald said in front of everybody that if I wanted it, I could have his old car, the 1958 Oldsmobile 88. Did I want it? I would die for it. I would soon be finished with driver's education in a couple of weeks, and all I had to do was pass the New York State driver's test. Donald said he would keep the car under his name because the insurance would be much cheaper. I was in heaven.

CHAPTER THIRTY-FOUR

January 1965: My 1958 Oldsmobile 88

I passed my driver's road test on the second try. On the first try, with the exam-
iner in my car, I passed a red light and he failed me. I took it again and passed.
I spent several days cleaning up my new used car. I simonized the black exterior,
shined up all the chrome, especially the bumpers that were a foot wide, eight
inches high, and a foot deep. There were two chrome fins on the back, which
merged into the rear taillights. I cleaned the inside. My mother helped me but
thought it crazy that her seventeen-year-old son owned a car. She changed her
mind when I drove her and my father to visit my Uncle Johnny in Mastic, Long
Island. She was in the backseat saying her rosary for the entire ninety-minute
trip. The car was a blessing for me since I was taking the subway all over the
Bronx and Manhattan to see my friends and go to work, and I had really given
up the chance to play sports other than track at high school. My car gave me a
lot more time and flexibility. Like on Saturday I could play softball with the
Melfords in the morning or afternoon and after the game go home, shower, have
dinner with my family, and go back down to Morris Avenue to hang out at the
club at night.

I was one of the few Melfords to have my own car although some of my
friends would borrow their father's cars. If the guys wanted to go someplace, my
car easily sat six, so we didn't have to take public transportation. A couple of us
started taking dates further up the Bronx to Fordham Road and beyond. In the
past, the Earl Theater and Addie Vallins on 161st Street was our idea of an uptown
date. Now we were going up the Grand Concourse to Fordham Road to the
Loew's Paradise Theater and Jahn's Ice Cream Parlor. We started going to the

cocktail lounges in Mt. Vernon and Yonkers on Saturday nights to see groups like the Ronettes, the Earls, and the Duprees.

By the end of January, when I got my semester report card, all my thoughts about school and education were shifting away from Cardinal Spellman to Hunter College. I was pretty sure that if I was accepted to Hunter, I would go at night and started to think about getting a day job come July. My father approached me about continuing to work with him after I graduated. I was skeptical so I spoke to my brother, Donald.

"Dad has approached me about working with him after I graduate. He even mentioned about buying a small van that I could drive and make local deliveries of his company's merchandize. He thought the money would be pretty good. And I could go to college at night," I told him.

Without hesitating a moment, Donald said, "Don't do it! Don't even think about it! Get a job like Peter in a bank; it's relatively easy and the short hours will help you get to class on time. And you won't be exhausted from doing physical work all day and driving around Manhattan."

As I have so many times in the past, I thanked my older brother for giving me good advice. A couple of days later, I spoke with my father and told him it would be too much running around and I would rather do something else. Then, I spoke to Peter about working in a bank and going to school at night. He thought it a good idea.

"As a teller in a bank, you start at 8:30 in the morning," he said. "The bank closes at 3:00 pm. All you have to do is prove your cash drawer and you leave. On slow days, you're out by 3:45. On busy days, like Fridays, you'll be there longer. I'll check out if there are any teller positions opening up in my bank."

The next night when he came home from work, Peter told me, "I have some bad news. Manufacturers Hanover has a strict policy. No employing immediate members of families, and that includes brothers. You're going to have to find another bank if you want to be a teller."

I figured I had some time to think this through. The idea of being a bank teller based on what Donald and Peter said appealed to me. Surely, in New York City there were plenty of banks.

CHAPTER THIRTY-FIVE

February 1965: Bombing North Vietnam

My last semester of high school was going well. Driver education was finished, so I had a little more time on my hands. I was into all my subjects except economics. I still found that boring. Brother Justice liked discussing current events especially civil rights, and Father Collins mentioned Vietnam at least once a week. He was passionate about what was evolving there and made copies of articles from the *New York Times*, which we read in class. In one article, I read that on February 7th, there had been an attack on Camp Holloway, a U.S. helicopter base located near the town of Pleiku in South Vietnam. There were about 400 Americans stationed at the camp, supporting South Vietnamese regular soldiers. The Soviet Union had just expanded its support and assistance to the North Vietnamese who were beginning a spring offensive. The attack on Camp Halloway was well planned and well executed. The airfield was severely damaged with mortar fire, leaving ten aircraft destroyed and fifteen others inoperable. There were American casualties: 8 dead and 126 wounded. Within twelve hours of the attack, President Lyndon Johnson ordered the bombing of North Vietnamese targets in Operation Flaming Arrow. Forty-nine U.S. fighter-bombers took off from the USS Coral Sea and the USS Hancock, and attacked North Vietnamese barracks in Đồng Hới, just north of the 17th Parallel. While the South Vietnamese celebrated the increase in American involvement, the North Vietnamese were not deterred. They launched another attack on a U.S. installation in Qui Nhơn on February 10th, resulting in the death of 23 more U.S. military personnel. In response, a combined force of about 160 U.S. and South Vietnamese fighter-bombers launched a larger attack against the North

Vietnamese, targeting Chap Le and Chanh Hoa, also located just north of the 17th Parallel. The Vietnam War was now escalating very quickly, and it was clear that the United States would be fully involved.

Father Collins talked with us about these events and questioned us about the escalation of the war. He asked us, "Do you see a parallel to the Korean Conflict? Do you think we can win a guerilla war?"

It was something we had just studied a week earlier. We had been studying the Korean War, so we saw it as history repeating itself. It was going to be difficult for the United States to win such a war. Father Collins was dismayed by the escalation and saw it as a "no-win" situation.

"What do you think would happen if the United States just pulls out of Vietnam all together and lets whatever happens happen?" he asked.

After a few seconds of silence in the class, I raised my hand and said, "The people of Vietnam would have to determine their own fate. And the South Vietnamese people will most likely have to side with the North Vietnamese."

Father Collins seemed okay with my response and went on to discuss the possibility of the Soviet Union or China becoming involved and somehow bringing Vietnam into their spheres of influence. He also made it clear that the two super Communist powers were not close allies. He also said that the United States involvement in Vietnam was going to be a very long affair with lots of casualties.

I went to work later that day and there were the guys in my father's warehouse talking about President Johnson's order to bomb North Vietnam. Besides my father, there were six other salt of the earth, blue-collar workers, most of whom were in their forties and fifties. There was Mac (Irish American), Eddie and Kemp (Black Americans), Ben (Italian American), Julie (Polish American), and Escobar (recent immigrant from Cuba). During lunch or when things were slow, they talked about everything. Sports and politics were their favorite subjects. Things could get heated at times and frequently who won the debate was whoever spoke the loudest. To a man, they were all for President Johnson's actions and their collective opinions basically came down to, "Bomb the crap out of North Vietnam!" A few days later, I was at the club with several of my friends. Their opinions were about the same as those of the workers in my father's warehouse. I wasn't sure if my friends were thinking that they might be fighting in Vietnam someday. I tried to steer them away from the dominant American position that we were saving South Vietnam and democracy for the world. Other than Frankie and Mickey, no one was buying what I was saying.

CHAPTER THIRTY-SIX

March 1976: Selma

N ew York City knows how to have a parade, and once a year, the St. Patrick's Day Parade takes over Manhattan. In March 1965, Cardinal Spellman High School was invited to be the lead high school in the parade in honor of New York City's Archbishop Frances Cardinal Spellman. The entire senior class was told that we would be marching in the parade. I suppose this was a good thing, but it meant hours of practice marching. The school had a band that marched at parades and other events, but the rest of us had to learn to march in step to the beat of the drum. We practiced outside around the track. On the day of the parade, we marched down Fifth Avenue. As we passed Cardinal Spellman standing on the steps of St. Patrick's Cathedral, it was obvious that he was quite proud of us and the school named for him. Life couldn't be better. At least, not on Fifth Avenue.

In Selma, Alabama, a different kind of march was being planned. After two failed attempts, civil rights leaders were planning a march on March 21st from Selma, Alabama, to the state capital in Montgomery to protest the state's voter registration system that discriminated against blacks. This was the third march in less than two weeks. During the first March on March 7th, Alabama state troopers wielding whips, nightsticks, and tear gas stopped the 600 marchers at the Edmund Pettis Bridge and pushed them back to Selma. During the second Selma March on March 9th, Dr. Martin Luther King, Jr. led more than 2,000 marchers across the Edmund Pettus Bridge but found the highway blocked by state troopers. King paused the marchers and led them in prayer, whereupon the troopers stepped aside. King then turned the protesters around, believing that the troopers were trying to create a situation that would allow them to enforce a federal injunction prohibiting the march.

On March 21st, 2,000 people set out from Selma once again, but this time, they were protected by U.S. Army troops and the Alabama National Guard forces that President Lyndon Johnson had ordered under federal control. After walking some 12 hours a day and sleeping in the fields along the way, they reached Montgomery on March 25. Nearly 50,000 supporters met the marchers in Montgomery, where they gathered in front of the state capitol to hear King and others address the crowd.

On Monday, March 22nd, several of our teachers had spoken to us about the Selma March. Brother Justice, in religion class, was moved by the previous day's events.

"I was so proud that at the head of the march were priests, ministers, and rabbis. And whites were well-represented among the marchers," he said.

I got the feeling that he wished he had been there. He took some time to tell us about James Reeb, a white Universal Unitarian minister who marched in the Second Selma March and who was beaten along with two other Unitarian ministers, Clark Olsen and Orloff Miller, on the night of March 9th. Reeb died two days later. I was touched by Brother Justice's story and the genuineness of his message that we were all God's children and needed to learn to respect and love one another. I think he got to most of us, but I wasn't sure. Our class had one black student, Lawrence, and I kept glancing at him as Brother spoke, wondering what this guy must be thinking.

That night after work, I brought the subject up with my father and brothers on the car ride home, and they, especially Donald, seemed sympathetic to the marchers. I discussed the Selma March with my Melford buddies too; I would say that some guys supported it, and some did not.

Between Vietnam and Selma, my head was filling up with ideas and conflicts. I was developing a set of values that needed more work but weren't necessarily in tune with those of my family and friends.

A couple of nights later, my brother Donald told Peter and me that he would be getting married to Dottie in October. Peter and I had been suspecting this for a while, but it still bothered us to know that Donald would be leaving us. He, by far, provided the most fun in the family, and we would miss him. Our home would not be the same. As we gave him hugs, I have to confess, my eyes misted up. Full-blown crying was out of the question.

CHAPTER THIRTY-SEVEN

April 1965: Hunter College

The first days of April were warm and welcoming. Easter was on April 18th and we started our spring break on Thursday, April 15th. Basketball with my brother Peter's friends was coming to an end, but the Melford softball team was having its first practices and was getting ready for yet another season.

On April 1st, I had received a package from Hunter College, saying I was accepted and that there would be a freshmen orientation session on May 4th at 3:30 p.m. I was ecstatic and thought about my meeting in December with the admissions adviser, Mr. Jaekel. He was correct in his assessment of my chances for being admitted. My brothers were happy for me. My mother and father were so-so. There were packets of forms and sheets I had to complete and bring with me to the orientation. In addition to basic information about who I was, there was also a form about intended major. It recommended that for certain subject areas such as accounting, you declare a major in freshman year. While accounting surely was in my family's blood, I decided then and there that I wasn't going to be an accountant, but I had no idea in what subject I would major, so I checked off the "Undecided" box.

I drove down to the club on Friday night, and found out that my buddy, Joey Fuzz was also accepted to Hunter College. After we congratulated each other, he told me he was going to attend full-time during the day. I envied him. Several other Melfords were receiving letters from college admissions offices. There was about five or six of us planning on going to college. A couple of the other guys were going to community colleges to specialize in a trade or career.

The following week at Cardinal Spellman, the students were talking about colleges and where they were going. Most were staying local, but some were going as far away as California. I couldn't relate to that mainly because I had only been in two states in my life, New York and New Jersey. After classes one day, I saw Father Collins in the hall. I had come to realize that he had made a significant impact on my thinking and my values.

He asked me, "What are your plans after high school?"

This was the first time I had a chance to discuss this with any of my teachers except the guidance counselor, Brother Andrew.

"Father, I just received a letter that I was accepted into Hunter College," I told him.

"That is a fine school. You will get a good liberal arts education there," he replied.

He went on to say that he had several students over the years who went to Hunter and that they were pleased with the educations they received. That night when I went home, I told my mother and father what Father Collins said about Hunter College. My mother seemed greatly relieved that a priest had blessed my college choice. My father said nothing.

For Easter, my mother baked the traditional pies and breads, and we had a good family holiday. My Uncle James turned up unexpectedly as people did in those days and we were glad to see him. It had been a while since he visited and once my grandmother on my father's side died, we never went out to Brooklyn to visit with him or his sister, my Aunt Lena. They had a very different view of things, especially my uncle who talked about opera and life in Brooklyn. He had the perfect Brooklyn accent—"boids" for "birds" and "pernts" for "points." There had been a falling out between my mother and Aunt Lena when my grandmother (my father's mother) died. I never really understood it. My brother Donald said it had something to do with Aunt Lena converting to Christian Science and she doubted whether my grandmother had the proper medical attention before she died. My mother also couldn't accept that there was no funeral mass, no wake, or other type of service. My grandmother had been buried immediately after she died. Given my mother's deep devotion to the Catholic faith, I could see how this would upset her even to the point that she never spoke to my aunt again. In any case, it was a good to see Uncle James and it was a good Easter.

CHAPTER THIRTY-EIGHT

May 1965: Freshmen Orientation

I was looking forward to orientation at Hunter College on May 4th. I spoke with Joey Fuzz, and we decided we would try to meet before the orientation in front of Gillet Hall on the campus since Joey would be coming from Cardinal Hayes High School and I would be coming from Cardinal Spellman. The orientation was presided over by several deans, faculty, and student government leaders. The auditorium was packed. The women students wore skirts and blouses while many of the men wore "Joe college" sweaters. with a stripe or two on the arms. Speaker after speaker reminded us how fortunate we were to be admitted to the college. The audience, in fact, did represent a select group of students, the vast majority of whom had excellent grades needed to be admitted to the tuition-free college.

The Dean of Academic Standards warned the incoming students that they would have to work hard to maintain their academic standing if they wanted to graduate in four years. She also invoked the traditional scare in a menacing voice. "Look to your right and look to your left, one of you will not be here one year from now." Fuzz and I looked at each other in horror. While the cliché was meant as a tactic, the fact was that many of us would likely fail out in our first year. The Dean went on to say that the faculty maintained very high grading standards and were not at all timid about giving students Cs, Ds, and Fs. Joey Fuzz and I looked at each other again. This was getting scary. She moved on to describe the academic program, spending time clarifying the general education requirements of sixty-plus credits. I was more comfortable now and I listened attentively. In the packet of materials that was sent to us back in April, one of the handouts had outlined these requirements. I understood them better than I thought I would—four courses in English, two in American history, one in mathematics (unless you planned to major in a science), four in a foreign language, etc. Then, she addressed another issue that was important to me. She cautioned that students should start thinking about their majors, which they would have to declare no later than the first semester of their junior year. As confident as I was about the general education requirements, I still had no idea what I was going to do about a major.

The last speaker was the Registrar. He told us we would be mailed all our registration materials in early August and that we would be assigned a day and hour to come in to register. He strongly suggested that we decide beforehand what courses we wanted to take and warned us to have back-ups "in case" our first choices were already closed because as entering freshmen we would be the last group of students to register. To soften the blow of this last piece of information, cookies, coffee, tea, and fruit juice were provided while several student musicians played guitars and harmonicas and sang folk rock songs such as *Mr. Tambourine Man, Like a Rolling Stone*, and *The Sound of Silence*, finishing with *Blowin in the Wind*. This was not the type of music in the jukebox at the Melford club. I drove Joey Fuzz back to Morris Avenue and we talked about the orientation.

"Fuzz, it sounds like a very competitive place!" I said.

"Yeah, and did you get a load of what the guys were wearing? And all the tennis courts?" he replied.

"Yep. It wasn't Morris Avenue, was it? And what did you think about that music at the end?" I went on.

"They should have played the Drifters or the Temptations," Fuzz replied.

"Fuzz, I envy you that you're going full-time during the day even if they played folk music. I am not sure about my decision to go part-time at night," I told him.

Fuzz said immediately, "So go during the day."

"I keep thinking about it!" I replied.

We got to the club, hung out for a while, and then I drove home. All that night, I kept thinking about Hunter, coursework, competition, and the folk-rock music. I talked with my brothers. They said not to worry. They had the same type of orientation at Fordham minus the music.

Later in the month, I started looking for a job at a bank hoping to start in July. A new bank had just opened a few months earlier off 233rd Street and Baychester Avenue, about three blocks from where I lived. The name of the bank was Federation Bank & Trust Company. I thought if I could get a job working there, a lot of my traveling logistics would be solved.

I asked my brother Peter, "Do you know anything about the Federation Bank & Trust opening down the street on Baychester Avenue?"

"No, but I'll find out for you tomorrow," he said

The next night when he came home from work, he told me, "Federation is a small bank and has sixteen branches in Manhattan, the Bronx, Brooklyn, and Queens. Go into the branch on Baychester Avenue and ask one of the managers or officers if they are hiring and see what they say."

And that is exactly what I did a couple of days later. I went in, and on the left was a line of five teller stations and on the right were three desks, where I presumed the managers were. I walked to the right and one of the men at a desk, John Marzullo, asked, "Can I help you?"

"Hi, I'll be graduating Cardinal Spellman High School down on Baychester Avenue in June and was thinking about working in a bank," I replied.

"Have a seat. Are you planning on going to college?" he asked me.

"I'm going to go at night to Hunter College," I said.

"We're hiring, but you have to apply through the Personnel Office in Manhattan," he told me.

He gave me his card and wrote on the back the name and address of the Personnel Manager, a Mr. James Stark.

"Write a brief letter to the Personnel Manager. Tell him that you want a job, working here at the Baychester Avenue branch and tell him that you already spoke to me," he said.

I said, "Thank you!" and we shook hands.

I wrote the short letter stating who I was, that I had just graduated Cardinal Spellman High School and was going to Hunter College at night and wanted to be considered for a job as a teller. I had my brother Peter look at what I wrote, and he thought it was good. I mailed it to the address in Manhattan and waited to hear back.

CHAPTER THIRTY-NINE

June 1965: Graduation

As I was getting ready to take my last final examinations at Cardinal Spellman, I received a letter from Mr. Stark asking me to call his office to make an appointment for an interview. I took this as a good sign. I called his office and I spoke to his assistant, who said they would need an entire afternoon or morning.

"I'm getting ready to take final exams. Could Mr. Stark wait until later in the month?" I requested.

"No problem!" she said.

We set my interview for 1:00 pm on the afternoon of June 23rd. I thought it would be a lucky day because it was my brother Peter's birthday.

During the week before the 23rd, I was taking Regents and final exams. I didn't find any of the finals particularly hard. I was relaxed and already accepted to college and unless I failed a course, I was set academically going into next year. I passed everything.

On June 23rd, I went into Manhattan to the Federation Bank & Trust's offices, which were in the Colosseum at 58th Street and Columbus Circle. I went up to the 23rd Floor and went into the Bank's complex of offices, and saw a receptionist who directed me down the hall to Mr. Stark's office.

"May I help you?" said Mrs. Ellis.

"Yes. I have an appointment with Mr. Stark," I said, and gave her my name.

"Take a seat. Mr. Stark will be right with you," she said.

Mr. Stark came out of his office in about ten minutes, extended his hand and said, "I'm glad to meet you!"

He asked me a few questions, which focused on why I wanted to work at Federation Bank & Trust Company. I described in some detail my plan for going to Hunter College at night and the advice my brother Peter gave me.

"Have you applied at Manufacturers-Hanover Trust?"

"No! It has a strict personnel policy of not hiring immediate family members, including brothers," I told him.

"How were your grades in high school?" asked Mr. Stark.

"Pretty good. I have an 88 high school average," I replied.

"What do you plan to major in college?" he asked me.

"I have two years to decide, but maybe economics," I lied.

"What kind of work do you want to do?" he asked then.

"I'd like to start as a teller. That's what my brother did," I replied.

"I want to give you a series of tests to determine your aptitude for working in the bank and the type of positions that you're best suited for," he told me.

"Fine!" I said in reply.

"Are you available later this week?"

"Next week would be better since my last day of classes at Cardinal Spellman is Friday," I said. He shook my hand, and ushered me out of his office to Mrs. Ellis, who set my appointment for Tuesday June 29th at 1:00 pm.

My graduation was on Sunday June 27th, 1965, at 2:00 pm in the afternoon. My mother, father, and brothers came. Cardinal Spellman was there and said a few words. As I walked up the aisle to receive my diploma, I was confident that I had received a good education. I learned literature, mathematics, and languages. I enjoyed most of my subjects, especially Latin. It is frequently said Latin's grammatical structures and vocabulary help one understand English better. This is true. I also enjoyed translating text and stories that were written thousands of years ago. Although my thoughts were not fully formed, studying other languages such as Latin and Spanish gave me insights into other cultures and an inkling that there's a larger world out there with different ways of speaking, hearing, and seeing things. I was grateful to the faculty especially Brother Peter, Brother James Paul, Brother Thomas, and Mr. Conte. Above all, I appreciated Father Collins and Brother Justice who taught me to be aware of and question the world around us.

On June 29th, I returned to the Federation Bank & Trust's offices at the Colosseum. I was given a series of tests. The first was a basic aptitude test. The second was general banking practices that required reading material and then answering questions about different courses of action. The third and last series of tests related to the mechanics of being a teller. It consisted of reading passages about serving customers, handling cash, and simple bookkeeping problems. I figured I did well on them. Mr. Stark asked me to wait in the outer office while he reviewed my tests. He came and invited me into his office about twenty minutes later.

He congratulated me, saying, "You did very well on your tests, and we would like to offer you a teller's position."

"Thank you. That's great news," I told him.

Then he said, "The only opening we currently have is at our main branch here in the Colosseum. What do you think?"

Although I had hoped to be working up at the Bronx Baychester Branch, I said, "That's fine."

He told me that my pay would be sixty-five dollars a week and I could start on July 6th. We shook hands on it.

CHAPTER FORTY

July 1965: Federation Bank & Trust

O n July 6th, I started working at Federation Bank & Trust Company. I had been told by Mrs. Ellis to come to her office to fill out some paperwork. The main or Colosseum Branch of the bank was on the ground floor 23 floors below the Personnel Office. I saw Mr. Stark who asked me to come inside and talk with him for a few minutes. He congratulated me again and expressed how happy he was that I would be working at Federation Bank & Trust.

"You'll start working as a teller in a week or two and until then we would like you to work in our Securities Department. The work is not very difficult, and you will not have any problem with it," he said.

I had no idea about what securities were, but I said, "Fine."

After I finished filling out my paperwork, I reported to a Mr. Hinkley, the manager of the Securities Department whose office was one floor down from Personnel. He welcomed me and explained what they did in his office and told me that I would be tallying the interest on bond coupons that were due and making sure that they balanced against the department's ledger. It wasn't complicated. I was given stacks of coupons and other bond paper that were organized by the issuers. I tallied the interest on each issuer's stack of bonds, produced a simple tally report, and then compared my figure to a ledger figure that had been produced for anticipated revenues. In almost every case, the numbers tallied. It wasn't a big office, with only about six people doing various jobs. There were two young women about my age working there, and during the break we introduced ourselves. Joan and Linda were summer workers, both of whom were going to college in Massachusetts. They had been friends since high school. Linda invited me to go to lunch with them. We talked about the bank. I told them my plans and how a teller's schedule fit going to school at night. Joan seemed to know a good deal about Federation Bank & Trust Company and Linda not so much.

At the end of the day, I went home and found myself very tired. We talked about my new job at the bank during dinner and rather than take a ride down to Morris Avenue, I decided to watch the Mets on the TV with my father. My father was a diehard Mets fan who, coming from Brooklyn, would never root for the Yankees. We talked a bit and then he said something very unusual.

He said, "I'm going to miss you in the warehouse."

He rarely ever expressed sentiments to me during my entire life. It was not part of his make-up. It was my mother and brother Donald who gave me the most congratulations, sympathy, or encouragement. I didn't know what to say, so I said, "I am going to miss the warehouse too."

While the work there had been generally boring, I made enough money and I had the freedom to come and go and fit in my school schedule and other things, as I wanted to do. My father and I talked some more, and he told me about his father who was a tailor. This was also something he had never done before. My grandfather had died many years before I was born, and I never knew anything about him. I realized that my father was seeing his youngest become an adult and that an important phase of his life was coming to an end. I kissed him goodnight and went upstairs to my room. The Mets were getting better and beat the Cincinnati Reds 6-3 on home runs by Ed Kranepool and Deron Johnson.

My brother Donald was still driving my father and brother to work in Manhattan, and they were glad to have me along for the ride. The second day in the Securities Department was a repeat of the first. Joan, Linda, and I had lunch again. We were talking about Federation Bank & Trust, and I told them how my brother Peter was an officer at Manufacturers Hanover Trust Company and that it was he who suggested that working as a teller would be very convenient if I was going to school at night. Linda asked me what I was majoring in.

"I don't know yet," I told her.

"I'm in pre-law for now but I am not sure I really wanted to be an attorney," she said.

"I'm majoring in international finance," added Joan.

"So that explains why you know so much about the bank," I said.

"She knows so much about the bank because her father is the president of the bank," added Linda.

"What?" I asked in surprise.

Linda repeated, "Joan's father, Mr. Del Giudice, is the President of Federation Bank & Trust Company."

"I had no idea I was in such high company," I said.

Joan laughed.

I continued to work in the Securities Office for the next several days, and the following week on July 13th, I started work as a teller. On the last day of working at the Securities Office, Joan, Linda, and I went out for a drink after work to the Colosseum Café, which was right across the street. I didn't see either of them very much afterward because as a teller, I had a very limited forty-five-minute lunch that started at ten thirty in the morning. I quickly learned the teller business, working in the Savings Department, which was the entry level at the main branch. On the bank floor were the paying and receiving tellers, the note tellers, the loan tellers, and branch officers, each in their own little areas. I was the low man on the totem pole. A couple of weeks later near the end of July at about three thirty in the afternoon and after the bank had closed for the day, Joan came into the bank with her father and couple of other people whom I think were senior officers. All eight platform managers—vice presidents, assistant vice presidents, and assistant managers—went over to say hello to Mr. Del Giudice. While all the employees were observing the homage being paid to Mr. Del Giudice, Joan saw me, came over, and gave me a big hello and a kiss on the cheek. After they left, half of the branch employees, including Mr. O'Brien, one of the vice presidents, came over to ask how I knew the president's daughter. I said, "I worked with her a few days once," I shrugged.

On the weekends, my friends and I traveled around in my car to single's bars such as Maxwell's Plum and Fridays in Manhattan and the Riviera Lounge in Westchester. We made several trips to Clay Cole's Rock and Roll Shows at Palisades Amusement Park in New Jersey. We loved the groups like Dion and the Belmonts, the Skyliners, and the Mystics. My car also added a whole other dimension to dating since it was a good place to make out with a girl.

My life at the bank and the "hot spots" of New York was going well, but it was becoming painfully obvious to everyone that Vietnam was not going to be a quick skirmish with a weak enemy. In late spring, President Johnson had launched a "multi-year campaign" of sustained bombing in North Vietnam and the Ho Chi Minh Trail in Operation Rolling Thunder. At the same time, U.S. Marines landed on beaches near Da Nang, South Vietnam, as the first large contingent of American combat troops to enter Vietnam. On July 28th, the president ordered an increase in U.S. military forces in Vietnam, from the 75,000 to 125,000. Johnson also said he would order additional increases if necessary. He pointed out that to fill the manpower needs, the monthly draft calls would be raised from 17,000 to 35,000. We eighteen- and nineteen-year-old boys were listening carefully.

CHAPTER FORTY-ONE

August 1965: Wildwood Days

On August 1st, I got a call from J.R. We were very close as childhood buddies, but once we moved from 152nd Street, that had changed. Our parents continued to visit each other regularly and I would get news about him from my mother. J.R. had graduated high school in 1964 and was working with his brother-in-law. He must have been making a good salary because he told me he had bought a new Chevrolet Impala. He and a couple of friends of his were going to Wildwood, New Jersey, the next weekend, and he asked if I wanted to come with them. There would be four of us and we would share expenses, mostly the motel bill. I knew one of his friends, Bob, but didn't know the other fella, Phil. A weekend on the beach sounded good. I asked the head teller, Jimmy, if I could have that Friday off since I had started working immediately after graduating and hadn't had any vacation time; he was okay with it.

J.R. picked me up on Friday morning. Bob and Phil were with him. J.R. said we were going to stay at the Baywood Gardens Motel, the same place that he and I had stayed with my brothers seven years ago. Bob and Phil had never been to Wildwood, so J.R. and I relived our weekend on the beach, the boardwalk, and the Wildwood Diner. During the almost four-hour drive to Wildwood, we talked a lot about sports. J.R. and I both loved the Yankees. When we were younger, his father would take us to afternoon games at Yankee Stadium. Bob and Phil were New York Mets fans. This made for lively discussion during the car ride since the Mets had been one of the worst teams in baseball ever since they were established in 1962. In 1965, the Yankees were good but not great. They still had all-stars like Mickey Mantle, Roger Maris, Elston Howard, Whitey Ford, and Bobby Richardson. The Mets were playing with a lot of expansion players and having a losing season. During the ride, we went through every position and compared ball players. It reminded me of when I was younger on 152nd street and my father and his friends would argue about the Yankees, the Brooklyn Dodgers, and New York Giants. Who was better? Pee Wee Reese or Phil Rizzuto? Bill Skowron or Gil Hodges? Yogi Berra or Roy Campanella? And of course, the granddaddy of all arguments, who was the better centerfielder: Willie Mays, Mickey Mantle or Duke Snider? The baseball discussions with Bob and Phil were a good way to fill the time. We kept our debate going the entire weekend.

We arrived in Wildwood at about two o'clock and went straight to the Baywood Gardens Motel. Nothing had changed—two-story pink and white building surrounding a small pool. After checking in, we grabbed a bite at the Wildwood Diner and then to the beach where we laid in the sun and went for dips in the ocean to cool off. I had become a fan of Ian Fleming and was reading *You Only Live Twice*. James Bond was in Japan.

Our bathroom was a little tight but had two shelves to the side of the sink where the four of us put our toiletries—razor, shaving cream, deodorant, and aftershave. Nine Flags had just come out with a new line of colognes that came in these small round vials with a little neck that fit neatly with the other items on the shelves. The exception was this decanter-size bottle of something called Khalifa (or as we called it Kha-li-FAH) that Phil had brought. It might have been too heavy for the shelves, so Phil put it right on the vanity. He used so much of it that our room smelled the whole weekend like a house of ill repute.

That night, we walked the boardwalk and went into a small club. Saturday was more of the same. The next night after dinner, two attractive girls were sitting on a bench across from the motel. They looked like they were waiting for someone. It was about nine o'clock and J.R. decided to go talk with them. I was watching this encounter from the balcony of our motel room when J.R. motioned me down. June and Kim were a little older than we were. Kim had a boyfriend who was supposed to meet them more than an hour before and hadn't shown up. They were from Medford, Massachusetts, just outside Boston. J.R. and Kim were doing most of the talking, and you could see that there was something brewing between them. After an hour or so, J.R. went back to our room to tell Bob and

Phil that we were going to hang out with June and Kim for the evening. That was fine with me and seemed to be fine with the girls, who by now had figured that they had been stood up. We took June and Kim to a club, had a few beers, and danced a little bit. J.R and Kim were really into each other. When the girls went to the ladies' room, J.R asked me, "Do you mind if I take Kim for a ride in my car?"

"Not at all. Go for it!" I replied.

Ten minutes after the girls returned, J.R. and Kim let us know that they would catch up with us later. June and I were enjoying each other's company and without J.R. and Kim, we started talking about a lot of different things. June was a couple of years older than I was, so I fudged my age. Since she graduated high school, she had been working as a salesperson in a department store. The evening was going nicely when she asked if I wanted to go for a ride. It seems that between the girls, she was the one with a car. We ended up driving out of town to a beach just past Wildwood Crest. She had a blanket in the car, and we went and sat on the sand. It was close to midnight. She was very easy to talk to.

"I want to go to college, but I think I want to leave Medford first. I really think I would like to go to California. I have a friend who lives in Redondo Beach and she keeps telling me I should come out," she said.

"I'll be going to college at night but not sure what I want to do yet. I doubt I would ever leave New York City. I have family and friends who were close to me," I said.

"I have an older brother, Brad, whom I adore. He's the only one I would miss if I left Medford," she said then.

I moved my arm over her shoulder, and she didn't seem to mind. She got a little closer, and I looked at her and we kissed. It was special—on the beach, the sound of the ocean, and the stars above. We kissed some more, and she lay down on her back, I was to her side, but I could feel her body. It was warm and soft. I touched her hair, her face, and her back. She had on a blouse and a light-yellow sweater. I slipped by hand under her sweater and blouse and caressed her breasts. Instinct and desire moved us. We stayed on the beach for the rest of the night.

As daylight was breaking, we started kissing again but we both decided that we had to get back to our friends. She drove me back to Baywood Gardens and told me she had a great night. I know I did. We exchanged addresses and promised to keep in touch.

When I got back to our motel, J.R. and Bob were awake, and Phil was just getting up.

J.R. immediately said, "Where the fuck were you?"

"I went to the beach with June."

J.R. "And what did you do?

"We talked about friends, families, colleges, and California. Where did you go last night?" I asked.

"I went to the beach with Kim."

"And what did you do?" I asked.

"We talked. The same as you!" he said.

J.R. and I burst out laughing and smirked at each other. Bob and Phil knew they missed something good.

It was Sunday morning and J.R. thought we would leave to go home around three o-clock in the afternoon. We all went for breakfast at the diner and then headed to the beach. I laid down on the blanket thinking about June. I fell asleep and woke up about three hours later. It was time to go home.

Back in the Bronx, J.R. dropped me off, and I thanked him for a great weekend. For the next several years, I would go down to Wildwood for a weekend now and then with different friends, but none compared to this weekend with J.R. and the girls from Massachusetts. A couple of weeks later, J.R. called to tell me he was joining the Army Reserves and would be going for his six-month active duty in October. June and I wrote to each other several times into the fall, but we never saw each other again. In her last letter, she said she was planning on moving to San Diego.

On August 6th, 1965, the United States Congress had passed the Voting Rights Act, yet another feather in President Johnson's legacy on civil rights. What should have been a great celebration for him and the country was lost a few days later when on August 11th, the Watts neighborhood in Los Angeles exploded in riots and bloodshed. Los Angeles police had pulled over a black motorist for reckless driving, and the incident escalated into a brutal pushing and shoving match between the police and the driver, his mother, and brother. The rioting that followed this incident would go on for five more days. When it ended, 34 people were dead, 1,032 injured, 3,438 arrested, and more than $40 million of property was damaged. Many were claiming that the riot had been sparked by police racism. I was wishing I could hear what Brother Justice would be saying about it.

Of the remaining Melfords who had graduated high school in June, five of us would be going to college and the rest would be going to work or into the military. P.J. enlisted for a four-year tour with the Army. Nino enlisted in the Air Force. All of us not attending college full-time assumed we would be drafted within a year or so. The Selective Service policy gave deferments to all full-time college students with the assumption that they could be drafted when they graduated. The membership in the Melfords was dwindling and had become less than half of what it had been a year ago

CHAPTER FORTY-TWO

September 1965: College Life

At Hunter College, registration was a sea of humanity with students waiting on long lines to get the courses they wanted. As an entering student focusing on general education requirements, I had a lot of flexibility, but I did want to fit in nine credits at night. The evening bell schedule essentially ran from 5:00 to 10:00 pm. Thankfully, I was able to register for English Composition I, American History I, and Introduction to Philosophy, all required courses taught by Mr. Tolk, Professor Weiss, and Professor Choi, respectively. Mr. Tolk was an enthusiastic teacher of writing, who was well organized and could communicate what he knew. The requirement for the course was to write seven essays, one due every other week. Professor Weiss, likewise, was very enthusiastic and a devoted scholar of history. Every reading assignment examined an historical event from some critical perspective. He emphasized throughout the course that we always needed to know the writer's perspective and viewpoint about the event or period. He reminded me a bit of Brother Thomas at Cardinal Spellman High School. Professor Choi was a very soft-spoken Korean who communicated his thoughts on philosophy in such a quiet tone that we had to listen very carefully to what he was saying. He assigned a significant amount of dense reading including Plato, Hegel, Marx, and Engels.

I would be attending Hunter four nights a week, Monday through Thursday with Monday and Wednesday being my late nights, when I would be finishing at 10:00 pm. On Tuesdays and Thursdays, my classes ended at 8:00 pm. Every day, I would work at the bank from 8:30 am to 4:00 pm., took the subway home, had a bite to eat, and then drove to Hunter College in the Bronx for classes. On

Fridays, I would stop with co-workers at the Colosseum Café across the street from the bank for a drink. The bartender, Philly, was one of the nicest people I ever met in my life. He was about 60 years old, with white wavy hair and a big smile, and could chat with customers about almost any subject. He always wore a tie and a blue or red pinstripe dress shirt under his white bartender's apron. If he liked you and knew you were a regular, you put five dollars on the bar when you walked in and you drank all night. Philly liked me.

At Hunter College, I was developing friendships with several students. Will lived in the same neighborhood as I did in the North Bronx, and we played basketball together at P.S. 87 at night when I first moved to Baychester Avenue. Will went to Mount Saint Michael's High School, not too far from where we both lived. He was in the philosophy course with me. Donny went to Cardinal Spellman. I never had any classes with him there, but we recognized each other from the school, and we were taking the English Composition I course together. Anderson was a heavy-set, blonde, jovial guy who was fun to be around. He was working for IBM in Manhattan and part of a small department that planned company conferences and other events. This was what he wanted to do as a career. Hunter College had no such major for him, but he just wanted a bachelor's degree in any subject area to move ahead in what he was doing. And then, there was Magic, a friend of Mickey at Cardinal Hayes High School. Magic was smart but was into drugs. We used to sit next to each other in Professor Weiss's class and if the class was going slowly, he would reach into his pocket and take out a handful of pills of every color. He would catch my eye, but I stayed away and told him I had to drive home. I liked Magic but he very much wanted someone to get high with and I was not that guy.

Once classes started, my time with the Melfords had diminished. Saturdays and maybe Sunday evenings were the only days I was going to the club. I set aside most of Sunday for reading and homework. On Saturday, September 25th, I went out with J.R., his friends Bob and Phil, and a couple of other guys whom I did not know. J.R. was leaving on Wednesday to do his six-month active duty in the Army Reserves. We went for dinner and a few drinks at Faiella's Restaurant in Pelham in Westchester. The owners were from Morris Avenue and were childhood friends of my mother who use to live next door to us in 300 on 152nd Street. When we got there, one of the owners, Jean, who I had not seen in several years recognized me and came over and immediately asked, "How is your mother?"

"She is doing fine but misses the old neighborhood," I said.

Jean said, "We all miss the old neighborhood."

I explained that we were there for J.R.'s send-off to the Army Reserves. She mentioned how some of the people from Morris Avenue, all of whom were her and my mother's age, came to the restaurant.

"The Russos are regular customers. And please give your mother my regards. I highly recommend the veal dishes," she said.

She bought us a round of drinks and after several more, our little party for J.R. ended at 11:00 pm. We said our goodbyes. J.R. and I gave each other a hug, the type you give someone you knew your whole life.

"Be careful and I'll see you in six months," I said.

At home, plans were being made for Donald's wedding. This was going to be a typical Italian celebration, with about 150 people coming. The marriage ceremony would be at Saint Philip Neri Church on the Grand Concourse, near Bedford Boulevard. The reception would be at Alex & Henry's on Courtlandt Avenue in the South Bronx. Donald's friend Augie was the best man, and Peter and I were ushers along with two of Donald's other friends. My mother was excited about the whole affair and was constantly talking about it. As usual, my father didn't show any emotion. Peter and I were still thinking about Donald leaving us.

CHAPTER FORTY-THREE

October 1965: Donald Gets Married

On Saturday, October 16th, Donald and Dottie were married at St. Phillip Neri Catholic Church. It was a fine affair with family and friends. We got to see relatives who lived in New Jersey and on Long Island on my father's side, whom we had not seen in a while. The church service was about twenty minutes and was just the matrimonial rite, not a mass. Donald's best man was Augie and the ushers were Peter, Donald's friends Johnny Boy and Dino, and me. I didn't know the bridesmaids at all. Alex & Henry's did a great job on the reception. Following in my father's footsteps, Donald had started a side business, doing income tax returns, and one of the owner's sons, Alex, Jr. was his client. Alex and his father went out of their way to make sure everything was perfect. The highlight of the entertainment was my Uncle Johnny doing a Louis Prima rendition of *That Old Black Magic*, followed by Donald doing *Blueberry Hill* ala Fats Domino. Uncle Johnny also sang the World War II favorite, *I'll Be Seeing You (in all the old familiar places)*, which teared up a few people. One of the musicians, Carmine, was my Aunt Zina's brother, and the band was ready for both. Her father was a musician from way back in Sicily who taught his sons to play the trumpet. When the reception ended, all of us in the bridal party and two other couples went to Manhattan to the Copacabana. Dino had a friend who worked security there, and he was able to reserve front row seats for us to see Tony Bennett. I spent the evening with one of the bridesmaids, Tina, who was several years older than I was and closer to Donald in age. We danced and drank, and I took her home. She lived just off Fordham Road in the Bronx. We kissed a bit and I said I would be in touch. I never saw her again. It was about 5:00 am when

I got home. Peter's car was already in the driveway. Donald and Dottie stayed at a hotel and left for Hawaii on Monday for their honeymoon.

The next day, Peter and I talked about Donald and the wedding. While we both lamented his leaving our family home, we were happy for him. Donald bought a house only about three blocks from where we lived, so we could visit him anytime we wanted. He continued to drive us to work every day. Peter now had his own room with my mother's altar all to himself and we had one less car in the driveway.

CHAPTER FORTY-FOUR

November 1965: Vietnam Escalates

On November 14 and continuing for three days, the news media were awash with reports of the Battle of the Ia Drang Valley in the South Vietnam Central Highlands. Nearly 300 Americans were killed and hundreds more injured. It marked a major escalation in the war. Up to that point in the conflict, the fighting had been carried out largely by the indigenous guerrillas—the Vietcong—against the Army of the Republic of Vietnam (South Vietnam). Most of the fighting had been at the small unit level, typically involving platoons, companies, or at most, a single battalion, on each side. After the clash in the Ia Drang Valley, while small unit fighting persisted all over South Vietnam, major conventional campaigns, would pit multiple regiments and even divisions of the U.S. Army and Marine Corps against the regular army of North Vietnam.

The following week, and just before Thanksgiving, all three of the faculty in my classes at Hunter College took time to talk about the Battle of Ia Drang Valley.

Professor Weiss said, "What we are witnessing are possibly the most significant events in American history since World War II."

Professor Choi said, "Southeast Asia would dominate the news for years to come and that America should not underestimate North Vietnam's resolve."

Mr. Tolk shared a Rudyard Kipling poem from the book, *The Naulahka: The Story of East and West*, written in 1892. The poem concludes with the lines

"It is not good for the Christian health,

To hustle the Asian brown;

For the Christian riles, and the Asian smiles,

And he weareth the Christian down.

With the name of the late deceased;

And the epitaph drear:

A fool lies here,

Who tried to hustle the East."

Mr. Tolk's interpretation of these lines was that America was the fool trying to hustle in Asia. He had us write an essay due the following week on "What America's involvement in Vietnam should be."

On Thanksgiving, in addition to my father, mother, and brother Peter, Donald was there with Dottie as well as my Uncle Tony and Aunt Jean. While nibbling on appetizers, I gently brought up Vietnam. My Uncle Tony, who was a World War II veteran and had seen action with the 1st Army, expressed skepticism about the United States sending soldiers to Vietnam to be involved with a ground war and even hand-to-hand fighting. He said quite candidly, "This is going to be another Korea! We're going to fight; our soldiers are going to get killed, and then we're going to pull out."

He certainly did not buy into the domino theory of stopping the spread of communism. My father agreed with him and expressed concerns about whether President Johnson knew what he was doing.

After dinner and after our company left, I went upstairs and started writing my essay for Mr. Tolk. I used my Uncle Tony's comments as a starting point, as I tried to compile my thoughts that had been developing for the past year or so going back to my high school classes at Cardinal Spellman with Father Collins. It was one thing to think about things and mull them over in your head and something else altogether to put your thoughts on paper. I started to understand that writing was a window into my mind. The thoughts that came and went had to be sorted out, grouped, and evaluated before I could write down what I truly believed. This essay began to clarify for me my antiwar views of America's involvement in Vietnam.

The following Monday evening, Mr. Tolk got each of us to briefly discuss our essays. Most, but not all, students were decidedly against the war so there was a lot of give and take. This was the first of many such class sessions I would be engaged in at Hunter College over the next several years.

CHAPTER FORTY-FIVE

December 1965: We Lose Our Lease

The semester was drawing to a close, and I was barely keeping up. It was especially the writing assignments that ate up huge chunks of time. I had to set aside several hours on a Saturday or Sunday to write the essays for my English Composition course. I could essentially fit in the readings for the other two courses whenever I had some free time, but I couldn't do that for the writing assignments. I had to think about the topic for a week or so, and then write in longhand and rewrite and maybe rewrite again on the weekend and then finally type it out. Despite this bi-weekly trial, I did enjoy writing and organizing my thoughts, which were getting deeper and more critical.

The Melfords had a small Christmas Party on Saturday, December 18th, for just girlfriends and invited guests. I took Matts' sister, Marie. We had gone on several dates, but we were not a steady couple. The party was fine, with jukebox music, sandwiches and other finger food, and drinks. By now, I was moving away from beer to liquor, mostly scotch and water. There was a lot of talk about Vietnam. Many of my friends were gung-ho, and I could see them either joining up or welcoming being drafted. I was one of the few old neighborhood guys who thought the Vietnam War was wrong. After the party, I drove Marie to a quiet lover's spot in Mosholu Park. The whole evening was a good way to start the Christmas holidays. Except for the war talk, of course.

I had my first final exams coming up on Wednesday and Thursday evenings and spent all of Sunday reading and getting ready. Fortunately, there was no final exam in Mr. Toth's English Composition I class. He was going to take the average of the seven essays that we had written during the semester. I had already turned in my term papers to Professors Weiss and Choi. We would have one more set of class meetings after the Christmas break when we would receive our final exam and term paper grades.

As always, Christmas at our house was very traditional. But we didn't put up any lights outside because Donald was no longer living with us. Donald put the lights up on his new house. Donald and Dottie and my Uncle Tony and Aunt Jean came over on Christmas Eve and Christmas Day. My Uncle James took the subway from Brooklyn to be with us on Christmas Day. I had a full work schedule but no classes the week of December 26th, so I planned to spend a couple of nights down at the club. We were talking about having a New Year's Party just for guests similar to the Christmas Party.

On Friday night, December 30th, the night before the party, when I got down to the club after work, I could tell something had happened. Several of the Melfords were there and they were not happy. Salvo was explaining, "Guys, I was told by the landlord this morning that our lease for the club will not be renewed starting in January. We have a week to clear out our furniture and everything else."

There was talk of trashing the place, but cooler heads prevailed. But some of us wanted to know why we were being evicted. Salvo said, "Mr. Zangelli did not give a reason. He just wants us out." We discussed several possibilities like our late parties were too noisy or the jukebox music was too loud and discarded all of them. It just didn't make sense to us. About two weeks after we vacated the premises, The Hollows Club moved in. The Hollows Club was on the other side of Morris Avenue and was a seedy place where what remained of the old-time petty crime guys hung out. They must have approached Mr. Zangelli with an offer he couldn't refuse, to pay a much higher rent to move into our nicely renovated club. In any case, the Melford Club was gone. We talked about maybe trying to secure a lease somewhere else on Morris Avenue, but the spirit was gone as well. Our membership had been dwindling as guys moved, went into the military or off to college, or were too occupied with work to spend time at the club. It wasn't just an end to a physical space but the end of our place and time. The Melfords had a great run, but now we would have our memories.

CHAPTER FORTY-SIX

January 1966: Final Grades

I had the last of the Fall semester classes during the first week of January 1966. Our professors returned final exams and term papers. I received "A's" on both the final exam and term paper in Professor Choi's philosophy class. Mr. Toth handed us a summary of the grades on the seven essays we wrote during the semester. I had a "B" average. In Professor Weiss's course, I had an "A" on the final exam and two grades on my term paper A/C. He wrote in the margin, "I am giving you two grades. The A indicates that what you say is fine and the C indicates that how you say it could use improvement." After class, I went to see him and ask for further clarification. He repeated what he wrote in the margin and said, "You need to improve your writing. Let me suggest you read *Elements of Style* by Strunk and White. If you want, you can rewrite your paper and hand it in again by next Monday and I will regrade it."

I bought *Elements of Style* that night at the college bookstore before going home. I read the 70-page book in two sittings and rewrote my paper. The main lesson I took from Strunk and White was to write in clear straightforward declarative sentences and minimize adverbs and adjectives. I left the rewritten paper in Professor Weiss's department mailbox with a postcard, asking if he would send me my grade. A few days later, I received the postcard and I had an A/A with a note: "Now you are writing. Good Work!" When I received my first transcript, I had received "A's" from Professors Weiss and Choi and a "B" from Mr. Tolk. I was confident that I could do well in college. For the spring semester, I enrolled in three courses—American History II, British Literature I, and Mathematics and Logic. My schedule would be the same and I would be attending classes four nights a week.

With the club gone, we started hanging out at Mickey's uncle's bar on 146th Street, just off Morris Avenue. It was a place to have a couple of drinks and joke around a bit, but it wasn't ours. I saw Joey Fuzz and asked him how he did at Hunter.

"I am dropping out," he replied.

"Why?" I asked, surprised.

"I don't like the students. They're too competitive in class and I just don't enjoy being there. I pretty much gave up on it in November," he said.

I think I understood what he was saying, and I didn't try to persuade him to give it another shot.

He asked me, "How did you do?"

I said, "OK. I passed everything."

I liked Joey Fuzz. We were life-long friends and he was smart, but the Hunter environment was too much for him.

Things were going well for me at the bank too. I was transferred from the Savings Department to the Paying and Receiving Department. I was also assigned the job of "coin teller" for the Manhattan and Bronx branches. This meant I had to make sure that they had enough pennies, nickels, dimes, and quarters. Every week, I would receive requests from the branches, order enough coins from the Federal Reserve, and ship them to the individual branches. Paddy, who was in charge of the safe deposit boxes assisted me in machine rolling the loose coins into wrappers. He loved doing this task and I was happy that he did. I also started dating Linda, one of the young women who worked in the Loan Teller Department. We met on Friday nights at the Colosseum Café. So rather than a drink or two with co-workers, we were there until 9:00 or 10:00 pm. She lived on Long Island, which was a bit of trip for me, but I had the car. Then we started going out on Saturday nights for a movie or to a club. She loved going to The Beach House in Long Beach. Giuseppe also started going out with a girl from Queens, and we double-dated a couple of times. I was seeing the rest of my friends from Morris Avenue even less.

CHAPTER FORTY-SEVEN

February 1966: Giuseppe Drafted

I n February 1966, I was back in the swing of working and going to school at night. My new professors were quite different in style and temperament from last semester. I had Mr. Tate for British Literature I. He was impeccably dressed usually, in a blue suit, light shirt and tie. He was very well organized, and had a certain amount of material he was determined to teach every evening. The problem was that he was boring. He would stand in front of the blackboard and lecture us. Every lesson was the same format. We analyzed portions of classic works like Chaucer's *The Canterbury Tales* or Spenser's *The Fairie Queene*. The latter I should have really liked but I didn't. If Magic had been in this class, I would have surely been tempted to take a couple of his uppers. Professor Armstrong was a first-rate history teacher. She too was well-organized, and we focused on the twentieth century, World War I, the Great Depression, World War II, the Cold War, and the present day. She was passionate about her subject, and I sensed I would learn a good deal with her.

Miss Silver was the wild card. She was young, in her twenties, and at first, I didn't know what to expect from her in the math course. She was a bit abstract and had her back to us most of the time as she wrote on the blackboard to explain math principles and logic trees. She also had a persistent cold or allergy and kept a tissue in her hand throughout every class. We had short tests every couple of weeks. I generally got grades in the 70s. I was a bit concerned until David one of the students sitting next to me told me he was getting 50s and 60s. After the second test, David asked Miss Silver in class about grading. "Don't worry about grades. I mark on a curve at the end of the semester." I did not quite know what marking on a curve meant. David explained to me, "The absolute scores on the tests will be curved so that the highest scores will be 'A's', the middle scores 'B's', and lower scores 'C's'. The lowest scores will be 'F's'. Do you get it?"

"No," I said. At Cardinal Spellman High School, you got the grade that was a grade. A 70 was a 70. An 80 was an 80. What David said helped but since I didn't know what grades the other students were getting; I still did not know how I was doing in this class. It was unsettling. In any case, I kept attentive and generally understood much of what Miss Silver was saying or coughing.

By the end of the month, there was really bad news for me. My best friend, Giuseppe received his induction notice and would be going into the Army in March. He had gone for his pre-induction physical in December, and we knew it was only a matter of months before he would be drafted. He wanted to be a paratrooper, so he was ready and maybe even happy to be going into the Army. Giuseppe and I had done so much together and in grammar school, we were inseparable. I would miss him, and I would pray that nothing would happen to him.

At the end of February, my brother Peter said he got a call from Johnny Boy. His brother Joey V had just finished his two years in the Army, and he was inviting a few family friends to a little get together in March to welcome his brother home. He was hoping that Donald, Peter, and I would come. It was going to be a Saturday in the latter part of March. I was always happy to see Joey V.

CHAPTER FORTY-EIGHT

March 1966: Joey V's Welcome Home

We had a small farewell party for Giuseppe at Mickey's uncle's bar on March 12th. He would be reporting to Fort Jackson, South Carolina on the following Monday. There were about eight of us there and we did a lot of reminiscing. The stories kept getting longer and crazier. I mentioned to the guys that Joey V had just came back after two years in the Army. Salvo said he saw Joey and spoke with him. "Joey was acting strange and I think maybe had been smoking some pot." At the end of the evening, we all hugged each other and said our goodbyes. I must say I didn't enjoy the night at all. I didn't like that Giuseppe was leaving and I was bothered by the Joey V story. I didn't see any of my Melford friends for a couple of weeks. I was busy with school and dating Linda. My friend Will at Hunter told me that a couple of his friends got together at Mt. St. Michael's gym on Sunday mornings to play basketball. It sounded like a good idea. I had passed on playing with Peter and his friends at night this year because I didn't have the time and would conflict with my class schedule. Playing with Will and his friends would be easier because Mt. St. Michael was so close to my house. I needed to get out and release some energy on the basketball court.

On Saturday night, March 26th, Peter and I left our house together to go to Joey V's welcome home party. Donald couldn't go because his income tax business had started up and he was just too busy at the end of March. On the way, I told Peter what Salvo had said about Joey, and Peter was surprised. We were going to meet at the Step-In Tavern down on Morris Avenue, have a couple of drinks, and then go to the Courtlandt Steak House. It was a busy Saturday night at the Step-In. Johnny Boy had invited about eight of us. When we got there, Johnny Boy gave us a huge hello and hug. I hadn't seen him since my brother Donald's wedding. Our families were always close, and we were like family. There were also a couple of Johnny Boy's cousins there, who didn't live on Morris Avenue but whom Peter and I had met at some family functions. Joey V was already at the bar and we gave each other a hug. He'd had a couple of drinks, but I could tell he was happy to see me and my brother.

"How are your mother and father? And your brother Donald?" he asked.

"They're fine. What about yours?" I replied.

"Good. I'm working with my father for now but I'm thinking about applying to the Fire Department," he said.

"I saw your mom, dad, and Lena in the fall at Donald's wedding. How was the Army?" I asked.

"OK but not great. I ended up stationed in Germany for a year," he replied.

"Germany sounds better than Vietnam!" I said.

"I don't know. At least there's some action in Nam," he replied.

We talked a bit more and he kidded me about the time when I was in second grade, and I was fighting with Louie and Larry outside of Our Lady of Pity School. "I will never forget how you saved my ass that day." I said. "And then I got a beating from Sister Mary Vincent the next day."

"It figures. You get beat up by the two guys and then you get beat up by the nun. There's no justice in this world, is there?" Joey V replied with a laugh.

On the far end of the bar, there were a few guys from The Hollows Club. Ever since they took over our club, I had an intense dislike for them. They were there in their sports jackets and fedoras and looked like a crew of ginzo clowns. Later in the evening, two younger fellas came in and they started yelling at each other, so the bartender went over and told them to cool it. Johnny Boy saw them too and thought that maybe we should start heading for the Courtlandt Steakhouse. Just as we were finishing up our drinks, The Hollow Boys and the two other guys started arguing again. Before you knew it, one of the younger guys took out a gun and started waving it around, threatening The Hollow Boys. Somebody threw a punch at the guy with the gun and it went off as he was falling. Johnny Boy was hit in the leg. A second later, Joey V ran at the guy with the gun and another shot went off, hit Joey right in the chest, and he went down too. The guy with the gun and his friend ran out of the tavern, leaving both brothers on the floor bleeding badly. I couldn't believe I was seeing another shooting like the time in Dave's Bar when Dave got shot. The bartender got towels and tried to stop the bleeding from Johnny Boy's leg. Joey V wasn't moving at all. I was kneeling by him, and my brother Peter was with Johnny Boy when the police got there. They had already called for an ambulance, which arrived within minutes. The ambulance personnel put a tourniquet on Johnny Boy's leg and carried him out on a stretcher and took him to a hospital. There was nothing they could do for Joey V. The bullet had hit him right in the heart and he died probably instantly. The cousins who came to the party said they would go and tell Johnny Boy's and Joey V's father, mother, and sister. Peter and I were devastated. I couldn't imagine a greater tragedy for the Vitales.

The police had taken the names, addresses, and telephone numbers of everybody who was in the Step-In Tavern during the shooting. Two detectives came up to our house on Baychester Avenue on Sunday and asked what we saw on Saturday night. They asked if we knew the guy with the gun or his friend. We had never seen them before. I called Mr. Simpson, my manager at the bank, and asked if it was okay to take a few days off. He had read about the shooting in the newspapers and couldn't believe I had been there. He said I should do what I had to do. It was OK.

On Thursday, there was a two-day wake followed by a funeral on Saturday at Our Lady of Pity Church for Joey V. Most of the people who attended, including my family, were so numb, they had difficulty expressing their grief. When I saw Johnny Boy and Joey V's sister, Lena, I went to her. Her crying and sense of loss were beyond me. I felt so bad for her. At the funeral, my mother wept uncontrollably throughout the mass. All of the 152nd Street friends were there. We all had tears in our eyes. The Vitales were a good family. They did not deserve this.

We found out a couple of weeks later that the police had arrested the guy who did the shooting. The argument had been over money and loansharking. Donald, Peter, and I went to visit Johnny Boy several times over the next couple of weeks. He was recuperating, but there was some nerve damage, and he would walk with a slight limp for the rest of his life. Mentally and emotionally, Johnny Boy would never be the same. I thought: "There's no justice in this world, is there?"

CHAPTER FORTY-NINE

April 1966:
Getting Back to My Life Slowly

I took a week off and returned to work on April 4th. When several people at
work asked me about the shooting, I said, "I'd rather not discuss it." The week
of April 4th was spring break at Hunter College, so I didn't have classes. I was
hoping that being at work would take my mind off what happened to Joey V and
Johnny Boy at the Step-In Tavern. I kept thinking that the bullets could just as
easily have hit my brother Peter and me, rather than Joey V and Johnny Boy. And
I hated the guys from The Hollows Club even more now than before. They were
a bunch of losers whose petty crimes ended up in taking the life of a friend,
devastating his family, and scarring it for life. My brother Peter was bothered by
what had happened, too. He would come home from work, have supper, and go
to his room for the rest of the evening, without saying much of anything. Our
normally festive Easter Sunday was a quiet affair at our house. It was just the
family and my brother Donald and Dottie. There was no joking or kidding
around, which was so common among us brothers. I was also staying away from
Morris Avenue. I didn't want to see the Step-In Tavern.

The week of April 11th forced me back into my normally busy routine of
work and school. Schoolwork made me think about other things far away from
Joey V, Johnny Boy, and the Step-In Tavern. My readings and other assignments
were emotional therapy. On Friday night, April 15th, I went out for drinks after
work. I had not gone out with Linda in a while, and I had not discussed the
Step-In with anyone at the bank. Someone must have said something to Philly,

the bartender at the Colosseum Café. Whether it was the booze or just that I liked Philly a lot, I started telling him what happened on March 26th. My co-workers gathered around to hear what I had to say. We stayed there drinking until about 11:00 pm. When I went to pay my tab, Philly said, "It is on the house!" I smiled, nodded, and thanked him for the free therapy session.

On Saturday, I drove down to Morris Avenue to Mickey's uncle's bar. Mickey, Salvo, Joey Fuzz, and a couple of my other friends were there. They seemed very glad to see me. Over drinks at the bar, I told them the whole story. They were not as close to Joey V and his family as I was, but they were saddened by his death. They also expressed their hate for The Hollows.

"A couple of nights after the shooting, someone threw a garbage can through the window of The Hollows Club," Mickey said. "They fixed the window, and a few nights later someone threw a garbage can through the window again."

Salvo called them, "A bunch of motherfuckers who should rot in hell!" They were.

Talking with my Melford friends was therapy of a different kind. I went home that night feeling better.

CHAPTER FIFTY

May 1966: Another Semester Ends

At Hunter, the semester was coming to an end. I was doing well in Professor Armstrong's history class. I wrote two papers for her, one on the Great Depression and another on American foreign policy in Southeast Asia. I tried to make the case that countries such as Vietnam and Cambodia would be better off aligning politically with China rather than the United States or Russia. My logic was so-so, but I enjoyed writing a narrative that was counter to the American position. Professor Armstrong liked it and gave me an "A." She also commented on the "crispness" of my writing. Thank you, *Strunk and White*. My British literature class with Mr. Tate was another matter. By May, I was dreading going to class, especially the double session on Wednesdays. He was beyond boring. I did the bare minimum. I wasn't sure where I stood with Miss Silver in math. I thought I understood much of what she presented in class, but I continued to get 70s on her tests. We had a difficult final exam, but I believed I passed. We met with our teachers one last time to receive final papers or exams. When the class met with Miss Silver, she explained how she marked on a curve. I didn't understand everything she said but somehow our grades had been distributed along a curve, with 65 being the lowest and 115 being the highest. When I got my final exam, I saw that my 78 had been extended into a 113. Next to the grade was a note saying, "Very good work and it was a pleasure having you in this class." I ended up getting "A's" in history and math and a "B" in British Literature.

Back at the bank, I received a call from Mrs. Ellis in the Personnel Office on May 24th, asking if I could meet with Mr. Stark the next day. I said, "Sure!"

"Come by around ten o'clock in the morning," she said.

The next day, I met with Mr. Stark, and he asked, "Do you know anything about computers?"

I said, "No!"

He said, "Nor does anyone else in the bank."

Where was he going with this? It seems Federation Bank & Trust was going to convert their data processing operations into a new network computer operation. I understood the data processing piece of what he said because, as a teller, I used to receive IBM cards and printouts from the Data Processing Department on a regular basis.

"IBM will have the contract to develop the online system, and they want to train some of the people at the bank to help install and operate the system. Would you be interested in being part of this implementation?" he asked me.

"Yes!" I said without knowing what exactly I was getting into.

"I need to give you a brief test to determine your aptitude to do computer work," he said.

"Fine," I replied.

He took out a small booklet and gave it to me. The front cover said, "Property of IBM." There were about twenty pages of paragraphs and diagrams followed by multiple-choice questions. He took me back to Mrs. Ellis and asked her to have me take the test. The test was a lot of logic questions, not unlike some of the material covered by Miss Silver in her math and logic course. It took me about an hour to complete. I returned the test to Mrs. Ellis, who told me, "Mr. Stark will get back to you in a day or so."

When I got home that night, I asked Peter what he thought about it. He said, "It's a good opportunity. All of the banks are doing the same thing."

I met with Mr. Stark the next morning.

"You did very well on the test, and we will make arrangements for you to go for training in June."

"OK," I replied. "Where will this training take place?"

"IBM has a training center in Lower Manhattan. Mrs. Ellis will be in touch," he told me.

CHAPTER FIFTY-ONE

June 1966: Computers

Sure enough, I received a memo from Mrs. Ellis to report to the IBM Training facility on Worth Street in Lower Manhattan at 8:30 am on Monday, June 13th. When I got to the Training Center, there were twelve other employees from Federation Bank & Trust there. We assembled in a small classroom, which was adjacent to a computer room.

Mr. Caramonte welcomed us and said, "I am here to assist you in any way I can to help you become more familiar with computer technology and to develop your skills to a level that will be a real asset to your company as it moves to convert its operations."

He put a slide on the projector and explained that we would be taking three workshops:

1. The Essentials of Computer Technology

2. Database Management Systems

3. Computerized Banking Systems

He immediately segued into the first workshop.

Computers operated on the binary system with bits (on–off switches) and bytes (eight bits). I loved the term "EBCDIC," pronounced Eb-ci-dik. It means Extended Binary Coded Decimal Interchange Code, which is used to represent characters of the alphabet and digits. Hardware consisted of input devices, output devices, and the all-important central processing unit with its control, arithmetic/logic, and memory units. Caramonte had excellent illustrations, showing the basic computer system and its components. He explained how sequential magnetic tape and random-access magnetic disk storage devices worked. I understood everything he was saying. The next day, he distinguished hardware from software and made the point that the software directed the hardware. He went on to explain different types of computer programming languages. He showed us code or sets of instruction in Common Business Oriented Language (COBOL) and Formula Translator (FORTRAN). In these languages, the logic construction was the same but the names and methods of executing instructions were different. He even had us do simple coding problems. Some of the people in the workshop became frustrated, but Mr. Caramonte explained that the objective was not to make us proficient computer programmers but to help us understand and appreciate the precision with which computers worked. On the last two days, Mr. Caramonte described the computer system that IBM was developing for Federation Bank & Trust Company. There were to be a series of databases for customer accounts, personnel records, financial information, and other administrative functions. He went into good detail on the customer accounting database. Again, I could understand all of what he was saying as he explained relational database systems, indexed sequential organization, and query languages. Finally, he explained how we would be responsible for working at the individual branches to assist the staffs in understanding and using the customer account systems. I couldn't believe it. I had received an education in eight days that opened the world of technology to me. I had known absolutely nothing about computers, and now I was intrigued with what I had seen and learned. I also knew that a lot of my co-workers were going to become very dependent on me as the new computerized system was deployed. The time had come to unlearn a lot of the manual systems that had been used for years.

CHAPTER FIFTY-TWO

July 1966: Summer and School

As the Spring semester ended, I had been debating whether to take a course or two during the summer. I decided to take what I hoped would be easy courses that were part of Hunter College's general education requirements. I looked at the schedule of classes and I saw I could take the two-credit health education course and a half-credit swimming course back-to-back for four nights per week for six weeks. I registered for them and they were exactly what I wanted. The health education course, taught by a Miss Lenihan, covered topics like nutrition, emotional well-being, and sex education. There was one textbook, one paper to write, and one final examination. The swimming course was a piece of cake. I already knew how to swim, as did the other students in the course, so the instructor, Professor Guten, turned our ninety minutes together every night into playing games such as water polo. It was a great way to spend a hot summer evening.

I hardly ever went down to Morris Avenue to see my friends. Monday through Thursday nights, I was in school. On Fridays, I became part of the regular crowd from the bank that went to the Colosseum Café for drinks. Most Saturdays and Sundays, I was still dating Linda from the bank. One of the other bank tellers, John Tronto, two years older, invited me for a couple of weekends to a beach house he was renting with friends on Long Island near the Hamptons. I was not thinking about Morris Avenue.

My pleasant and busy summer of work, school, and beach was disrupted on July 15th, by a notice from my draft board to report to 39 Whitehall Street near Battery Park in Manhattan for a pre-induction physical on July 29th. I was expecting this but seeing my name on draft board stationary caused instant anxiety. I saw myself drafted, going into the Army or Marines, fighting in Vietnam, and worse.

I reported, as instructed, for one of the most unpleasant experiences of my life. Hundreds of us completely or partially stripped of our clothes were put in lines to move from one station to another, and up and down flights of stairs, to have every part of our bodies examined. You waited on a line to answer questions, you bent over, you coughed, and you had some device attached to or probed into your body. The individual examinations were very quick but waiting on the lines took forever. I was moving along routinely with everyone else until one doctor took my blood pressure and checked my pulse.

"Please step out of the line and take a seat over there," he told me.

He pointed to a bench directly opposite his desk. About fifteen minutes later, he motioned for me to come over and he took my blood pressure and pulse again. He directed me to take a seat again on the bench. This went on two more times.

Finally, he asked me, "Are you being treated for high blood pressure?"

"No," I replied.

"Your blood pressure is borderline high for the Army," he said.

"Really?" I asked, surprised.

"Do you take prescription medicine?" he asked then.

"No," I replied.

"Do you use drugs?" he went on.

"No!" I said.

"Do you smoke marijuana?" he asked.

"No!" I replied again.

"Do you drink a lot?" he asked next.

"Not too much," I said.

He then took my blood pressure one more time and twisted his lips in a quizzical way.

"Are you sure you don't take drugs?" he asked me again.

"Not at all!" I retorted.

"Do you take any prescription medicine?" he asked then.

"No!" I replied.

"I am going to recommend that you go to St. Alban's Naval Hospital in Queens for five days of tests. You'll hear from us in a week. You can get back in line now," he said finally.

I got back into the line and finished my physical at about 4:30 in the afternoon. I went home and told my parents and brother what happened at Whitehall. I didn't know if this was good news or bad news. They weren't sure what to make of it either. I had always assumed that I was in good health. I only went to a doctor when I was sick, and that wasn't very often. Donald and Peter had never gone for pre-induction physicals because both had documented health issues that precluded them from going into the draft. Donald had rheumatic fever as a child and Peter had a herniated disk in his back. In high school, I had perfect attendance. I played basketball and softball, I ran track, and I was in good condition. Wasn't I?

CHAPTER FIFTY-THREE

August 1966: Barracks Life

In the first week of August, I received a letter from my draft board, directing me to report to Ward K at St. Alban's Naval Hospital for five days of testing, starting at 9:00 am on August 22nd.

I arrived at St. Alban's Naval Hospital, as instructed, and was directed by the military police (MP) at the gate to report to Chief Petty Officer John Bentley in Ward K. Ward K was a barracks. It was a wooden, one-story building, which contained ten beds, a bathroom, and the chief petty officer's office. Four of the beds were occupied when I arrived. I went immediately to see Chief Petty Officer Bentley.

"Welcome to Ward K," he said.

"Thank you," I replied.

Smiling, he said, "You must really be looking forward to this."

"Yep. You have no idea," I said and added, Am I supposed to call you 'Sir'?"

"No. You are a civilian and not in the Navy. While you are here, you will be given a blood pressure test every four hours," he said.

"Even at night or early in the morning?" I asked, curious.

"Every four hours," he repeated, as he put a wrist band on me that had my name, my date of birth, and my rank, "Pre-inductee."

"Am I allowed to have visitors?" I asked him then.

"There is a visitor center near the main entrance, but no visitors were allowed in the ward," he told me.

There were five beds on each side of the ward. I was assigned the fourth bed on the left. I hung my clothes in the closet next to the bed. I didn't have to wear a hospital gown. Once I settled in, a male nurse came in and took my blood pressure at 10:00 am.

"Your blood pressure is normal. I will be back at 2:00 pm," he told me.

"Thank you," I replied.

I decided to go and introduce myself to the other guys in the barracks, all of whom had been wounded in Vietnam but were able to walk, in one case with the assistance of a cane.

Danny the fellow in the next bed was in the Army. He was about ten feet from a bomb explosion and was hit in the left eye with shrapnel. There was no visible wound, but he had lost most of his vision in that eye. He had been at St. Albans for a week. Next to Danny was Paul. He was a marine who was with his company during an attack. A firebomb hit about ten feet from him, and he was suffering with burns on thirty percent of his body. "I am happy to be alive," he said.

Carl was directly across from me. He was a marine who had received multiple gunshot wounds in his right leg and was walking with a very noticeable limp. Next to Carl was another marine, Stan, who had lost the lower part of his leg after stepping on a landmine and got around on a cane. Of the four of them, I felt most sorry for Stan, who was the least talkative. Danny and Paul were very sociable and gave me the lowdown about life in the ward, like lights out, mess, and where we were allowed to walk. They treated me as if I was one of them. They wanted to know what I did, if I had a girlfriend, and, of course, what my plans were. We got along fine.

On Tuesday morning, another fellow came into the ward and took the bed to other side of me. I introduced myself and he said, "Hi, my name is Ian Chaiet." It turned out he was here for the same reason I was. His blood pressure was higher than normal during his pre-induction physical. He was a few years older than any of us in the ward were, except for Chief Bentley—maybe in his early to mid-twenties. We spoke some more, and he said, "I had a student deferment until last year when I graduated from Columbia University."

He asked me what I did.

"I work in a bank during the day and go to Hunter College at night," I told him.

"That must be quite a grind," he replied.

"You organize your schedule and get used to it!" I said.

"A couple of friends of mine had just started a counter-culture newspaper," he told me

"What do you mean by counter-culture?" I asked him.

"Basically anti-war," he said.

We talked some more, and I found out that Ian was from Chicago, that his parents were rich, and that there was no way he was going to go into the military to fight in Vietnam.

"What is the source of your parent's wealth?" I asked.

"My grandfather on my mother's side was one of the founders of The Continental Baking Company in the 1930s. They invented the 'Twinkie' and made a fortune," he told me.

"My grandfather thought he was the luckiest man in the world when he got a job as a parkie after World War I, taking care of Crotona Point Park in the Bronx," I told him.

Ian laughed.

For the next three days, Ian and I had long conversations about Vietnam and civil rights. I told him about my family and my anti-war sentiments that had been developing since high school. I told him of Father Collins at Cardinal Spellman. It became obvious during our conversations that he was much better informed than I was, and he was on a mission to do something about the war. Ian ended up on the exact same testing schedule as me. Nurses took our blood pressure religiously every four hours. My blood pressure went up and down a few points on any given test. Ian's was much higher than mine was.

On Wednesday, Chief Bentley said he wanted to speak with me, so I went into his office. He asked me about my career goals and aspirations. I told him about my working in the bank and going to college at night and that I wasn't sure about what I was going to do in life.

"Have you ever thought about the military?" he asked.

"Half my friends had joined or were drafted, but honestly, I have no real desire to be in the military but if drafted, I will do my duty," I told him.

"What are you majoring in?" he asked then.

"I still haven't decided," I replied, explaining that I had just finished my freshman year and was taking basic general education requirements. He gave me a pitch about the U.S. Navy and what I could learn there. I listened carefully but wasn't really interested. I think he detected this.

As I got friendlier with the other guys in the ward, especially Danny and Paul, they became more open about how they felt about the military. Nobody there was gun-ho excited. Danny and Paul were quite honest and told me, "If you don't have to go in, don't go." They also did not have much good to say about their time in Vietnam. Danny especially, "There was a lot of 'Yes, Sir' and 'No, Sir' but nobody really seemed to know what was going on." Ian didn't converse with the other guys as much as I did. He read a lot, sitting in his bed or outside in the area behind the ward. But he and I spoke on a regular basis, and I was becoming more and more impressed with what he knew.

The food in the mess hall was bland and tasteless, and typical of hospital food. The guys in the ward complained about it, so I asked Chief Bentley if we could have food brought into us.

"I don't see why not since none of you are on a restricted diet," he told me.

I called Linda, my girlfriend from the bank. She lived about twenty-minutes from St. Albans, so it was easy for her to come over.

"Would you mind doing me a big favor by bringing a couple of large pizza pies over here?" I asked her.

The next evening at around six o'clock, Linda was driven over by her brother, and she brought three large pies with her. We met in the Visitor's Center and we talked for a bit. As I was walking toward the ward with the pies, there was a gate I had to go through, guarded by a couple of MPs. One of them, a marine, looked at me snidely and asked, "What is your rank?"

I told him quite proudly, "I'm a pre-inductee," and showed him my wristband.

I just kept walking and I don't think he could figure out anything to say or do to me.

I got back to the ward. Even though it was not very hot, the pizza was good. Danny was able to get a couple of six packs from somewhere. We took chairs outside behind the ward and had pizza and beer.

Friday came and I could leave after my last blood pressure test in the morning, which was at 10:00 a.m. There was a chart next to my bed, and when my last test was recorded, I asked the nurse, "How does it all look?"

"Your blood pressure is generally in the normal range but several times it spiked upwards about forty points," she said.

I packed my clothes and said my goodbyes, assuming I would never see these guys again. The last person I spoke to was Ian. We shook hands and he said, "We should get together some time in Manhattan. I live on Houston Street and my office is on Hudson Street."

He gave me his calling card and I gave him my work and home phone numbers. We said goodbye.

That weekend I saw Linda on Saturday night, but otherwise, stayed home and thought a lot of what I had experienced at St. Alban's. I also kept thinking about my conversations with Ian.

CHAPTER FIFTY-FOUR

September 1966: New Semester

In the fall of 1966, I found my work at the bank was getting interesting. While I was still basically a teller, I had to go to meetings each week about the conversion of the bank operations to the new computer system. I was getting quite an education about computers and implementing database systems. I listened attentively, took good notes, and was committing everything I was hearing to memory. There were meetings with the bank managers from the Manhattan branches as well. I was surely the most junior person there, but I knew a lot of details about the conversion, which were helpful to them.

School started again on Tuesday, September 6th. My three courses were British Literature II, French I, and Introduction to Psychology. I wanted to register for a course dealing with some aspect of computers. I searched the entire schedule but couldn't find anything. I had Professor Cohen for British literature, Miss Stern for French, and Mrs. White for psychology. My classes were again on Monday through Thursday evenings. I still got to work riding with Donald but on Fridays, I would more frequently take my car, have a couple of drinks at the Colosseum Café with people from the bank, and then drive to Morris Avenue and see the guys. I wasn't sure where I wanted my relationship with Linda to go, so sometimes I dated other girls I met at work or went down to the old neighborhood on a Saturday to hang out with the guys at Mickey's uncle's bar. On Sunday mornings, I played basketball with Will and his friends at Mt. St. Michael's High School.

At Hunter, I was satisfied with my professors. Professor Cohen loved talking about Keats, Coleridge, and Shelley. I appreciated his enthusiasm for poetry, but I really got into the course when we moved on to Charles Dickens, Rudyard Kipling, and a dash of John Stuart Mill. Mill was more of a philosopher than a literary type, but Professor Cohen had a deep respect, if not love, for his work. Mrs. White was very well organized and related a lot of the course to current events and things we saw or heard in the newspapers or on television. My only problem with the course was that she spent the first part of the semester on Sigmund Freud. I didn't buy into the five psychosexual stages at all. It was interesting, even provocative, to hear Mrs. White talk about them, but I couldn't accept that they were the basis for our psychological development. Miss Stern was young, probably younger than half the students in the class. She was an attractive woman with short brown hair cut at a diagonal across her forehead and narrow eyes. She always dressed in a light blouse and dark skirt. I had a little crush on her. Besides being attractive, she seemed very knowledgeable and in class would go off on short tangents on any number of topics. I took French because I had to complete four units of one foreign language for the general education requirements. I could have taken advanced courses in Latin or Spanish instead, but there weren't any Latin courses offered in the evening. I thought the introductory course in French would be less demanding than a more advanced course in Spanish. About three weeks into the course, I asked Miss Stern after class if she would like to go for a cup of coffee in the Student Union Building. She looked at me and said, "I can't right now but maybe at another time." That wasn't a complete brush-off, was it?

CHAPTER FIFTY-FIVE

October 1966: Ian

I had been thinking about Ian Chaiet since our meeting in August at St. Albans Naval Hospital and decided to give him a call. I called his work number and somebody else answered and said he would give him a message. About two hours later, Ian called back.

"I am really glad you reached out to me. Have you heard anything from your draft board?" he asked.

"No. How about you?" I asked him.

"Nothing. How about getting together for a drink?" he said.

I said, "I'd love to. How is your schedule over the next week or two?

I added: "I have classes Monday through Thursday, but I am free on the weekends. I get out of work on Fridays at about 4:30 pm."

"I am tied up this Friday but how about the 14th?" he inquired.

"Works for me," I told him.

"Is there was a nice place for a drink near you?" he asked.

"Yes, but there will be too many of my co-workers there. How about if I come down to you?" I replied.

"My favorite bar is the White Horse Tavern on Hudson Street," he said.

"That's fine with me. I'll meet you there about 5:30 pm on the 14th?" I told him.

"See you then!" he said and hung up.

The White Horse is one of New York's oldest taverns. I had never been there. It was crowded but not so much that you couldn't pick out someone if you had to. On the walls were pictures of writers including Dylan Thomas who had made the place famous and performers such as Bob Dylan and Mary Travers. I liked the feel of it and saw Ian and somebody else at a booth off to the right. I went over. Ian stood up and gave me a warm handshake. He introduced me to Scott, who worked with him at the paper and was a friend of Ian at Columbia. I sat down and ordered a scotch and water. Our conversation was easy and brisk. Ian and Scott talked a lot about their newspaper. I was really interested in what they were saying, their ideas, and the reason they felt the need for a critical voice to push against the Vietnam War, which was rapidly escalating.

Scott said, "There are already 400,000 American troops in Vietnam, with more on the way. It is a war we will never be able to win. Just ask the French who were there in the 1950s."

Scott was much more passionate about Vietnam than Ian was and saw the newspaper as their vehicle to oppose it. I listened intently because I didn't know as much as they did. Soon Ian changed the subject.

"How are your classes going at night?" he asked me.

"I'm taking the general education courses that are required of all of the undergraduates. At the pace I am going, I might be finished in about five years, maybe more," I answered.

"You should be going full-time. You will enjoy it more and get the most out of it," he said. "How much writing are you doing?"

"Every course has writing assignments. For the basic English composition course, I wrote an essay every two weeks and I'm actually starting to enjoy it," I said.

I told him about the paper for Professor Weiss and the Strunk and White episode, and the paper for Professor Armstrong on Vietnam and Cambodia. "I'm also getting all of this incredible experience working with computers at the bank." I described what I had learned about the essentials of computers and database design, and I could tell that something changed. These Columbia guys seemed to respect me for what I was doing and what I knew. The evening seemed to fly by. At about 11:00 pm, Ian said that he had to go to work the next day and that he had to call it a night.

"Tomorrow's Saturday." I said.

"Scott and I are working seven days a week right now, but let's keep in touch," he said.

Ian and Scott insisted on picking up the tab. I thanked them. As we went out the door, Ian's last words to me were, "Think about going to school full-time!"

I took the subway up to 59th Street to get my car from the parking garage near the bank. My head was spinning, not from the booze but from my conversation with Ian and Scott.

CHAPTER FIFTY-SIX

November 1966: Coffee with Rhoda

On a Tuesday, in the beginning of November, during a five-minute break in my double-period French class, I asked Miss Stern if she wanted to go for a coffee after class on Thursday. She gave me a long look.

"Is there anything in particular we need to talk about?" she asked me.

"No; I'm just being social and want to talk with you a bit," I told her.

"OK; Thursday then," she replied.

After class on Thursday, Miss Stern and I went to the Student Union for coffee. As we walked across the Campus, she asked how I ended up in her French class and I gave her the lowdown. At the Student Union, we each got a coffee and piece of cake and sat down at one of the tables overlooking the campus. I figured I could ask her a question or two, so I did. "You seem much younger than any of the other professors here at Hunter. When did you start teaching?"

"This is my first term teaching," she said. "My father teaches at Boston University and contacted a colleague who was able to get me a couple of adjunct positions here in New York. I just got my master's degree last June, but I hope to get a Ph.D. I'm also thinking about spending a year in Paris before starting a Ph.D. program. And what are your plans?"

"Good question. I work during the day at a bank, which I am enjoying and spend four nights a week here at Hunter," I said.

"What are you planning on majoring in?" she asked me.

"I wish I knew," I replied. "Both of my brothers majored in accounting, and all I know is that I don't want to be an accounting major."

Then, we talked about our families. She was born and raised in Boston. Her father taught literature and her mother was a musician. She didn't have any brothers or sisters. I told her about my father, mother, and brothers, and life in the South Bronx. It was clear that our backgrounds were about as different as they could be.

"One of the things I love about teaching at Hunter is that so many of the students are the first in their families to go to college. And going at night is not easy. I admire the students here who balance their time between work and school in incredibly busy days," she said.

I took that as a compliment. I decided to change the subject and told her about Ian and how he encouraged me to go full-time, but the financials didn't quite work out for me.

"It sounds to me like you have a family that will help you out. They always do and it would only be for a few years. You should think about it," she said.

"Yes, I know. I just have been following in my brothers' footsteps," I replied.

Then, Miss Stern said, "It has been pleasant having coffee with you, but I have to get home."

"Where is home?" I asked.

"Lower Manhattan," she said.

"I have a car and I could drive you." I hoped.

"That's kind of you but I can take the train. New York is lucky to have such a great public subway system," she replied.

"I know. I've been taking the subway to work and school since the eighth grade," I said and walked her to the train on Jerome Avenue.

"Goodbye; thanks for the coffee. And I'll see you on Tuesday," she said.

"Bye and thanks for taking the time to talk with me," I told her.

When I got home, my father was asleep in his chair with the television on. My mother was sitting next to him saying her rosaries, and my brother Peter was upstairs in his room. I gave my mother a kiss, which I did every time I came into or left the house.

"Are you going to be home for supper tomorrow night?" she asked me.

"No. Mom, I'll be going out with some friends from work," I told her.

"We hardly ever all have dinner together anymore," she said.

I detected the sadness in her voice, and I understood why. Other than Sunday afternoon, I hardly ever had dinner with the family anymore. For my mother, her family, her home, and providing for us was all that mattered. She missed not having us together and around her. I also think she missed Donald. He was her favorite, and deservedly so. He was the nicest and most considerate of us three brothers.

I went upstairs to talk with Peter. He was watching television.

"How are things going?" he asked me.

"Pretty good. You know how busy it is going to school at night," he replied.

"You must be used to it by now," he said.

I also told him how much I was enjoying doing the computer conversion at work. "My bank will be doing a similar conversion next year. Stick with it and they'll make you an officer when you graduate college," he said.

We talked some more about working in a bank. He was enthusiastic. He kept getting promotions and making more and more money. A bank career was working for him. But I was beginning to wonder if it would work for me.

CHAPTER FIFTY-SEVEN

December 1966: Induction Notice

On a Friday night in early December, I stopped briefly at the Colosseum Café after work but left at 8:00 pm and drove the twenty minutes up to the South Bronx. Salvo, Mickey, Georgie, and Joey Fuzz were at Mickey's uncle's bar. We talked about all sorts of things—what we were doing, sports, and girlfriends. I was floored when Salvo said, "The Step-In Tavern closed, and a delicatessen opened in its place. Dave's Bar has new owners, and no one has seen Dave."

I hadn't been to 152nd Street since Joey V and Johnny Boy were shot. Of course, we kept coming back to the Melfords. It wasn't long ago that we had twenty members and we were the talk of the Morris Avenue. Our parties attracted people from all over. Now the club was gone, and our buddies dispersed all over the county, the country, and overseas. I felt old with all the reminiscing of things that no longer existed. I left about midnight and headed home.

Most of the time, I was so absorbed with work and college that I had put the possibility of being drafted out of my mind. I thought maybe my blood pressure might make me ineligible. That wasn't to be. On December 13th, I received an induction letter from the Selective Service, ordering me to report on January 5th. If I wanted to appeal or seek a deferment, I could contact a Mrs. Catherine Reid, and there was the address and phone number of the local draft board on Grand Avenue and 174th Street. I called two days later and spoke to Mrs. Reid's assistant, who made an appointment for me for December 22nd at 1:00 p.m.

On the 22nd, I drove to the draft board. It was in a small building with one large open area and several small private offices. I spoke to the receptionist and she directed me to a room to the right. I went there and inside was a pleasant looking grey-haired woman who could be anyone's favorite aunt. I said to her, "Are you Mrs. Reid? I have a 1:00 pm appointment."

There was a chair beside her desk, and she motioned me to take a seat. She was looking through a folder with my name on it while speaking to me, "I gather your blood pressure is OK."

"I guess so. I'm not sure," I said.

"I also gather that you don't want to go into the army," she said.

"Yes," I replied.

"And what do you want to do?" she asked.

"I go to Hunter College at night and I'd like to keep going," I told her.

"How many credits have you completed?" she asked me.

"Twenty," I told her.

"And what do you do during the day?" she asked.

"I work at Federation Bank & Trust Company in Manhattan," I replied.

"What is your grade point average?" she asked.

"3.6," I told her.

"It sounds like you're a good student, but we don't give deferments for part-time study. If college is what you want to do, you should go full-time," she said.

"If I go full-time will I be granted a deferment?" I asked her.

"Absolutely!" she replied.

"But I won't be a full-time student until the spring semester," I told her.

"That's OK. You should take this application to your school and have it signed by the Dean of Students or the Registrar as soon as possible. As soon as you bring it back, you will have your deferment," she said.

I thanked her but I could not believe how well this went. I wanted to give her a kiss for being so nice. After my experience at Whitehall Street during the pre-induction physical, I had not been expecting such a nice person.

I got in my car right then and there, and drove to Hunter College. I went directly to Shuster Hall that housed the administrative offices. The Dean of Students Office was on the first floor, and I told the receptionist that I wanted to transfer from part-time status to full-time status, and I needed a form signed by the Dean of Students for my local draft board. She directed me to see Associate Dean Carl Phillips, down the hall. I had to wait about twenty minutes until I could tell him of my meeting with Mrs. Reid at my draft board and that I needed to have a form signed verifying that I will be a full-time student in the Spring.

He looked at it and said, "I am seeing a lot more of these lately. Wait here minute. I want to get a copy of your transcript."

He returned about ten minutes later with my transcript and commented, "All As and Bs. You are a good student."

He gave me two copies of a Hunter College form for transferring to full-time status. I filled it out. He signed both forms and told me to return one for Mrs. Reid. I thanked him. I couldn't believe how easy and quick it was to complete this paperwork. It was about 3:45 pm so I drove back to the draft board on Grand Avenue. I asked the receptionist to see Mrs. Reid. She told me I could go right into her office. Mrs. Reid was at her desk.

I said, "I don't know if you remember me, but I was here a couple of hours ago about a deferment."

I handed the signed form to her. She looked at it and told me that I will receive a notice in the mail in a few days granting my deferment. "I hope all this works out well for you," she added.

Thanking her profusely, I got out of there as quickly as possible and drove home.

When I got home, I gave my mother a hug and a kiss, saying, "Ma, guess what?"

"What?" she asked.

"I am going to be going to school full-time and I am quitting my job at the bank," I said.

"Did you tell your father?" she asked.

"No," I told her.

"Did you tell Peter?" she asked.

"No," I said again.

"Did you tell Donald?" she went on.

"No. You are the only one I have told yet."

I gave her another hug and went up the stairs to my room to get my books for my classes. I came downstairs and had a quick sandwich. My mother was looking at me and not sure what to think or say.

"Ma, just think I am going to be home more for dinner with you and dad and Peter," I said.

She smiled. I kissed her and gave her another hug.

It was the last night of classes for me before the Christmas break. When I got to French class, I told Miss Stern (or Rhoda Baby, as I thought of her) what I had done earlier in the day and she gave me a beaming smile. I asked her if she could go for a cup of coffee. After class, she and I went to the Student Union. Over coffee, I told her all about my day at the draft board, Mrs. Reid, and Dean Phillips. She thought it was a great decision.

"Will you be teaching any courses in the day next semester?"

"No, I decided to spend at least a year in Paris and maybe even complete my Ph.D. there. I leave in January. I was not one hundred percent sure, but I've thought about it and if I really want to be a French professor; I must live in France for some time. Anyhow, I have to go now," she said.

I walked her to the Jerome Avenue train station. I wanted to give her a kiss, but I didn't quite have the courage. I wished her all the best. She said, "You too!"

The next day was the Friday before Christmas, and there was a party after work at the bank. I was going to tell my manager and some of my co-workers that I would be leaving, but I decided to wait until the following week. It was a good party. I was looking at these people that I knew I would be leaving at the end of January, and probably forever. It is funny how life changes. People come and go but they influence who you are and what you become.

Christmas Eve and Christmas were celebrated as well as ever in our house. My mother started cooking and baking a week before. I saw my brother Donald on Christmas Eve and I told him about my plans. He was encouraging. He announced at dinner that Dottie was pregnant, so we were going to have the first of our next generation soon. After Donald made his announcement, I said, "Ma, you are now going to be a 'Big Momma.'" She smiled. To be a grandmother would be special. But a lot of the talk, especially between my brothers and me, was about college. My father listened. I was sure he was thinking carefully about it and had opinions but did not offer much.

Monday, December 26th, was a holiday, so on Tuesday, I went to my manager, Mr. Simpson, and told him I would be leaving at the end of January. "I am sad to see you go, but I presumed it was just a matter of time with the draft and all," he said.

On Wednesday, I met with Mr. Spear, who was coordinating the computer conversion at the bank and told him I would be leaving. He was more surprised than Mr. Simpson was.

"You have a really good aptitude for this computer stuff, and you should stay with it," he told me.

"Thanks. I appreciate all of the advice and help you've given me," I said in reply.

On Wednesday, I got a call from Salvo saying that a few guys and girl-friends were going to be at Mickey's uncle's bar on New Year's Eve for a small party and asked if I wanted to come.

"Sure, but I don't think I will be bringing a date," I told him.

The New Year's Eve Party was good but nowhere near the kinds of parties we had at the Melford's. We did a lot more talking, drinking, and very little dancing. "I heard The Hollows Club was closing up." Salvo said. "Since the Joey V shooting, there's been a lot of heat from the police who were watching their every move."

"Good riddance to a bunch of assholes!" I said.

When I left at about 1:00 am, I decided to drive up Morris Avenue to see what it looked like. I had not gone beyond 149th Street since Joey V was shot at the Step-In Tavern. As I drove up the avenue, I realized how things had changed since I was a young child. Gone was Almanti's Pastry Shop, Jerry's Pizzeria, and Paganelli's Drug Store. When I got to 152nd Street, Vincent's Butcher Shop was now a dry cleaner and the Step-In Tavern was a delicatessen. I turned up 152nd to see what my old block looked like. On the left side, there was a pretty big playground that extended all the way to 153rd Street. Further up from the playground was a construction site where a new elementary school (P.S. 1) was being built. On the right side, where my grandparent's house was and my mother, my uncles, my brothers, and I grew up, was an empty, garbage-strewn lot that stretched to 151st Street. Old tires, rusted steel drums, broken beer bottles, and other assorted debris covered the ground. I could see the lampposts in front of Our Lady of Pity Church and the boarded-up school halfway up 151st Street. As I came to the end of 152nd Street and made a left turn onto Courtlandt Avenue, I thought to myself that I would try to forget about what I just saw. I will always remember 152nd the way it was when I was a child.

CHAPTER FIFTY-EIGHT

January 1967: Full-Time Student

On January 3rd, I received a letter signed by Mrs. Reid from the local draft board that I had received a deferment from military service because I was a full-time student. It also stated that if for any reason, I did not continue attending college full-time, I was to notify them.

I had final exams the first week of January and received "A's" in English and French. I probably deserved a "C" in psychology but ended up with a "B." Mrs. White was a good teacher, but as I said, I couldn't relate to the psychology canon based on Sigmund Freud and skipped a lot of the readings.

I decided to give Ian a call to tell him that I was going to college full-time.

"This is great news. We should get together and celebrate. Scott and I discussed you a couple of times since we spoke, and we could use some part-time help here at the newspaper if you are interested," he said.

It felt good that he was so enthusiastic for me, and the possibility of working with him had my mind spinning a bit. "I'd love to work with you and Scott at the newspaper," I told him.

Ian told me he was going to San Francisco on business for a couple of weeks but that we could meet for lunch or dinner or just drinks when he got back to discuss it further.

Things were going well and the only problem I had was that my car, with the cold winter weather, would have trouble starting. I took it to Mike, Donald's mechanic, and he said that my car was getting old and I might consider replacing it. I had a few hundred bucks in savings, but not enough to buy a new car. I could consider a used car. The bank had a small repossessions department. I asked Mr. Simpson about it. He sent me to John Hincks, who told me that a 1964 Pontiac just came in two days ago and I could have it for about $1,600.

"Where can I see it?" I inquired.

"Come to my office, and we can walk to the garage where they keep the repossessions right now," he offered.

"OK. I will be there in a few minutes," I told him.

I looked at the silver blue Pontiac and liked it. My problem was I didn't know how I would pay for it.

With the semester ended, much to the delight of my mother, I was having supper with her, my father, and Peter. And Peter asked, "How is your car doing?"

"Not good. Mike told me I should probably consider getting a new one," I said and then told them about my conversation with John Hincks. My father looked up from my mother's homemade chicken noodle soup for a couple of seconds and went back to the soup. Out of the blue, my mother says to my father, "Amadeo, I think you should give him the money to buy the car."

My eyes almost popped out, and so did Peter's. My father in a very low voice almost a whisper said, "Let me think about it."

I was amazed and did not know what to say. The next night we were at dinner again and my mother asked my father again about the money for the car.

"Ok. I will give you $1,600 for the car, but if I should need help down at the warehouse, you will come and do some work for me."

"Our son is going to school full-time. He won't have time to work with you," my mother said.

He looked a little frustrated and pissed off but did not say anything. That meant I was getting the money.

Later that night, I was with Peter in his room and he said, "I can't believe that Dad is giving you the money for a car."

"I can't believe it either," I said.

"I tell you what, little brother, I spoke to Donald about an hour ago and we're going to chip in and cover your insurance for the next couple of years," he said.

I was beyond thankful. Three days later, I had a new car.

My last day at the bank was January 24th. My co-workers had a going-away party for me and gave me a Cross pen and pencil set. We said our goodbyes. We would never see each other again.

The next day, I went to Hunter College to register and while waiting on the registration line, I saw a "Help Wanted" sign looking for part-time students to work in the new college computer center. I wrote the phone number down and called the next day. I spoke with Mrs. Tina Best, who asked me if I had any experience. I told her what I did at Federation Bank & Trust and she seemed interested. Maybe even impressed. I had an interview on Monday, January 30th, with the director of the new computer center. Dr. Mannes and I had a good conversation, and I could tell he was interested in me. He offered me a part-time position at $2.50 cents an hour, which was $1.25 more than the minimum student's aid rate. He thought I could work 20–25 hours per week.

"How come the college doesn't offer any computer courses?" I asked him.

"If we get the computer center up and running, we'll have computer courses in the Spring or at the latest next fall," he said.

"Thank you. I'll take it," I told him.

I went off for to my first day of classes for the Spring 1967 semester. I was grateful for how things were turning out for me. I was going somewhere—to school full-time. I had the support of my family, as Miss Stern had predicted. I had been offered options of working in places that would be important for my personal growth and future. I was excited about working in a new computer center and maybe working with Ian and Scott at their "counter-culture" newspaper.

"Deo Gratias!"

FIFTY YEARS LATER

2017

My son, Michael and I enjoyed the baseball game. The Boston Red Sox took an early lead and were winning for most of the game, until the Yankees scored five runs in the bottom of the eighth inning. Aaron Hicks hit a three-run homer run to cap off the comeback. The Yankees would go to the postseason only to lose to the World Series Champions, the Houston Astros. Michael and I talked about the game on the way home, but my mind kept wandering back to 294 East 152nd Street, Morris Avenue, my family—all of whom were deceased—the Melfords, and Joey V, my very first savior.

Supplement–Real People and Places

Organized sequentially by chapter, below are brief descriptions of the people and places that are real in this novel. Anything not identified in this supplement as real, is fiction.

Introduction

Yolanda's Restaurant has been on 149th Street between Morris and Courtlandt Avenues since the 1960s and owned by the Calisi family.

Our Lady of Pity Church and School were on 151st between Morris and Courtlandt Avenues. The school was phased out in the 1960s. The church was deconsecrated by the Archdiocese of New York in 2017.

Judy's Florist, owned by the Mazzella family, has been on Morris Avenue since the end of World War II.

Colasacco's Sandwich Shop was on Morris Avenue but has been closed for many years.

294 East 152nd Street was bought by my grandparents in 1917, and three generations lived there.

Bronx Vocational High School renamed Alfred E. Smith High School was on 151st and 152nd Streets. Evan Hunter, the author of *Blackboard Jungle* taught there. Evan Hunter's real name was Salvatore Lombino. The movie by the same name was a major success for MGM in part because of its soundtrack and the song *Rock Around the Clock* by Bill Haley and the Comets.

Chapter One

294 East 152nd Street was exactly as described in this chapter. The apartments, basement, and backyard are accurate depictions.

The bathtub in the kitchen was a major accommodation that served multiple purposes besides bathing, as described in this chapter.

The first names of all the people in my family are their actual names. My grandmother was always referred to as "Big Momma." She spent hours every day embroidering altar cloths for Our Lady of Pity Church.

Lena and Ben were friends I played with as a child, but their names have been changed. Ben's family was the only black family that lived on 152nd Street.

Chapter Two

All the first names of my family mentioned in this chapter are actual names. The story of the immigration and early years in this country of my grandparents were told to me by mother and father when I was growing up. The occupations and backgrounds of all the individuals are as I remember them.

My uncles served in World War II and saw a great deal of action in Europe.

The RKO Royal Theater was located in the Hub, as described, and was one of the most beautiful theaters in the Bronx. It was designed by the architect Thomas W. Lamb, opened in 1913, and closed in 1965. The building was demolished in 1967 and signaled the end of one of the major entertainment centers of the Bronx.

Chapter Three

The descriptions of the buildings and grounds of Our Lady of Pity Church and School are accurate.

The names of stores and the descriptions of buildings on 152nd Street are real. Vincent's Butcher Shop on the corner of 152nd Street moved to Arthur Avenue in the Belmont section of the Bronx in the 1960s and is still in business today as Vincent' Meat Market.

The name of my kindergarten teacher has been changed, as are the names of all my teachers described in later chapters.

You will notice that as you read further into this book that surnames are rarely used. However, the Pesces and Russos are real and represented three generations of friendships with my family.

Chapter Four

I had a terrible stutter as a child, which disappeared because of the private lessons I received from my teacher Miss Cassidy.

The Frog Hollow Boys was the name of a club in the Bronx but the Hollows Club, as described in this chapter, is fictional.

The San Silverio street festival occurred in June on Morris Avenue every year and was comparable in popularity to other Italian street festivals such as San Gennaro in Lower Manhattan. A scaled-down San Silverio festival moved to the Morris Park section of the Bronx in the 1970s and then to Dover Plains, New York.

Chapter Five

The story about Sally is true but her name has been changed.

The story about the fight with Louie, Larry, and Joey V is true but the names have been changed.

Father Alexander was a real person, and most of us went to him for confession because he had difficulty speaking and hearing and always gave three *Hail Marys* for a penance.

I did receive my first Holy Communion and Confirmation, and Skippy was my godfather. I have the Waltham wristwatch he gave me in 1955 and it still works, and I wear it once a year.

Chapter Six

The story of my mother breaking my glass jar bank and using the money to buy me shoes is true.

The story of the ink spilling onto my lap is true.

Mrs. Gerson (name changed) was our music teacher and the sing-alongs, as described, were a regular routine in our class.

Playing softball in the parking lot of Yankee Stadium is true. New York Yankees Elston Howard and Ralph Terry did watch us one day.

Giuseppe is a real person and growing up, he was my best friend.

Chapter Seven

The incidents in Fourth Grade with Sister Mary Harold about punishments including sending me back to kindergarten happened, but names have been changed.

I did develop a serious hearing problem and had my tonsils and adenoids removed. My stay at New York Eye and Ear Hospital is true, but names have been changed.

The descriptions of the Hub, the Grand Concourse, the Bronx Zoo, and Times Square are exactly as I remember them. Many of the places such as the Concourse Plaza Hotel were very special and attracted famous people. One of the saddest chapters in Bronx history was that the Concourse Plaza where major league baseball players for decades had stayed throughout the summer season became a welfare hotel in the 1970s to provide housing for the homeless.

Chapter Eight

Nino (name changed) is a real person who bore the brunt of Sister Mary Christina's punishments.

The altar boy vignettes (the funeral mass, the *Good Night Sweet Jesus* benediction, the Holy Thursday mass, Dino falling down, and the choir scene with Father Emanuel) are true, but the names have been changed.

The scenes of the hot summer nights (jukebox music, my father and his friends playing pinochle, women sitting on our stoop, and kids playing Nevada's Lump) were real.

Donald graduating college and getting a new car as a gift from my father is true.

The trip to Wildwood, New Jersey, happened, but names have been changed.

Chapter Nine

The City of New York condemned the buildings on 152nd Street and 153rd Street, as described.

Jane Jacobs was a community activist in Manhattan and brought pressure on Robert Moses to abandon the Lower Manhattan Expressway.

Father Ernest did make a plea, as described, to Mayor Wagner and other city elected officials to spare our neighborhood from any further renewal projects.

Chapter Ten

The Halloween incident is basically true, but names have been changed.

The wake and funeral for my grandmother was, as described, in this chapter.

Chapter Eleven

The move to a new house in the North Bronx was, as described. I had my own room and we had two bathrooms, one of which was complete with shower and bathtub.

Playing basketball at P.S. 87 on Tuesday, Thursday, and Friday nights is true although names have been changed.

Reading a novel on the subway everyday became a passion for me.

The decision to go to Cardinal Spellman High School is accurately described.

Chapter Twelve

My first year at Cardinal Spellman High School was, as described, in this chapter. The names of all my teachers have been changed, and this is true throughout the chapters covering my time at Cardinal Spellman.

I did start working part-time with my father in my first year of high school.

Chapter Thirteen

The call from Jamey about my Morris Avenue friends starting a club was, as described, but names have been changed.

The vignettes about doing piecework and assembling bibles are true.

Chapter Fourteen

Club 19 was the first name of our club.

St. Rita Church and School did exist on College Avenue. In 2014, St. Rita's Church merged with St. Pius Church.

Chapter Fifteen

The incident at the New York City Department of Health including the fight and being escorted back to Morris Avenue in a police car is accurate, as described, but names have been changed.

Chapter Sixteen

The name of our club was changed to the Melfords, as described, in this chapter.

Chapter Seventeen

The story of Brother Arnold and the gospel of the mustard seed are basically true.

P.S. 1 is an elementary school built on 152nd Street and still operates.

Chapter Eighteen

The description of the Halloween Party at the Melfords Club is accurate, but names have been changed.

Chapter Nineteen

Father Collins (name changed) discussed civil rights issues in our class.

The scene in the gymnasium at Cardinal Spellman High School on the afternoon of President John F. Kennedy's assassination is accurately described.

Chapter Twenty

To Kill a Mockingbird, Fahrenheit 451, and *The Ugly American* were important books that started my reading more non-fiction.

Chapter Twenty-One

The events in the English class with Brother Thomas are true. Literature came alive for me under his tutelage. His leaving the order and our class in January was devastating to us.

Brother Crispus meant well, but his subject matter did not click with me especially after Brother Thomas had opened up exciting aspects of literature.

Chapter Twenty-Two

Dave's Bar was a real place, but the name has been changed. It became one of our favorite places to go for a drink. We always felt welcome and among friends.

Chapter Twenty-Three

The blind date and fight scene with Jamey and Matts are a composite story with some of the elements being true and some fiction.

Jamey's decision to join the Air Force was true and bothered me a great deal. I saw the future that night for my friends and me, and it was not going to be pleasant.

Chapter Twenty-Four

Everything is this chapter is true.

Chapter Twenty-Five

The shooting in Dave's Bar is true but the names were changed.

Chapter Twenty-Six

Parts of this chapter are composite sketches.

Father Collins left an impression on me when he discussed the deaths of Andrew Goodman, James Chaney, and Michael Schwerner.

Chapter Twenty-Seven

I was becoming more aware of current events especially issues related to civil rights.

Several of the Melfords started dating girls from New Jersey. One of the Melfords ended up marrying one of these girls. The names of the girls and the town have been changed.

Chapter Twenty-Eight

The weekend to Long Beach, Long Island is accurately depicted.

The day trip to Glen Island happened, including the fight on the way home.

My discussions with Jamey and Giuseppe were real.

Chapter Twenty-Nine

Father Collins discussed the Vietnam War on multiple occasions.

The story of Brother Kenneth is true.

I took and passed driver education with Mr. Conte.

Chapter Thirty

My thinking was not at all clear about what I was going to do after high school. I was sure I was going to go to college. After my discussion with the guidance counselor, Brother Andrew (fictional name), I did not think I was going to follow in my brothers' footsteps and go to Fordham University and major in accounting.

Chapter Thirty-One

The incident with Frankie is a composite story. Parts are fiction although the part about Larry and the gun is true.

Chapter Thirty-Two

The way the decision to go to Hunter College unfolded is essentially accurate. Fuzz was going there was important to me. I also liked the Bronx Campus and the convenience of taking courses there or at the Main Campus on 68th Street. And at $12.00 semester, I would not have any money issues.

Chapter Thirty-Three

Donald did give me his car.

Chapter Thirty-Four

My own car was an important turning point in my life. It would give me great flexibility to combine school, work, and seeing my friends.

Donald's advice about not taking my father's offer to continue to work with him in the warehouse was golden.

Chapter Thirty-Five

Because of Father Collins (fictional name), I started reading more about the Vietnam War. My father regularly read the *Daily News*, and a copy of it was always lying around our house. I started reading the *New York Times*, which in 1965 cost ten cents for the daily edition. In comparing similar articles in the two newspapers, I began to understand how the news represented points of view.

Chapter Thirty-Six

I did march with the seniors of Cardinal Spellman High School in the St. Patrick Day's Parade.

Chapter Thirty-Seven

I was accepted at Hunter College and decided to attend in the evenings.

We did not see my Uncle James very often, but we enjoyed his company. I loved his Brooklyn accent and throughout my life for fun, I would duplicate it with people especially if they were not from New York City. I also came to admire him because with a very limited education, he had an extensive knowledge and a love of opera.

Chapter Thirty-Eight

The freshmen orientation at Hunter College was, as depicted.

Federation Bank & Trust Company was a New York City bank and had a branch on Baychester Avenue near where I lived. It merged with Franklyn National Bank in 1967.

Chapter Thirty-Nine

My interview and meetings at Federation Bank & Trust Company are accurate. The names of the individual have been changed.

Chapter Forty

My first job out of high school was at the Federation Bank & Trust Company. My first few days at the bank were, as described in this chapter. All the names have been changed.

Chapter Forty-One

The trip to Wildwood, New Jersey, is true. All names have been changed.

J.R. and I did meet two older women and separately had wonderful evenings with them.

Chapter Forty-Two

My first semester at Hunter College is a composite of courses, faculty, and students I had including Magic and my other fellow students. All the names have been changed.

Saying goodbye to J.R. for his Army Reserve commitment was difficult. J.R. and I were very good friends and spent a lot of time together when we were younger, especially playing sports. In softball, he was the shortstop on our team and was as good as anyone from the Morris Avenue in that position. I played alongside of him at either second or third base. I was always sorry that we drifted apart.

I became a regular customer at the Colosseum Café, going there most Friday nights and occasionally for lunch. Philly was the evening bartender and was the best in his business. The Colosseum Café still exists in its original location although the ownership has changed.

Chapter Forty-Three

The basic description of Donald's wedding is accurate although parts are fictional. Peter and I would surely miss our older brother.

Chapter Forty-Four

The Battle of the Ia Drang Valley in the South Vietnam Central Highlands was the topic of class discussions at Hunter College, with many of the students decidedly against America's escalating involvement.

Chapter Forty- Five

Our eviction from the Melford club is accurately depicted. It was an immensely sad day. For me, without the club, I sensed immediately that there would be changes to the dynamic of my friendships and relationships.

Chapter Forty-Six

The exchange with Professor Weiss is true, but it happened later in college. With him, I came to understand and appreciate writing like never before. I still have the copy of *Elements of Style* by Strunk and White on by bookshelf at home.

I felt very sorry for Joey Fuzz (fictional name). He was a good friend whom I knew since I was five years old. I always thought he was smarter than I was, and it was sad that things did not work out for him at Hunter College.

Chapter Forty-Seven

As indicated in this chapter, I had no idea what grading on a curve meant.

Giuseppe going into the army was devastating news for me. We were like brothers, and throughout our lives, we did so much together. As indicated in this chapter, I was also concerned that he was bit too gung-ho and I feared for his safety.

Chapter Forty-Eight

Some elements of this chapter are true but most of it is fiction. Names have been changed.

Chapter Forty-Nine

Most of this chapter is fiction.

Chapter Fifty

This chapter represents a composite of stories—some fiction and some non-fiction.

Chapter Fifty-One

This chapter represents a composite of stories—some fiction and some non-fiction.

Chapter Fifty-Two

My experience during the pre-induction physical at Whitehall Street is accurately described. It was determined that I had fluctuating blood pressure.

Chapter Fifty-Three

My visit at St. Albans Naval Hospital for five days of blood pressure testing is true, including the pizza story. Names have been changed.

Chapter Fifty-Four

The instructors in this chapter are accurately described; however, all names have been changed. I did have a crush on Rhoda Stern.

Chapter Fifty-Five

This chapter is mostly fiction.

Chapter Fifty-Six

This chapter is mostly fiction.

Chapter Fifty-Seven

Catherine Reid at my draft board was a real person.

I transferred to full-time status, as described.

Chapter Fifty-Eight

I did work in the computer center at Hunter College in the Bronx, soon to become Lehman College; however, my first position was in the Business Office.

My father bought the repossessed Pontiac for me.

Fifty Years Later (Year 2017)

The Yankees beat the Boston Red Sox, as described.